GODS & SNIPERS

DAVID HEALEY

INTRACOASTAL

GODS & SNIPERS

By David Healey

Intracoastal Media digital edition published 2019. Print edition published 2019. ISBN 978-0-9674162-0-5

Cover art by Streetlight Graphics

BISAC Subject Headings:

FIC014000 FICTION/Historical

FIC032000 FICTION/War & Military

"There's nothing so much like a god on earth as a General on a battlefield."

—From *The Killer Angels* by Michael Shaara

CHAPTER ONE

ON THE DAY that Caje Cole lost his sniper rifle, it finally rained. After a spell of summer heat and drought, the skies opened up and drenched the French countryside. Lightning laced the sky and thunder rumbled deep as any distant German 88. An autumn chill rode in with the rain and wind.

It was September 1944. The fight to push the Germans out of France had been tough and bloody. Even the rain couldn't wash away the many signs of war in the wrecked vehicles, burned villages, and fresh graves in the fields.

The wet weather also kept Allied planes grounded, which meant that German tanks could operate unimpeded, roving the French countryside. Sherman tanks were suddenly scarce, forced into inaction by a lack of fuel. For the men on the ground, four men knew their business, though, and Cole was nominally in charge.

Officially, they were attached to an infantry regiment, but the truth was that they were on their own. That was just fine with Cole. Their mission was simple. Whenever they encountered a German sniper, they were to take him out.

It was an important task. A single enemy sniper could hold up an entire company. Worse yet, a sniper might move unseen along a unit's flank and pick off soldiers as the unit advanced. The Germans had a regular training program for snipers and were quite adept at the tactics involved. German snipers learned about camouflage and were equipped with the best telescopic sights available. On the U.S. side, snipers were men who fell into the job and didn't receive any real training, putting the Americans at a distinct disadvantage.

At this late stage, most of the German snipers tended to be fanatical teenagers—often members of the Hitler Youth—who had been given a modicum of training. They had been taught to shoot but not to survive. Cole and the others didn't much like killing kids who couldn't have been much more than fifteen or sixteen, but even these kids could be very deadly with a scoped Mauser in their hands.

Unlike adults, these boys didn't understand the rules of engagement. One minute, they would surrender, and then the next minute, they would pull a Luger out of nowhere and start shooting. Crazy kids. It was best not to take prisoners.

They had not encountered any Germans today, but that didn't mean the Jerries weren't there.

Up ahead, he saw a blur of movement through the curtain of rain. Cole raised his fist, signaling a halt. They crouched, ready to fire. Cole put his rifle to his shoulder and peered through the telescopic sight, but all that he could see was more rain.

A voice called out, "Who the hell are you?"

The voice belonged to an American. Cole looked back at Vaccaro, who nodded, then stood up with his rifle raised over his head. Cole stayed on the rifle, eye to the scope, just in case.

Vaccaro shouted into the rain, identifying themselves. "Sniper squad," he added.

They waited a moment, and then several figures began to emerge from the rain, weapons at the ready. The rain made it difficult for anyone to see. It also made everyone wet and miserable. When they saw that the snipers really were Americans, the other soldiers visibly relaxed. Cole counted two dozen men, including a sergeant and a captain. They all moved off the road together into the shelter of some over-hanging trees, trying to get a break from the rain. As if matching the mood of the landscape, the leaves had turned a sickly yellow in the fall temperatures. The branches broke up the downpour just enough that they could all light cigarettes.

"You see any Germans, sir?" Vaccaro asked the captain.

The officer shook his head. "Not yet, but you can be damn sure they're out there. This rain is giving them a chance to regroup. How about you? You see any Jerries?"

"Not today," Vaccaro said.

He nodded at Vaccaro's rifle. "Snipers, huh?"

"Yes, sir. There's been quite a lot of on-the-job training involved."

The captain fixed his gaze on Cole, who still hadn't said a word. Cole was still keeping watch down the road because no one else seemed to be paying attention. The war didn't take smoke breaks. "You don't say much, do you?"

"No, sir," Cole drawled.

The captain's name was Norton. He took a deep drag on his cigarette. He looked to be in his mid-twenties, making him just a shade older than most of the soldiers. He was six feet tall with the dark good looks of an actor, like he could be Ronald Reagan's younger brother. The trouble was that Captain Norton knew he was everything that his men were not and he expressed that in his supercilious tone. Cole had a natural dislike of uppity folks and had gotten on the wrong side of a few officers like that.

"I'm not a bad shot myself, you know, as long as I've got a decent rifle," Captain Norton said. "I was one of the alternates on my team at Harvard for the '38 Olympics in the military patrol competition. Some people call it biathlon. You ever do much of that, soldier?"

"Ain't never heard of it."

"Basically, it's an athletic competition involving skiing and shooting."

Cole said, "If we come across any Krauts looking to challenge us to an athletic competition, I reckon I'll let you know. Sir."

Vaccaro made a noise that could have been a groan, but that was possibly indigestion. It was true that Cole didn't say a whole lot, but when he did say something, he often managed to say the wrong thing. Especially where anyone higher ranking was concerned. It seemed like Cole couldn't help being ornery.

Norton flicked away his cigarette and stared hard at Cole. "What's your name, Private?"

"Cole."

"No wonder you don't talk much, Cole. You sound like a goddamn hillbilly. What do you think about that?"

Cole took his time answering. A tense silence had fallen over the squad. The sound of rain on their helmets grew louder. "Whatever you say, sir."

"Are you a good shot with that rifle?"

"I done some good with it."

"Yeah? Give it here a minute."

Cole hesitated.

"I said to give it here. That's an order," Norton snapped, his voice carrying too far, even with the muffling effect of the rain. If there were any Germans around, he had just alerted them. He held out his hand for the rifle.

Faced with a direct order from the captain and with the squad looking on, Cole had no choice but to hand over the sniper rifle that he had carried since Omaha Beach. "It's a Springfield, sir."

"I can see that," Captain Norton said, taking the rifle. He worked the action. He put the rifle to his shoulder and peered through the telescopic sight. "Not a bad rifle. Not the best I've seen, but not bad. I'll tell you what. I'm going to hang onto this, Cole. We've got an extra grease gun around here some-where, and you can have that. Sergeant Woodbine? Where's that M-3?"

Captain Norton slung Cole's rifle over his own shoulder and stood there, as if expecting an affirma-tive answer from Cole. Cole's face was so hard to read that it was like wet stone in the rain. It was so quiet that the individual raindrops on the sickly leaves overhead sounded as loud as drumbeats.

Vaccaro broke the silence. "You can take my rifle,

sir. Or I can give Cole mine. I can take the grease gun."

"No, we'll give the grease gun to the hillbilly," Captain Norton said. "Later on, he can maybe shoot some squirrels with it. You don't have a problem with that, do you?"

Cole stiffened. "No, sir."

But Captain Norton wasn't done with him. Now he was glaring at the Confederate flag painted on Cole's helmet. "In case you haven't heard, the South lost the war. This is the United States Army, goddammit, not the Stonewall Brigade. I want that covered up."

"Yes, sir."

Norton indicated the men behind him with a thumb over his shoulder. "Your squad is with us now. Your vacation days are over. You'll have to pull your weight for a change. Let's get ready to move out."

A sergeant stepped forward and handed the M-3 to Cole. All he said was, "Here you go," but with his eyes and body language, he managed to convey the fact that he thought the captain was being unreasonable. Not that anything could be done about it.

Cole hefted the grease gun and yanked back the cocking lever so hard it was a wonder that it didn't snap off in his hand. Cheaply made out of stamped metal, the entire gun was mass-produced junk intended as a disposable weapon. Its chief attribute was that it could spew a great quantity of lead at close range. It was nicknamed a grease gun because it looked exactly like what you'd expect in a mechanic's garage if you needed to lubricate a chassis.

Though cheaply made, the M-3 had its uses. The thirty-round magazine was loaded with .45 ACP, which made it a deadly weapon at very close range. The gun basically sprayed bullets. Beyond a couple hundred feet, hitting anything was mainly a result of the number of bullets heading at the target rather than marksmanship.

By comparison, Cole's Springfield rifle could reach out across a vast distance. He wasn't scared of getting close to the Germans, but it just wasn't his style.

The grease gun's muzzle wandered in the direction of Captain Norton. The captain had moved away to light a cigarette and didn't notice.

Vaccaro put a restraining hand on Cole's arm and muttered, "Don't go shooting him now. I'd hate to be on your firing squad."

Giving Vaccaro a look with his hard eyes, Cole lowered the weapon. Cole had strange eyes that were so clear they could have been made out of ice. Vaccaro knew those eyes could see like an eagle's, but a cold hatred burned in them as well. Hit with that glare, Vaccaro actually took a step back as if Cole had pushed him.

"City Boy, I'd a thought you'd volunteer for my firing squad," Cole said. "But I can tell you that if anyone is gonna get shot around here, it ain't gonna be me."

"That's what I'm afraid of," Vaccaro said.

They fell in at the end of their new squad and moved out along the muddy road. Their new squad was a little sloppy, but the rain seemed to have washed away the Wehrmacht. The soldiers walked unchallenged down the muddy road, each step carrying them closer to Germany.

But the war was still out there, somewhere. The chatter of rapid fire carried toward them across the fields and they all tensed up. Out of habit, Cole went to put his rifle to his shoulder, ready to return fire, and remembered that he was now armed with an M-3.

Vaccaro was watching him. "Want to switch?"

"Hell yeah, but ain't no sense rocking the boat no more. I reckon the captain done made it clear that he wants me to have this here grease gun," Cole said. The firing in the distance tapered off, so he lowered the grease gun and spat. "Fine weapon that it is."

"You'll get your rifle back," Vaccaro said, although he didn't sound convinced. "Give it some time."

Cole said, "One thing about me, I ain't nothin' but patient."

Vaccaro shook his head. Sure, Cole was patient

when he was behind a rifle scope. But at other moments, he was impulsive. And he was vindictive pretty much *all* of the time. Cole got even, no matter what, and no matter how long it took. A story had gone around that in boot camp, Cole had put up with a bully just long enough to jump him one night and damn near beat him to death with a can of beans stuck inside a sock. You were better off staying on Cole's good side.

"It's the part about you being patient that's got me worried," Vaccaro said.

CHAPTER TWO

FAR BEHIND THE FRONT LINES, General Dwight D.
Eisenhower lit another cigarette and studied the map
spread on the wall at Supreme Allied Command
headquarters. The situation changed daily, even
hourly, and his aides struggled to keep up by moving
paper icons around the map. The cardboard cutouts
of planes, tanks, and soldiers resembled nothing so
much as paper dolls and would have seemed outright
silly if they had not represented the placement of
battalions and bombing runs. The map represented
where men lived and died on an hourly basis.

"What's on your mind, von Rundstedt?" Ike
muttered to no one in particular.

"Sir?" an aide asked, hurrying over because he had
heard Ike's voice. "Did you need something?"

Ike shook his head and exhaled a stream of

tobacco smoke. "Just thinking out loud," he said. "If you were the Germans, what would you do?"

"Sir, I'd give up."

Ike barked a laugh. "In that case, you have more sense than the entire German High Command, son."

Ike's smile faded as the aide moved away. Given that the Germans weren't likely to surrender, what would Rundstedt do?

Currently, Rundstedt was the overall commander of German forces. The Germans had been through so many leaders in France that one almost needed note-cards to keep up. First there had been Rommel, certainly a capable and competent soldier, but he had been badly wounded when Allied planes strafed his car. Next was Kluge, then Model, and finally Field Marshal von Rundstedt. Ike considered that it would be reassuring to think that the Germans were scraping the bottom of the barrel in terms of commanders, but he knew better than to underestimate Runstedt. This last general, born in 1875 into a family of Prussian aristocrats, was practically a relic from another era, but in a sense, he was the last general standing after defeats, battlefield deaths, and the summertime plot against Hitler.

It was true that Runstedt had been dismissed from command after the failure to halt the Allied invasion of Normandy back in June. However, he had since been recalled to overall command of

Wehrmacht forces in the West. Intelligence reports indicated that Hitler trusted Runstedt, implying that the general wouldn't take much initiative but that he would follow Hitler's orders.

Nonetheless, Ike definitely wanted to know what was on the field marshal's mind. And if Runstedt had been in the room with him, Ike would have asked him another question that echoed the one posed by his aide: "Why don't you just give up and save both sides a lot of lives and misery?"

Of course, Ike knew that decision wasn't Runstedt's to make. It was Adolf Hitler's. The German people called him *Der Führer*, which translated to English as, The Leader. At this point in the war, he had consolidated power to the point that he called all the shots on and off the battlefield.

There had been intelligence reports of a cabal that had attempted to kill Hitler with a bomb back in July. If only they had succeeded, Ike opined, peace talks would likely be underway. Alas, the assassination attempt had not been successful.

Since then, Hitler had wrested many command decisions away from his generals because he no longer trusted them. Several high-ranking officers had been arrested and killed. Others were forced to commit suicide, Kluge among them. Only the most loyal generals, such as von Runstedt, had survived the putsch.

Runstedt had refused to take part in the plot against The Leader. Perhaps like some, he had feared that Hitler's death would launch a civil war between the SS and the Wehrmacht at a time when Germany could ill afford it. He wasn't a terribly imaginative commander, but he was a capable organizer. Under his command, the German military continued to fight like a punch-drunk boxer.

Ike knew that Hitler would never surrender and that many more thousands of soldiers and civilians—perhaps tens of thousands or hundreds of thousands—would die before the war was over. The Leader encouraged every last German soldier to fight to the end for the Fatherland, and far too many had taken his wishes to heart. The savage fighting across Normandy had been testament to that.

IKE SIGHED and lit another cigarette. He now smoked more than two packs a day and lived off tobacco, coffee, hot dogs, and a nightly allotment of two fingers of bourbon.

As Allied Supreme Commander, the fifty-four-year-old commander was a gifted organizer, and often as much of a referee as a general. He managed to balance the demands of politicians with personalities no less forceful than FDR and Winston Churchill.

Churchill, in particular, was an old soldier at heart who had his own ideas about how to win the war and how it should be fought, most of which were quite astute. The problem was that the goals of the fading British Empire did not always align with American ones. The resulting tensions provided Ike with many headaches.

Then there were the generals.

In all honesty, the generals were his most vexing problem. For starters, he had to juggle the disparate personalities of Omar Bradley and George Patton. Both were good generals with very different personalities and approaches. Neither man was necessarily fond of the other as a result. However, their disagreements were nothing compared to those with the British General, Montgomery. Monty was a prickly character and nobody's fool. Also, he saw the British as the ones who should take the lead role in the victory in Europe, not the Americans. Theoretically, at least, Ike could dismiss any general who got out of line, but finding replacements for the likes of those men would be impossible at this stage of the war. When God had made Patton, for example, he'd broken the mold.

Despite all of these challenges, slowly but surely it was all coming together for the Allies, but the war was far from won.

Still, Eisenhower was nothing if not an optimist at

heart, and now, looking at the maps with its martial paper dolls, he could not help saying it aloud to himself, "By God, we've got them on the run."

A defensive war was not an approach that the Germans favored. Their early military success had been built around the concept of the Blitzkrieg or Lightning War intended to overwhelm an enemy's defenses. Their tactics included the concept of *Schwerpunkt*, or the point of main effort, which was where the main attack centered. Imagine the point of a spear and you got the idea of German strategy. For much of the war, the tip of the spear was all that Germany had needed.

Since this doctrine was not suited to defensive operations, German tactics changed. One thing about the German military was that it managed to be highly adaptable.

Confronted by defensive wars in the Eastern and Western Fronts, German tactics changed significantly during 1944 to something that might be called the rubber band defense, in that the front lines became very fluid. The front line became less important to hold. If the Allies overran the forward positions, the secondary line of defense would halt the enemy advance and the Germans would counterattack with a mobile force deployed just to the rear of the secondary line of defense. It wasn't enough to completely stop the Allied advance, but it was an effective strategy to bleed the Allies dry.

There were some in the German high command who saw these tactics as shameful, considering that these were the tactics of retreat. But by 1944, with the notable exception of Hitler himself, most German officers knew that the military simply didn't have the men or materials for anything but this more elastic approach.

WHILE THE GERMANS FALTERED, the Allies pressed their advantage. Led by the Third Army under fiery General George Patton, American troops had dashed nearly 400 miles from the Normandy beaches and across France, culminating in the crushing blow to German forces at the Falaise Gap. D Day had been the foothold, but the fighting at Falaise had finally broken the German hold on Normandy.

In all honesty, Ike had not expected the Germans to collapse so quickly. Consequently, the Allied advance had outpaced its supply lines. The roads and bridges that the Air Corps had bombed so effectively to thwart the Germans now meant difficulties in transporting Allied supplies. The famed Red Ball Express had trucked supplies to keep up with the troops on the front, but it was not enough. Simply put, Allied forces were spread too thin.

In some sense, it was a good problem to have. Reluctantly, though, Ike had called for Patton to halt. Ike could not send Americans yet deeper into enemy country without fuel, ammunition, food, or adequate medical care. The situation left American troops too vulnerable to counter-attack if the enemy regrouped. The Germans were notoriously good at that.

German forces were quickly coming to what would become known as the West Wall. They had lost France at great cost. Between the D Day landing on June 6 and early September, it was not unreasonable to state that the Germans had lost more than 300,000 men. That was nearly half the 1944 population of Boston or the entire population of Columbus, Ohio.

While the human losses alone were hard to bear, the Germans also had lost hundreds of tanks and almost countless vehicles and horses, not to mention artillery captured or destroyed by the Allies. There were no replacements for those men or for that equipment. War was a meat grinder. Every man they lost, every tank destroyed, practically every shell fired, could not be replaced—or not replaced easily. The Allies were wearing down their enemy through sheer numbers and seemingly endless resources. In a single year, American factories produced thousands of Sherman tanks.

As for the Luftwaffe, it was now mostly like an eagle with clipped wings, having only about 650 serviceable planes of any kind. With the Luftwaffe outnumbered ten to one, the skies over Europe mostly belonged to the Allies.

But the numbers on paper did not tell the only story. Working in the Germans' favor was the fact that conditions by mid-September were not conducive to air operations. Rain, sleet, and heavy fog kept the planes grounded. The grounding of the planes enabled the Germans to re-organize. Just when it seemed that they were at their lowest point, when they must surely be beaten and the war must be over, they had a talent for managing to mount an active defense. Grudgingly, Ike also had to admit that the Germans made far fewer tactical mistakes than the Allied forces. But they had no cushion.

The Germans were far from beaten and the fighting was far from over. After the mostly flat countryside of coastal and central France, they were now in terrain that favored defense, with hills, forests, rivers, and even the old fortresses of the Siegfried Line. If Normandy had been the Atlantic Wall, then this was Germany's West Wall. Rather than giving up, as Ike had hoped, the enemy only seemed to be fighting harder.

The main goal of concern right now was not the Rhine, but one of its tributaries, the Moselle River. Currently, the bloodiest fighting of the autumn campaign was about to take place on the banks of the Moselle.

Both the Germans and the Americans needed to get across the waterway *and then* make their way to the Rhine. The Germans were mostly on the other side of the Moselle by now, which meant that they had destroyed or were trying to destroy the Moselle bridges. This meant that U.S. Forces must build pontoon bridges, which was a time-consuming task usually undertaken under fire.

The Supreme Allied Commander thought about all of the German tanks, artillery, and machine guns being brought to bear against Allied troops that the Germans now saw as invaders. With no way to go but forward, American troops would have to brave the maelstrom and ford the Moselle River as the first step toward invading Germany itself.

"God help them," Ike said.

CHAPTER THREE

THE NEXT MORNING, Cole and the rest of the squad woke up wet to the bone from the rain. Even the leather of their boots was soaked through. They heard firing in the distance, and the thump of bigger guns that might be tanks or artillery.

"Beautiful morning," Vaccaro said, tugging at his poncho. "What do I want for breakfast? Maybe eggs and bacon, or a nice fresh bagel. How about you, Cole? Bet you could go for some squirrel stew or whatever it is you hillbillies eat for breakfast."

"Biscuits and gravy," Cole said quietly. Between his knees stood the stubby machine gun, as sheltered from the weather as possible. It was against Cole's nature not to take care of any weapon, even one that he didn't much like. "Wouldn't that be somethin'? My mama made biscuits and gravy when we had flour and milk. When pa didn't drink up the money. Everybody got one biscuit and one ladle of gravy and we thought we was kings and queens." Cole shook his head at the memory.

Coming from Cole, that had been quite a speech. Vaccaro seemed about to say something mocking but fell quiet, looking at the far-away look on Cole's lean face. Vaccaro had never worried about getting enough to eat, but he could see echoes of hunger in Cole's lean frame. He finally said, "There's not gonna be any biscuits and gravy this morning. There's not even gonna be any hot coffee."

Sergeant Woodbine was moving among the men, reminding them to put on dry socks if they had them and to oil their weapons. It was a fact that an infantryman had to take care of his feet first and foremost. Wet boots, wet socks—it was a surefire path to blisters or even trench foot or frostbite once the weather turned cold.

Captain Norton sat apart from the men, under the relative shelter of a tree branch over which had been rigged a canvas tent half. Of course, Norton hadn't done the rigging himself but had made his men do it for him.

Leaning against the tree was Cole's rifle. Norton hadn't bothered to make sure that the Springfield stayed dry. There is was, getting wet in the rain, and it was only with a huge effort that Cole didn't walk over there and set him straight. The lazy son of a bitch didn't deserve a pop gun, much less Cole's rifle.

The captain was huddled over a tiny stove, apparently intent on making himself a hot cup of coffee. The men had to make do with canteen water or attempting to dissolve a packet of instant coffee in a cold cup of water. Captain Norton didn't seem too concerned about rusty weapons and wet feet, so it was hard to say whether Norton had ordered Woodbine to check on the squad or if he had elected to do that himself, which was just the thing a competent sergeant would do.

"You boys good?" Sergeant Woodbine asked, approaching them.

"I could use some bacon and eggs," Vaccaro said. "And some hot coffee. Maybe I'll go ask the captain to share."

Woodbine snorted. "You go ahead and do that," he said. "Just don't ask me for help getting his boot out of your ass."

The sergeant moved off, his comment showing that he didn't necessarily hold Captain Norton in high regard.

Everybody knew that there were good officers and bad officers. But a good sergeant did his duty regardless. He owed the men that much. A few minutes later, when Norton gave the order, Woodbine got everyone up and moving.

In the dawn light, the unit continued moving east. The unit had been cobbled together and it showed in the way that the men drew invisible lines among themselves. There seemed to be a grudging silence hanging over the men. This came from being a unit that was cobbled together, an end result that was more like hamburger or sausage than steak. Cole and Vaccaro, along with the two men from their original squad, had slept apart from the others and eaten their rations together. The other men did the same.

Normally, soldiers from different units got along well enough, even if they didn't work together with the easy familiarity of men who had fought side by side for weeks. These men lacked cohesion. They were missing that element of trust, a bond of brotherhood, that only came from weeks together in the field.

Soldiers from different units were normally happy to trade anything, especially news and Army gossip. But Captain Norton's actions in taking away Cole's rifle had driven a wedge between the two groups. It was bad enough that there were Germans to worry about without dealing with the whims of bad officers, but that was the Army for you.

Cole pushed his thoughts aside and focused on the countryside around them. No sense letting himself get killed over being distracted by Norton. The grease gun wouldn't be much of a defense until the Germans materialized within spitting distance, but his eyes never stopped searching the roadside fields and woods for any threat.

His eyes felt gritty from lack of sleep. Captain Norton hadn't bothered to post a guard. When Sergeant Woodbine had suggested it, the captain claimed it wasn't necessary. Cole and Vaccaro had taken turns sleeping during the night. No matter what the captain said, Cole knew that the Germans wouldn't mind cutting their throats during the night, never mind the fact that they were retreating.

The rain had let up, so that was something.

Summer was giving way to fall. They could feel it in the chill mornings and in the way that the shadows stretched long and dark by late afternoon. Fall always had been Cole's favorite time of year in the mountains.

They were heading east toward the Moselle River. Trouble was, so were several thousand Germans. They couldn't exactly complain that they had not run into any Wehrmacht troops, but the thought of entire German divisions on the move made them uneasy. At any moment, they might run into a rear-guard unit—or worse, into a panzer.

Signs of the Germans were everywhere. They passed the ruins of several tanks, reduced to blackened hulks of steel thanks to the P47 Thunderbolts constantly hunting for German columns. They also encountered more than a few dead Germans. Some wore the headgear of tank crew members, and their bodies tended to be badly burned. Either their comrades had been in too much of a hurry to bury them, or maybe there hadn't been anyone left alive to see to the task. The lucky ones now lay in fresh graves in the nearby fields, marked by makeshift crosses.

Some of the men in Captain Norton's unit paused to plunder the bodies. The smell was awful, but that didn't keep them from searching for prized SS insignia or possibly a Luger. Cole and the others looked on with disapproval. Norton should have put a stop to it, but he himself couldn't seem to resist doing his share of plundering. While his men scoured the remains of a tank, Norton bent over a body and removed the dead German's *Hundemarken*—the Wehrmacht's version of dog tags.

"That's pretty low for an officer," Vaccaro muttered.

"I reckon he's a ninety-day wonder," Cole replied, referring to the three-month training program that turned recent college graduates into officers. "Not much better than a shavetail."

A shavetail was derogatory slang for a new lieutenant that referred to an old Army term for untrained mules, back when they had pulled supply wagons. Norton was actually worse than a shavetail because he seemed to know just enough to be confident in his own abilities, and thus, all the more dangerous.

As a result of this fascination with collecting souvenirs, their pace through the countryside was slow and Norton's men were paying more attention to the dead Germans than they were to the possibility that live Germans could appear at any moment and turn them into dead Americans.

Norton's sergeant drifted toward Cole and the other snipers. He was a big man, well over six feet tall, and the fact that he stooped constantly to make himself less of a target gave him a lumbering appearance.

"Dumbasses," he said, nodding at the men poking at the German bodies. "One of those Krauts is gonna be booby-trapped, and then that'll be the end of that."

"Captain ought to put a stop to it," Cole said.

"You try telling him," the sergeant said. He spat. "He ain't gonna listen to me."

"Then he sure as hell won't listen to me," Cole said. "I don't reckon we hit it off too good."

The sergeant made a noise that could have been a laugh, if there had been any mirth in it. "The name's Woodbine," he said.

"I'm Cole. That there's Vaccaro."

"I've been in France since Utah beach. How about you boys?"

"Omaha," Cole said.

Sergeant Woodbine gave a low whistle. "Omaha, huh? I understand that was some shit."

"Didn't nobody get a welcome mat put out for them that day, no matter what beach you was on." Cole thought about Jimmy Turner, just nineteen years old, machine-gunned by the Germans despite Cole's efforts to keep him alive. "We done lost a lot of good men that day."

"You'd be right about that," Woodbine said. He lowered his voice. "Listen, that business about the captain taking your rifle away ... well, it just isn't right, but there's not a damn thing I can do about it. Norton makes his own rules."

"Ain't your fault," Cole said. "It is what it is."

"Still, it doesn't mean I agree with it. I said something about it, and he told me to go to hell. You said your name was Cole?" His eyes went to the Confederate flag that Jimmy Turner had painted on Cole's helmet. The sergeant's eyebrows went up in recognition. "Say, you're that sniper, aren't you? The one that was in the newspaper? I remember the helmet from the picture."

Cole looked away. "I don't know what you're talkin' about."

The sergeant snorted. "Ha! Just how many guys

named Cole are there walking around with sniper rifles?"

Vaccaro spoke up. "It's him, all right, Sergeant. You won't find a better shot in the whole damn Army."

"Which makes it even dumber that Norton took your rifle away," Woodbine said. With a frown, he reached into his pocket and produced a roll of medical tape. He tore off a couple of strips and gave them to Cole. "Norton wanted you to cover up that flag, so I'd do just that if I were you. If Norton is happy, then we'll all be happy."

Cole slapped the tape haphazardly across the front of the helmet. "Officers always reckon they know better."

"They do now, don't they? He—" Woodbine started to say more, but was cut short when Cole grabbed the sergeant by the shoulder and shoved him toward the ground. Half a second later, a mortar round exploded in the road ahead. The screaming that followed told them that someone had been hit.

"Germans!" Norton shouted.

Vaccaro snorted. "What the hell did he expect? Vikings?"

They scrambled behind the wrecked hulk of a tank. A couple of bullets pinged off the blackened armor. Captain Norton ran to join them, crouching behind the wrecked tank and figuring out what to do next.

After these many months in France, Norton's men were far from being greenhorns. They hadn't frozen in the road but had scattered toward whatever shelter they could find. The trouble was that they were keeping their heads down, not bothering to shoot back. The man who had been hit by mortar shrapnel lay writhing in the road. There was no hope of helping him, not with the Germans shooting at them.

"I want fire superiority!" the sergeant bellowed. "Take out that mortar position!"

Now that a command had finally been given, the men in the squad responded, opening up on the Germans after the initial moments of confusion.

From the rate of fire from the Germans, it seemed that the GIs had run into a small squad tasked with holding up any pursuing Allied forces. This was definitely not the entire Wehrmacht, but a smaller unit left behind to fight a rear-guard action. That much was a relief. The German position was anchored by an armored Kübelwagen, flipped on its side. Its location at a slight bend in the road gave the Germans a commanding view of any movement on the road. It was the perfect setup for an ambush, and the Americans led by Captain Norton had walked right into it.

Another mortar pounded the road, showering

their hiding place with mud. The Germans kept up a steady rifle fire, their shots pinging off the wrecked tank.

"I never thought I'd say it, but it's a good thing the Jerries know how to build a tank," Vaccaro said.

"Can't be more than half a dozen Jerries," Cole replied. "But they got us pinned down right good. I can see that mortar crew from here. Give me your rifle a minute. Let me see if I can pick 'em off."

Grinning, Vaccaro started to hand Cole his scoped Springfield.

"What the hell are you doing?"

They turned to find Captain Norton glaring at them.

"Sir?"

"That's your weapon, soldier," he said to Vaccaro. "You keep that rifle unless I tell you different. Private Cole has his own weapon."

"Yes, sir." With a glance at Cole, Vaccaro took the rifle back. Here they were, pinned down by a handful of Germans, and Norton still had it in for Cole.

It turned out that Norton wasn't finished. "Besides, he's not the only one around here who can shoot. Now, get the hell out of the way."

Norton put the sniper rifle that he had taken from Cole to his own shoulder. For Cole's part, it was like seeing another man with your girl. Norton propped it against an edge of the tank's hulk. The

Germans were no more than 200 feet away. Even without a scope or binoculars, they could just see the steel-gray helmets of the German mortar crew in their dug-in position. Not that the Germans were an easy target.

As they watched, Norton took a long time lining up the sights. Meanwhile, the Germans got off another mortar round, showering them all with mud and whistling shrapnel.

Finally, Norton fired.

"Did I get one?" he barked excitedly.

"No, sir," replied Sergeant Woodbine, who was watching the German position through binoculars. "Maybe try again?"

"You bet your ass I'll try again."

Norton took his time, but his second shot missed, too. He fired again. He hadn't bothered to time his shots to coincide with a mortar round, so that the Germans quickly identified his position. Rifle rounds ricocheted off the ruined tank, so close that Norton had to duck his head. Out in the road, they could hear West calling for help. Bullets erupted in geysers all around him; it was a wonder that he hadn't been hit again.

"Sir, you want me to try?" Cole asked the captain. "I know I can pick 'em off from here."

Norton turned on Cole, his face livid. "God-dammit, Cole! This rifle isn't zeroed in properly. You call yourself a soldier? I ought to transfer you to mess duty."

Cole had a lot to say in response, but he kept his mouth shut. Besides, they had bigger things to worry about. The Germans continued to keep them pinned down. Peering out, Cole could see West writhing in the mud.

"Aww, to hell with it," Cole announced. "You boys cover me."

Without another word, he dashed from behind the wrecked tank, holding the grease gun at hip level and keeping his finger on the trigger as he ran. The burst of fire wasn't accurate, but it was enough to make the Germans keep their heads down.

He reached West and bent down to help him up. West was too big for Cole to carry, but he got West's arm across his shoulder and managed to half drag, half carry him toward the relative safety of the wrecked tank. Bullets whipped the air and another mortar round hit the road.

"Let 'em have it!" Sergeant Woodbine shouted.

The Americans emptied their M-1s at the Germans, firing furiously enough to buy Cole and West precious seconds. They tumbled behind the panzer, West grunting in agony from the pain of his wounds.

Immediately, Vaccaro went to work on West,

giving him a shot of morphine, dousing his wounds with sulfa powder, and wrapping them tight.

Norton sat with his back to the tank, clutching the sniper rifle, and looking white-faced. When the Germans had returned fire, a couple of rounds from their Mausers had passed close enough to his ear that he felt the air vibrant. His legs had involuntarily turned to Jell-O.

"We'll have to work around them, sir," Woodbine said. "There can't be more than a half dozen Jerries up there, but they've got that goddamn road covered."

"Don't you think I know that?" Captain Norton snapped.

The sergeant clapped his mouth shut. "Yes, sir."

Norton started to organize the encirclement, but Cole interrupted.

"Sir—"

"Goddammit, Cole! What the hell is it now?"

"It's the Germans, sir. They ain't there no more."

Norton risked a peek around the tank. The hole that had held the mortar team appeared empty. The soldiers behind the Kübelwagen also seemed to have disappeared.

"They're gone," Norton said. "Guess we chased them off."

Cole wasn't so sure. The Germans would likely set another ambush ahead. "The thing about Krauts is that the ones you don't kill today, you just have to fight tomorrow."

Norton glared at Cole. "You've got this whole war figured out, huh? Good for you. Now shut the hell up and get a move on."

CHAPTER FOUR

MAYBE CAPTAIN NORTON didn't want to hear it, but Cole was right about someone just having to fight the Germans later on. The Germans who slipped away from Captain Norton's squad went down another road, eager to escape rather than fight. But when they heard a vehicle approaching, they quickly set up another ambush, knowing that it was more likely to be an American vehicle than one of their own.

In a Jeep rushing toward the unseen Germans sat Brigadier General Winston Bell Tolliver III, known to his friends and family as "Bean" Tolliver because he'd been the smallest and youngest in a family of large male relatives. It wasn't really right to say that Tolliver was sitting in the Jeep. In reality, he held on for dear life in the passenger seat of the Jeep hurtling down the dirt road. Jeeps did not have seat belts, so it was either hold tight or get bounced out into the muddy road. The general kept banging his shins painfully against the metal dashboard.

Despite his nickname, Bean Tolliver was actually of average height and build, though starting to go soft in the middle. With fifty on the horizon, the general had a touch of gray around the temples, and the hair on top starting to go thin. His balding head was hidden beneath a pristine steel helmet emblazoned with a single star. Just last year he had started needing glasses to read fine print, but he kept those tucked into a pocket.

He was a staff officer assigned to Eisenhower's HQ, playing a key role in logistics. The bulk of his job was to oversee the ordering of supplies from tires to gasoline to spare parts for shipment to France. Once those tires and gasoline and spare parts arrived, it was someone else's problem to get them into the field. Here in Normandy, the Red Ball Express had mostly taken care of that.

Tolliver was good at this job, but it wasn't exactly the sort of role that left one covered in glory and bedecked with medals. Despite the stars on his collar, Tolliver sometimes felt that he didn't quite measure up to combat officers.

His uniform had managed to maintain a few of its creases even after a couple of days in the field. Unlike General Patton, he was not armed with a pair of pearl-handled revolvers. He did, however, carry the standard issue Browning 1911. Tolliver rarely had need of a sidearm but thought it would be wise to take one along as he headed into Indian Country.

As the war seemed to be winding down—some claimed the Germans would be done by Christmas—anyone and everyone who could finagle it was trying to get some sort of field command, or to at least get close enough to the fighting to hear actual shots exchanged in anger. The desire to own some piece of the actual war also fueled quite a market in battlefield souvenirs. He'd even heard of a German *Stalhelm* bring swapped for a bottle of Kentucky bourbon.

Once peacetime arrived, there would be a lot of jockeying for the limited number of leadership roles, and those with some form of field command would be better positioned to survive the culling that was sure to take place once the war was over and the Army didn't need so many officers.

Tolliver, though, was thinking that he might be fine with getting out of the Army after this war. His brother-in-law had a large Ford dealership near Washington, D.C., and had already offered Tolliver a job as the general manager. Tolliver was mulling it over. It was strange to think that by next summer, he might be back in the States, ordering tires and gasoline and spare parts for civilian cars and trucks.

Maybe it was foolishness or curiosity, or equal

parts of both, but he'd had a desire to see some of the war before it moved into its final stages. When the opportunity presented itself to get out in the field, General Tolliver had jumped at the chance. He had wrangled a trip into the field to check on the supply chain first-hand, instead of relying on the written reports typed by his clerks.

His was a military family in many ways, but Tolliver had never actually seen any combat. Hell, he thought, he'd scarcely ever been close enough to the fighting to hear artillery. The thought made him a little ashamed. And so he'd pressed this Jeep and young driver into service to see a little of the war before it was over.

Tolliver couldn't help comparing himself to his grandfather, Confederate Colonel Amos Tolliver, who had been a real soldier, fighting at Pickett's Charge and Gaines' Mill, among other places, until he had finally fallen, mortally wounded, in an inconsequential skirmish known locally as "The Battle of Gifford's Field." Tolliver was something of a Civil War history buff and he had visited the field, which he imagined had looked very much the same eighty years before. Back then, the field outside Richmond grew a ragged crop of cornstalks as Union troops closed in on the Confederate capital.

It was exciting to think of what he had seen through his eyes. Had he ever met General Lee or

Stonewall Jackson? Colonel Tolliver was forgotten to most, and he certainly had not been famous in his day. There weren't any mentions of him in most of the history books.

His grandson knew the feeling. As an obscure brigadier general working to supply the troops, Tolliver's name would not have rung many bells with Eisenhower, who mostly dealt with the likes of Bradley, Patton and Montgomery. To be sure, they were a handful.

The Jeep caught the edge of a shell hole and bounced, forcing Tolliver to get a grip on the Jeep. Again, his shins whacked painfully against the metal dash. With just 60 horsepower, the four-wheel-drive Jeep wasn't fast, but it churned up the muddy road. As for the name, Jeep, nobody was sure where that had come from, but it had certainly stuck. The sturdy vehicle was helping them win the war, but it wasn't about to be confused with a Cadillac.

Like his grandfather, General Tolliver would have much preferred riding a horse, but that was modern warfare for you, all gasoline and gears rather than saddles and hooves. Tolliver knew what kept a modern Army going because he had written requisition orders for most of those supplies.

"Which way, sir?" the driver asked, coasting the Jeep to a stop at a crossroads that lacked any sort of road sign.

The young driver was clearly anxious, his eyes darting around at the woods and fields for any sign of Germans. Did the driver, who was hardly more than a teenager, know something he didn't?

The truth was, Tolliver didn't have a clue which way to go.

He wasn't particularly worried—not yet, at least. The Germans were supposed to be done and gone, but they apparently hadn't gotten that particular memo. Already this morning, they'd had a close call when they had spotted a German tank in the distance. Fortunately, the tank either hadn't seen them in turn or had not been interested in something as inconsequential as a lone Jeep. Still, the sight of the panzer had left them both shaken. That was a little too close for comfort.

In avoiding the tank, however, one wrong turn had led to another. It had been a compounding of errors that led them to this anonymous crossroads. The retreating Germans had removed all the road signs or pointed them in the wrong direction in an effort to confuse the Allied advance.

He hadn't counted on getting lost. In fact, he was more than a little embarrassed about it. He was supposed to be a general, after all. The young soldier kept his eyes on Tolliver, waiting for some kind of instructions. Out of the corner of his eye, Tolliver saw that the kid gripped the steering wheel so tightly that his knuckles were white.

His driver wasn't annoyed. He was scared.

They had lost contact with the American advance more than two hours ago, and it was just possible they would round a bend in the road and come upon an entire SS regiment. If that happened, Tolliver's field trip would get unpleasant in a hurry.

"Just let me, uh, get our bearings," Tolliver said.

"Yes, sir."

Tolliver took out his map. He sighed, and reluctantly, he fished out his glasses in order to read the tiny place names. The fact that the glasses made him look like an old man likely did not inspire much confidence in the driver.

This was already the fourth time he had looked at the map in the last hour. The problem with a map was that it was really only useful if you knew where you were in the first place. Tolliver didn't have any idea. *Goddammit*. The muddy roads and brown fields were all starting to look the same to him. They had gone down one unmarked road and then another, until they had ended up at this spot—wherever the hell that was.

The landscape around them consisted of low, rolling hills covered in pastureland and patches of woods. It was pretty country, or it would be if it hadn't been so gray and overcast. One good thing was the Army Air Corps was grounded, meaning that their Jeep wouldn't be mistaken for a Kraut vehicle and strafed into oblivion. Up ahead, bigger hills began and marched toward Belgium and the Ardennes region. Somewhere up in those hills was the Moselle River, and beyond that, the Rhine itself.

As he studied the map, turning it one way and then another in hopes that it would reveal their location, he felt his driver's eyes studying him doubtfully. The kid seemed to be wondering just what sort of general he was driving around.

"Sir?" the driver asked again, one foot on the clutch, the other on the brake. He seemed anxious to get going, rather than to idle here like sitting ducks at this godforsaken crossroads.

Tolliver wasn't going to pretend to know something he didn't. "Son, if you have any idea where we are, I hope that you will speak up."

"I'm sorry, sir." The driver looked at him nervously. "I haven't got a clue, sir."

Tolliver glanced at the sky to get his bearings from the sinking sun, then waved his hand at the road that led west. Generals made decisions, he reminded himself, even when they were supply officers. He forced himself to grin, putting a brave face on it. "The Moselle River must be in that direction. We're bound to run into our boys before we get there."

He didn't add, *unless we run into the Germans first*, but they both seemed to be thinking it.

"Yes, sir," the driver said without much enthusiasm, and put the Jeep into gear. They jostled along in silence for several minutes.

"What's your name, son?

"Smith, sir. Ralph Smith."

"How old are you, Ralph?"

"I just turned twenty, sir."

Tolliver shook his head and said, "I've got socks older than you. Where you from?"

"Connecticut, sir."

"The land of Mark Twain," the general said.

"If you say so, sir." The young soldier looked confused. A thought seemed to come to him. "But wasn't *Huckleberry Finn* set on the Mississippi River?"

"Ah, you're a reader."

"We had to read it in high school, sir."

"You're right that *Huckleberry Finn* is set on the Mississippi River, but Mark Twain lived in Hartford, Connecticut, for more than 20 years. That's where he wrote the book, you know. He lived right next door to Harriet Beecher Stowe, who wrote *Uncle Tom's Cabin*."

"*Uncle Tom's Cabin*? I've heard of it, sir, but I haven't read that one," he said.

"It's not a very popular book where I'm from," said Tolliver, who had grown up in Virginia. "That book caused a lot of trouble. You might even say that it helped to start the War Between the States."

"Yes, sir."

Their conversation seemed to have reached a dead end, but the road stretched on ahead. Tolliver felt like an idiot for having dragged this kid out here and gotten them both lost. For what purpose? If Tolliver was being honest with himself, he had to admit that he had come out here mainly to satisfy his curiosity about the front—and perhaps so that he could lay some claim to having seen something of the war beyond stacks of forms on his desk.

The fact that Smith had to swerve around a large crater left by a German shell more than likely saved them both from being killed instantly when a burst of fire raked the road, just where the Jeep would have been a second before if Smith hadn't jerked to the wheel to the right.

Directly ahead of them stood a low stone wall. Behind it, Tolliver caught a glimpse of several square helmets and the flash of muzzles. They were taking fire. Shocked, Tolliver realized that these were Germans.

The driver slewed the Jeep sideways, trying to get turned around, but the muddy road didn't cooperate. The vehicle moved sluggishly, more like a ship turning than a race car. Then the tires lost any purchase and spun hopelessly in the mud. They were sitting ducks for the Germans. Desperately, the driver worked the gears and hit the gas, but they were stuck fast.

"Out!" Tolliver ordered.

They both jumped out into the mud, putting the Jeep between themselves and the shooting. Beside him, the kid was wide-eyed with terror.

Tolliver was sure that his own expression wasn't much different. They both hunkered against the Jeep as shots ripped the air overhead. The Jeep shuddered and clanged as bullets struck it. Thank God for Detroit steel, Tolliver thought. Lucky for them, the Germans didn't seem to have a machine gun.

Gunfire chattered, still chewing up the Jeep, but the sturdy vehicle was good at stopping bullets.

The young soldier had remembered to grab his M-1. Tolliver saw the driver start to straighten up, getting ready to return fire. In his mind's eye, he could see what was going to happen if that kid stuck his head up. That was too much of a target for the Germans to miss.

Tolliver pulled him back down by the back of belt. "Hold on, son. They'll cut you down right quick. Sit tight."

He didn't have a plan yet, but sitting here getting shot at wasn't much of one. He chanced a look around the back end of the Jeep. The Germans were taking cover behind a low stone wall beside the road.

"We need to get into those woods. Those Germans are retreating, and they'd be happy to see us high-tail it out of here. I'll cover you."

He already had the 1911 Browning in his hands. It didn't have the range or accuracy of a rifle, but there was a reason why a .45 slug was nicknamed a flying ashtray. You had to respect a big, fat bullet coming your way.

"Sir?"

"Go!" he shouted, and opened fire from the back end of the Jeep, gripping the pistol in two hands and aiming each shot. The general's desk job did not require much shooting, but Tolliver had grown up around guns and still hunted on occasion. He was a good shot. Each fat slug hit the top of the wall sheltering the Germans and sent shards of stone flying. The Germans kept their heads down under the sudden barrage of .45 slugs.

He glanced over his shoulder long enough to see the driver cover the distance to the woods in seconds, running like a rabbit, God bless him. Then the kid threw himself down on his belly in the underbrush. Tolliver hoped to hell that the kid remembered to cover *him*. He crouched, then took off running for the woods. He saw with satisfaction that the driver was shooting back. The young soldier had remembered his training.

Tolliver got in among the cover offered by the low

shrubs, and then they both moved deeper into the woods. It seemed to take him a long time to catch his breath after sprinting for the woods, and his heart hammered far out of proportion to the amount of exertion. Getting too old for this, he thought.

He sure as hell hadn't planned on fighting any Germans.

Honest to God, right about now, he missed his desk.

The kid was looking at him, still wide-eyed, shaken up and scared.

I may be nothing more than a bean counter, Tolliver thought, *but I owe it to this kid to try to get him back home after dragging him out here.*

He touched the young soldier's arm, reassuring him. "Sit tight," he whispered. "If those Germans do come after us, you know the drill. You move deeper into the woods, and I'll cover you."

"Yes, sir."

Tolliver hoped it wouldn't come to that. The magazine of his .45 was almost empty. What was he going to do, charge them while screaming the Rebel Yell? Charging the enemy hadn't been such a great idea in 1864, and it was an even worse idea in 1944.

Fortunately, he'd been right about the Germans not bothering to give chase. He could just see them through the trees. Once it was clear that the Americans had fled, they came out from behind the wall.

There were only a dozen of them, but that was enough. They walked over to the Jeep, seemed to debate taking it, but then headed down the road on foot in the direction that Tolliver had been traveling in before the ambush.

Tolliver was a little amazed, simply because he had not seen the enemy up close yet. Those were Germans, all right.

Once they were sure that the Germans had gone, Tolliver led the way out of the bushes. He and the driver were now scratched and muddy, but they were alive.

His driver walked up to the Jeep and whistled when he saw the bullet holes.

"Think she'll run?"

"Only one way to find out, sir. We'll see if she starts."

"Good idea." Tolliver clapped the driver on the shoulder. "That was a nice bit of driving, turning the Jeep like that. You kept us from being killed, I'd say."

"Thank you, sir." Though shaken, the kid still managed a smile.

As it turned out, the Jeep did start. But it was still stuck in the mud. With the kid behind the wheel, Tolliver got behind the Jeep and set his feet, then as the kid gave it some gas, he gave to vehicle a big shove to help the tires break free of the mud.

"Don't stop!" He waved the driver on and jogged alongside until he could pull himself into the Jeep.

"Where to, sir?"

He told Private Smith to return to the last crossroads they had passed and turn left. "With any luck, there won't be any Germans down that road," he said, wishing he felt as confident about that as he sounded.

CHAPTER FIVE

BROKEN AND BLEEDING, what was left of the German army was streaming toward the Fatherland. The squad that had ambushed Tolliver and his driver was just the remnant of a shattered unit. The entire German military had collapsed in the wake of the defeat at the Falaise Gap. The retreat was about as orderly as one could expect, considering that the fighting had decimated tens of thousands of soldiers. Huge numbers of German troops were either dead, wounded, or captured.

At Falaise, the Germans had been effectively trapped between British and Canadian forces to the north and American and Polish forces to the south, leaving just a narrow escape route. The image that it called to mind was that of troops pouring through a funnel—under fire all the way.

Devastating as the Falaise Gap had been for Wehrmacht forces, the Allies had also lost an opportunity to utterly crush the enemy. Logistics and communications had worked against the Allies, along with the reluctance to close the gap in such close quarters for fear of Allied troops from several nations accidentally firing on one another in what might be described as a circular firing squad situation. General Eisenhower had held back, determining that losses from friendly fire would undermine tenuous relations and the war effort far more than allowing the battered Germans to escape. For decades to come, historians would debate Ike's fateful decision.

Having passed through that gauntlet, the Germans' best plan now was to retreat in hopes of regrouping later. Although the Allies nipped at their heels and Allied planes harassed them, the retreat was orderly, led by battle-hardened NCOs and officers.

Some troops rode on horses. A few lucky ones—mostly the officers—rode in motorized vehicles. Most men had to rely on their own two feet to carry them toward the Moselle River, and then the Rhine beyond. They knew that they were not walking toward salvation, but toward a final stand. One last chance to save the Fatherland. The Allies were closing in from the west, and from the east came the hated Russians, flooding toward the Fatherland like an inexorable red tide.

* * *

RETREATING with the German forces was General Karl Unterbrink. The defeat at the Falaise Gap had left the military fragmented, flowing in motley units toward Germany in hopes of reorganizing. For now, these German troops counted themselves lucky to be alive.

The small unit that Unterbrink commanded was hardly large enough to be directed by someone of his rank. A general normally commanded a brigade or a division, not a collection of ragged *Soldaten*. There were remnants of units, and men in groups of two and three, all gathered together like metal filings to a magnet. As a general, it was Unterbrink who served as this magnet. Unterbrink was determined to be the commander that these hard-fighting men deserved.

This morning, he'd had sixty-three men. Yesterday, he'd had sixty-six. Sometime during the night, those three must have decided to take their chances in surrendering to the Allies rather than fighting it out to the last man.

Gefreiter Hauer had taken the head count. A sniper by training, Hauer had been with him since before the Allied invasion. Unterbrink had made

Hauer his de facto aide de camp and scout, answering only to the general. He was loyal as a Rottweiler and twice as vicious.

"Three less than yesterday," Hauer said. "The deserters can't have much of a start, sir. I can bring them back and shoot them in front of the others to set an example."

Unterbrink wasn't happy about losing three men during the night to desertion, but he put a brave face on it. "We are better off without them if they do not want to fight," he said.

He wore an officer's double-breasted greatcoat that was a bit too warm for the weather, but he knew that the days would be turning colder soon enough. Unterbrink didn't mind that; he had always liked the winter.

Even spattered with mud, Unterbrink managed to look dashing. Normally, the lapels of a general's coat had red facing, but Unterbrink had opted for a plain junior officer's field coat that made him less of a target for enemy snipers. He knew about snipers because he had put them to good use himself. Hauer was a case in point.

He had left the coat open just enough to make the two gold oak leaves and single gold bar combination on the collar of his tunic visible so that his rank was clear. He did not yet have a Knight's Cross at this throat, which rankled him a bit. He held out hope that the defense of the Fatherland would offer new opportunities to win one.

The coat was belted around the middle. For a man of fifty-two he was very fit, thanks to daily calisthenics that he kept up even during the retreat. On the belt he wore a holster containing a Luger. He wore an officer's Jodhpur-style trousers tucked into black riding boots. On his head, instead of the familiar *Stahlhelm*, he wore an officer's cap with goggles pulled up over the brim, nearly disguising the ornate braided officer's insignia known as "the cabbage patch" for its close resemblance to that humble vegetable.

Although Unterbrink had downplayed most outward displays of his rank to avoid becoming a target, there was no questioning that he had an air of command that had nothing to do with insignia and gold braid. He exuded authority.

"This way," Unterbrink shouted, standing in a Kübelwagen, the sturdy vehicle that was essentially the German equivalent of a Jeep. They had just emerged from a forested area into open ground surrounded by farm fields. He glanced at the sky, worried that Allied planes would appear at any moment now that his men were out in the open. "Hurry! *Hop, hop, hop!*"

He waved toward the right-hand road at an unmarked crossroads. He did not know the name of this place and it did not matter. The goal was simply to move west. A few modest houses stood nearby to create something of a crossroads village. A couple of young boys had come out to watch the soldiers go by, but no adults were in sight. The road to the left was blocked by the smoking ruin of a Panther tank. Two bodies lay just beyond it, still steaming like roasts taken from an oven. The smell of charred flesh hung over the crossroads. The general's stomach rumbled hungrily in spite of himself because the smell resembled roast pork. He found that reaction more curious than revolting. *Deep down, we are all beasts,* he thought.

The crossroads carnage was a horrific sight, but they were inured to it, having seen too many of their comrades killed. But these men were not defeated or beaten. They were soldiers. They would fight until the end.

Unterbrink loved them.

He was doing the best that he could for them, leading an orderly retreat, trying to get these men back to Germany.

He saw one young soldier struggling to juggle his gear, which included a haversack and Mauser K98, with the ungainly weight of a Panzerfaust. Unterbrink jumped down and went to sort him out.

"Here, give me that a minute," the general said, reaching for the Panzerfaust. The rocket-propelled weapon would make short work of any Sherman tanks that they came across, but it was an unwieldy burden, being a wooden stick nearly two meters in length with the heavy charge at one end. Unterbrink grabbed a length of rope from the car and tied it to both ends of the Panzerfaust to create a makeshift sling. He held the weapon while the soldier slipped it over a shoulder.

"Give that a try," Unterbrink said. "Keep it over your left shoulder like that, and you can still fire your rifle when you need to."

"Much better, sir."

Unterbrink climbed back into the Kübelwagen.

"Probst!" shouted a soldier going past, raising a canteen that likely contained something stronger than water.

The general grinned. "That's the spirit."

One of the men broke into song and the singing spread. The song was called "Erika." Popular since before the war, it was a rousing tune that stuck in one's head. The lyrics themselves were sentimental rather than martial:

BACK AT HOME, *there lives a little maiden*
  and she's called Erika.
  That girl is my faithful little darling
  and my joy, Erika!

                    .   .   .

Unterbrink felt a lump in his throat.

Sixty-three men. Such good men. He would command them as proudly as a division.

He watched them going by, singing now, carrying Panzerfaust over their shoulders, two MG-42 machine guns, ammunition. They might be short of fuel and food, but weapons remained plentiful. The soldiers' burdens were heavy, many were footsore or hungry, or they ached for their lost comrades. Energized by the patriotic song, they swung along the road with a new spring in their step.

The Allies had breached the Atlantic Wall and the Germans had lost the battle for France at the Falaise Gap. Their broken forces streamed toward Germany and what was called the West Wall—the Fatherland's last line of defense. There, what remained of the German military would make a last stand, trying to ignore the fact that the dreaded Russians were pressing toward Berlin on the Eastern Front. The Leader kept promising super weapons that would turn the tide. Unterbrink knew better. Victory or defeat would be in the hands of men such as these.

Battered and bleeding, the German nation was being forced to fight for its life on two fronts. Better than most, General Unterbrink understood that strategically, victory on two fronts was an impossible task. The best that they could hope for was to bring the enemy advance to a halt long enough to buy Germany time—or possibly a seat at the negotiating table.

Over the summer, a group of officers had tried to assassinate Hitler with a bomb. They had come close, but The Leader had survived to exact terrible revenge on the officers, along with their friends and families. Hundreds had been rounded up and shot. There were rumors of cruel punishments involving meat hooks and basement hangings carried out by the Gestapo, along with forced suicides.

Unterbrink thanked his lucky stars that he hadn't been part of that circle. Anyhow, if Hitler had been killed, there might have been a power struggle in the resulting vacuum just when Germany needed strength.

Hitler had consolidated power in the wake of the assassination attempt. The general thought that Hitler's command decisions were increasingly erratic and desperate, but Unterbrink kept such thoughts to himself. Besides, his war had come down to these sixty-three men and the need to get them across the Moselle River.

Off to one side of the crossroads, Hauer stood holding a sniper rifle. He was about average height but solidly built, like a heavyweight boxer. He was not singing but keeping watch over the neighboring woods and fields. Only when the last of the men had gone up the road did Hauer seem to relax.

The sniper's gaze fell upon the two young French boys who were still watching the last of the soldiers. One of the boys had started doing a goose step, marching back and forth along the road. The stiff-legged march had become familiar to French residents watching the German occupiers arrive. The retreating troops were not doing the goose step today. Clearly, the boy was mocking the Germans.

"What are you playing at?" Hauer demanded. "Do you think this is funny?"

Too late, the boys realized their mistake. The boys would have been better off running away, but they froze. Whether or not they spoke German didn't matter because they could understand the sniper's angry tone. Hauer walked over and cuffed the bigger boy violently in the head, knocking him to the ground. Hauer then kicked him savagely, causing the boy to cry out. Hauer would have kicked him again, but the boy was too quick and rolled away out of reach.

Coming to their senses, the boys ran off. The sniper started to raise his rifle to shoot them.

"Hauer, get in," the general said, fully aware that he had just spared the lives of the two French boys.

The sniper lowered his rifle and looked up. He had intense blue eyes. "Yes, sir."

Hauer walked over and got into the passenger seat. He set the rifle between his knees, within easy reach, the barrel pointing up. Unterbrink sat in the back seat, which was nearly overflowing with gear, from medical equipment to an iron curaiss from the Great War that Hauer had found in a barn. The Kübelwagen was one of only two vehicles available at the moment and had been pressed into service to carry whatever it could.

As he settled into the seat, Unterbrink could not resist a nervous glance at the skies.

"It looks like we have lost the Americans for now," the general said.

"They'll be right behind us. To be honest, sir, I'm more worried about their damn planes."

"Do you think that you can shoot down a plane with that rifle of yours?" the general asked.

"I can try." Hauer seemed to think it over, as if it was an actual possibility. "But I doubt it."

The general gave the sniper a sideways look, wondering if the man was serious. Shoot down a plane with a rifle? It would be just like the sniper to try. He liked Hauer's style, though; a few more like him, and the Wehrmacht might not be in retreat right now. Nonetheless, the general had to admit that there had been a few excesses along the road that had brought them here, and it was usually Hauer who was at the heart of them.

The young man had been a butcher before the war, and it showed in his occasional acts of brutality. He would have shot those two boys just now, for example. Unterbrink was usually willing to look the other way when the sniper went too far, so long as Hauer got results. As the situation became more desperate these last few weeks, the general had increasingly come to depend on Hauer when things became difficult. Hauer could be relied upon when there was hard, dirty work to be done. He could not but help to think of it as letting a dog off a leash. Hauer was his indeed his own personal Rottweiler.

Unterbrink lit a cigarette and sighed. He would have preferred a different war, and a different time. He often though of his ancestors, aristocratic Prussians who had served all the way back to the Napoleonic Wars. Their portraits had stared down from the walls of his ancestral home, proud men in immaculate uniforms shiny with gold braid and impressive medals. Those had been the days of swords and horses and black powder. Unterbrink was fighting in a war with tanks and planes and machine guns—and bloody butchers with telescopic sights on their high-powered rifles.

He pushed such thoughts aside. This was a time for action, not introspection. There would be plenty of time for that when the war was over—if they survived.

"We need to keep going. If we can just find a bridge across the Moselle, we'll be that much closer to the West Wall," Unterbrink announced. He unfolded a map, tapped it with a gloved finger. He continued after a moment, as if thinking out loud. "This place looks promising. Ville sur Moselle. It's just a few kilometers from here."

"Yes, sir. The sooner that we get across that river, the better," Hauer agreed.

"There will be antiaircraft guns and what's left of the Luftwaffe once we get closer to Germany, to give us some cover from these Allied planes," Unterbrink said.

Hauer glanced at the sky. Grunted. "Looks like rain. That would be a good thing for us! It would keep their planes grounded."

"Let's move out while we can." The general leaned forward and touched the driver's shoulder, and the Kübelwagen leaped forward.

CHAPTER SIX

Just a few miles to the north of Ville sur Moselle, American troops were preparing to fight their way across the river at the town of Dornot in order to establish a bridgehead.

Dornot was a good-sized village on the banks of the Moselle River. As a crossing point, it was less than ideal because any troops, tanks, or trucks would have to squeeze through the narrow main street in order to reach the river.

The road leading through the river valley wasn't much better, hemmed in on all sides by low hills, and currently a morass of mud from the cold, steady rain. And yet, more and more troops piled up on the muddy road, forcing the troops up ahead through the narrow places with the same physics as a tube of toothpaste. The problem was that as these troops pushed through, it became more urgent for the Americans to be able to get across the river.

In military parlance, a river crossing was known as a bridgehead. For American GIs, it was going to be a bloodbath.

And they knew it.

"I wish we'd get this over with," Private Robert "Frenchie" Tremblay said, the last word emerging an octave higher from his nervously constricted throat. Nobody bothered to kid him about it. They could actually see the Germans on the opposite bank of the river.

Waiting for them.

"I got to say, this is gonna be a bitch," said Private Marty Pulaski, crouched at his buddy's elbow.

The men had been in position since before dawn, waiting to pile into rubber boats for the attack across the Moselle. However, here it was past ten o'clock in the morning, and nothing had happened except that they had run out of cigarettes.

"It's a SNAFU, is what it is," Frenchie said. His nickname came from the fact that he spoke French fluently, thanks to parents who had grown up in Quebec before moving to the States for work. He spoke Canadian French, but it was clear enough for the locals to understand him. "Situation Normal, All Fouled Up. Nobody knows who's in charge."

Pulaski hid his grin at his buddy's definition of

SNAFU. Despite months of war and carnage, his friend couldn't quite bring himself to swear like a soldier. Frenchie was too much of a straight arrow for that. To Pulaski's way of thinking, the situation was more than Fouled Up—and the F-word that came to mind reflected that.

Soldiers loved a good rumor, and the hurried conferences they had witnessed between officers from various units seemed to back up what they'd heard. That would also explain the long wait. Two different units—one infantry, one armored—had ended up in this spot with orders from two different commanders. It was taking a while to wrangle out who was in charge and whether or not the attack should go forward even though it was evident to all that the Germans were dug in and ready for them.

Another rumor persisted that the Germans awaiting them were SS. The GIs had fought both SS and regular Wehrmacht in France. The Wehrmacht troops were not pushovers, but they had the good sense to surrender when things got rough. They didn't have a death wish. The SS troops fought to the last man. SS troops didn't expect to be taken prisoner, and they didn't *take* prisoners, either. If you found yourself surrounded, it was unlikely that you could expect any quarter from those SS bastards.

Unfortunately for the GIs, both rumors had a

basis in truth. There had been a real mix-up in the command structure that was causing confusion about the river crossing. If that wasn't bad enough, the German troops on the other side were, in fact, SS. The Americans would have to fight for every inch of that bridgehead against a determined adversary.

Both Frenchie Tremblay and Marty Pulaski belonged to Company F, 11th Infantry, which had seen its share of fighting during the months leading up to this point. They had lost close to 30 percent of their unit since the June landing, either wounded or killed. In fact, it seemed as if the time since D Day had been one long battle with a few snatches of sleep thrown in.

Some of the men couldn't take it anymore. There had been more than a few self-inflicted "accidental" shootings through a hand or foot—anything to get off the line. The Army kept that quiet. Then there were the genuine Section 8 cases where men had gone into catatonic states or simply balled up in a foxhole at the sound of a German 88 and then refused to leave. These guys weren't cowards—they had done their share, and then some—but something in their minds had snapped. They had reached the breaking point. The Army swept these cases under the rug because they were bad for morale.

Frenchie and Marty had been among the lucky

ones so far, but you wouldn't know it to look at them. Both young men had dark circles around their eyes from lack of sleep. Marty had developed a nasty-sounding wet cough as a result of the cold, rainy weather. Just the other morning, they had awakened to the sting of sleet pelting their faces. The men shivered and pulled their filthy uniforms closer.

It was only September, but winter came early to this part of Europe. So far, no winter gear had been issued. The supply lines were stretched too thin. The Army had enough trouble getting gasoline and ammo and medical supplies to the front, let alone warm socks. Many of those supplies were brought in by the heroic Red Ball Express, the nickname given to the supply truck drivers wrangling their way through the muddy roads all the way from the coast.

Like his buddy, Frenchie, Private Pulaski was looking out at the expanse of open water to the banks on the other side, knowing full well that the Germans were dug in and expecting them. This was not a scene for a postcard. The river was ninety yards wide here and six or seven feet deep, with a powerful current exacerbated by the recent rains. That current was deceptive because there were no rapids or anything else to disturb the surface. Instead, the current flexed like a smooth, brown muscle. The water had a dank, muddy smell that clung to the shoreline. From a soldier's point of view, the river was neither inviting nor scenic, but just another obstacle to cross.

On the other side of the river was a flood plain that stretched for around 400 yards before the land began to rise steeply. The only cover on the plain was provided by a patch of woods shaped roughly like a horseshoe. Just a mile from the river they could see the twin fortresses, Fort St. Blaise and Fort Sommy, part of the old Siegfried line of defense built by the Germans, that presided over the flood plain. Beyond those forts began the foothills of the Ardennes region, one of the most rugged and wild regions in central Europe.

Near these fortresses, German artillery had dug in to cover any river crossings by the Americans. The rugged terrain that provided good cover to ground forces, along with the wet weather, meant that the Army Air Corps no longer had all of the advantages. One benefit was that German armor seemed to be absent, having concentrated to the south to confront General Patton's forces.

Just then, a shell ripped in and struck just behind the American position. Dirt and debris showered the waiting troops. Moments later, another shell came at them from west of the river, this one hitting the poor guys anchoring the unit's right flank on the river bank.

Frenchie heard screams and saw the air fill with

clods of mud and chunks of what might be body parts. With the other men, he flattened himself against the wet ground, but the firing stopped.

"What a clusterfuck," Marty muttered. It didn't take a general to see that this was a lousy position. The riverbank offered minimal protection. Nobody liked being exposed to enemy artillery.

It didn't help that the Jerries still had a few stubborn pockets of artillery on *this* side of the river, which meant that the Allied forces were occasionally being shelled from both the front *and* the rear. While artillery had tried to soften up the German positions earlier that morning, it was hard to say how effective the barrage had been. The German positions were spread out and well protected by the fortresses or the low hills in which they sheltered. All in all, it was a hell of situation.

Finally, the order came to launch the boats. Marty and Frenchie slogged through the water to get the rubber boat away from the shore. They didn't have to go far because the banks of the Moselle dropped off steeply. This was an unforgiving river. They clambered over the sides into the boat and tried to find a comfortable way to sit.

"We're jammed in here like sardines," Marty muttered.

"More like sitting ducks," Frenchie said.

They both grabbed paddles and began to dig into the water. Their pace against the current felt agonizingly slow. Due to that current, Frenchie had no hope of landing directly across from their original position. Instead, their boat and all the rest had to settle for a point downstream.

Immediately, the ungainly, overloaded rubber boats came under enemy fire. Bursts from German machine guns swept the river. Tracers lit the gloom. The men in the boats kept low, but the rubber sides didn't provide any protection.

Mortar rounds burst periodically, erupting in fountains of water and shrapnel. Even boats that didn't lose all the men aboard to a burst of machine gun fire were shredded and began to sink. Loaded down with gear and ammunition, the men who found themselves trying to swim for it didn't stand a chance and quickly slipped under the surface. Those who could grabbed hold of a passing rubber raft, although the drag of the men in the water further slowed the progress of the boats.

All that Marty and French could do was to keep paddling frantically. The boats ahead of them got chewed to pieces, but their own boat somehow managed to slip through—so far.

Survivors from the shredded boats grabbed the sides of their raft. One of those guys tried to eel his way over the side into the raft and Marty reached back and clanged the guy over the helmet with his paddle. "Hang on and kick, or we ain't gonna make it!" Marty shouted as the chastened soldier slipped back into the river.

Finally, the first of the boats reached the far shore and the men scrambled up the steep, overgrown riverbank. Sporadic artillery fire came from the American side, but it was enough to silence the German guns. Shells were in short supply, however, and it was not long after the big American guns stopped that the German firepower started back up.

Ashore, it was like D-Day all over again.

Men made themselves as flat as possible as the mud erupted all around them, churned by machine gun fire. They heard the distinctive ripping sound made by the deadly German MG-42 guns that let loose with twelve-hundred rounds per minute.

"Move it!" a sergeant shouted. "You want to die, you stay right here!"

Screaming, his own rifle held ready although he had nothing to shoot at yet, Frenchie ran forward. They struggled across the open ground with tracers hissing around them and occasional bursts of mortar shells. The terrified troops had nowhere to go but onward. Finally, some of the men reached the relative shelter of the copse of trees midway between the river and the German fortifications.

Frenchie fell down beside Marty, panting with exhaustion, spent both physically and emotionally. Overhead, bullets snicked away at the autumn leaves, sounding like steel sleet. It seemed impossible for them to go on, and yet they must. Already, the sergeant was rallying them for a push toward the forts. They had a lot of ground to cross, all covered by enfiladed machine gun positions.

Frenchie felt someone grab his arm.

"It's been nice knowing you, Frenchie," Marty said. "Write to my parents, will you?"

"Don't talk like that, goddammit," Frenchie said, his own rule about swearing forgotten. "But listen, if I get killed, you'll do the same for me, right?"

"Sure I will," Marty said. Every soldier knew that his number might be up at any moment, but the two of them had been in so many scrapes together that they almost took it for granted that they would get out of this one alive. That outcome seemed even more uncertain. "Now, let's go tell those Germans to shove it up their asses."

At the urging of their sergeant and a lieutenant— their captain hadn't made it off the boats alive—the young GIs sprang up and joined the others running at a crouch toward the nearest fort.

On the way, they passed a group of five dead civilians, including two women, all lined up in a row where they had been mowed down.

"What the hell?" Marty wondered.

"Must be SS that done that," the sergeant said. "They shoot anybody who looks like French Resistance."

The unit moved on. To their relief, the German firing subsided as the Americans advanced and hit the enemy positions with mortars and grenade launchers.

But the Jerries had hardly rolled out the welcome mat. The GIs were faced with rows of barbed concertina wire, which they slowly hacked their way through using the few pairs of bolt-cutters that were available. Others wrapped scraps of cloth or webbed utility belts around their hands and simple yanked a path through the tangles of barbed wire, so desperate that they ignored the vicious slices to their hands and wrists and faces.

The wire wasn't the worst of it. At the edge of the barbed wire was a moat. The bottom was filled with yet more concertina wire, along with rusty metal spikes. These Krauts really knew how to make a guy feel unwelcome. They smelled gasoline, too—the sheen in the bottom of the moat was definitely not water. If the Germans fired just one tracer round into the moat, the Americans would be caught in the resulting conflagration.

Frenchie had thrown himself down into the dirt

at the rim of the moat, bracing himself for what was coming next.

Nobody was giving any orders to cross, though, because on the other side of the moat rose the sheer walls of the fortress itself. Even if they made it across the moat, scaling those walls would be impossible without ropes and ladders, and maybe an engineering platoon to help. They would die like bugs hitting a windshield on a summer night.

"Fall back to the river!" the sergeant shouted. "We're here to secure a bridge, not sack a fort."

For the first time that day, Frenchie felt a sense of relief. Apparently, the Germans had fled the fort, which was so imposing that, defended or not, the only way forward was to go around it. The GIs had succeeded in driving off the Germans and securing a river crossing. Their job now would be to get back down to the river and dig in until more troops could be brought over. Having wrested the riverfront from the Germans, their job now would be to hold this position.

Cautiously, the GIs reversed direction and returned using the path that they had so laboriously cut through the tangled barbed wire. To the south, they could hear sporadic firing in the distance, a reminder that they were not the only ones at war this day. Frenchie was glad to be headed back toward the relative safety of the riverbank.

"Guess we showed them," Marty said.

But Frenchie and the other GIs could not have been more mistaken. They had just cleared the barbed wire and reached open ground again when the Germans counter-attacked.

CHAPTER SEVEN

TRAP, Frenchie thought, as soon as the first tracer rounds from an MG-42 arced across the sodden ground, cutting the Americans to pieces.

Frenchie threw himself flat and stayed there, too terrified to move a muscle as the sound of "Hitler's Buzzsaw" filled the air.

He saw immediately what had happened. The Germans had not abandoned the fort in the face of the attack, as the Americans had thought. Instead, the Germans had slipped out unseen to flank the attackers—and even to hit them from the rear. The men had been so intent on going forward that no thought had been given to the fact that the fort might have been a ruse.

It was all a trick, a devious trap set by the SS troops, and the Americans had fallen for it.

They were now caught in a crossfire of tracer rounds coming at them from three directions.

Men fell all around him. He looked around for Marty and saw his own fear and confusion mirrored on his buddy's face. Just behind Marty, a man in a panic ran back into the concertina wire and was trapped like a fly in a spiderweb. He seemed to dance on imaginary strings as bullets riddled his body.

Frenchie froze. He couldn't even see the enemy to shoot back or pick a direction to shoot toward. German fire seemed to be coming at them from everywhere at once.

The lieutenant was trying to organize the retreat from the fort. He started to yell something, but the side of his face exploded. He staggered, then fell over sideways.

"Fall back!" the sergeant bellowed, then waved for the men to follow. Frenchie felt like he was pinned to the ground. *Get up*, his mind shouted. But his muscles refused to move. He felt Marty grab his shoulder and start to drag him away. That snapped Frenchie out of it.

He ran with the others for the river, recrossing the open field and heading toward the copse of trees that provided the only cover along the way. They ran like rabbits, gear flapping, helmets askew, boots slipping in the mud. One or two men dropped their rifles. Tracers darted from those trees ahead, which meant that Germans had slipped in behind them to occupy the horseshoe-shaped grove halfway back to the river, which they had thought of as their fallback position. The Americans had nowhere else to go. If they stayed out in the open, they would all be cut down.

Led by the sergeant, they stormed right among the trees and overran the nest of German machine gunners. They were so close that Frenchie had a glimpse of the twin lightning bolts on their uniforms. So, the bastards were SS. Would they surrender or put up a fight?

Frenchie was no more than a few feet away and he got a good look at their faces. They looked even younger than him, just a bunch of kids, but they sure as hell didn't look scared. They greeted the Americans with outraged shouts. The Germans gave no thought to surrendering. Instead, they grabbed their *Schmeisser* submachine guns and opened fire.

Frenchie fell to one knee and jerked the trigger of his M-1 as fast as he could without even aiming. There were bullets flying everything, but when he saw one of the SS soldiers double over, he was pretty sure that it was his bullet that had done it. He had to admit that it felt good to get even.

One of the SS soldiers was a tough bastard who refused to go down. He tossed away his empty *Schmeisser*, then raised a pistol and shot one of the

GIs. Seconds later, a burst from a grease gun killed him. With the SS soldiers dead, the grove of trees, at least, was back in American hands—never mind the fact that they were flanked on both sides. They could see the boats pulled up on the riverbank a few hundred feet away, but the safety of the other shore was as far out of reach as the stars or the moon.

If they left the cover of the woods, the Germans would turn them into hamburger.

But retreat was not an option. First and foremost, they had orders to secure and hold the bridgehead. That meant holding this grove of trees and the river-bank beyond at all costs.

The sergeant gave orders to dig in, using the clump of woods to anchor their position. These men had some experience digging foxholes. A hole in the ground had saved their asses more than once. They broke out their folding shovels and quickly got to work. Their line was in a rough horseshoe that approximated the shape of the grove. There weren't enough men left to dig a line of foxholes longer than 100 yards wide and roughly as deep on both sides. All the time that they were digging, they were also under fire.

Marty slid into a foxhole alongside Frenchie, who was still making the hole deeper. "I just hope the Jerries don't get behind us," he said, nodding at the terrain sloping gently to the river. "It's all over if they do."

Fortunately, there were some troops on the far shore to provide covering fire to their rear—if they didn't end up shooting their own guys in the process. All in all, it was a precarious situation for Frenchie and the others to be in. It wasn't even much of a bridgehead. But orders were orders, so they would defend that ground like they were at the Alamo.

Momentarily, the firing stopped. Frenchie kept digging. He heard orders shouted in German—the Jerries were that close—and then the firing started up all over again, heavier and more intense this time. He dropped the shovel and grabbed his M-1 just in time.

The Germans came at them from three points of the compass—north, east, and west, laying down heavy rifle fire. Once they were close enough, they threw a few stick grenades.

Though outnumbered, the Americans had some advantage in firepower. Their M-1 rifles were semiautomatic, while the Germans were mostly equipped with the bolt-action Mauser K98. That was a good rifle but had a slower rate of fire. Frenchie squeezed off five quick rounds, aiming at a German he spotted running at them in a crouch. He reloaded without bothering to see if he had hit the soldier.

Frenchie was no killer, but he sure as hell didn't want to be killed, either, and the Germans seemed intent on doing just that. It was kill or be killed. He picked out another target and felt the rifle jolt against his shoulder. All the shooting had left him beyond deaf—all that he could hear was the ringing in his ears. The recoil was the only way he knew that the rifle had fired.

The German attack melted away. His heart pounded and his head rang, but he felt elated to be alive. Maybe these SS bastards weren't as tough as everybody said.

He turned to say as much to Marty.

His friend lay slumped in the bottom of the foxhole, his eyes open but sightless. A fat hole was visible at the top of his helmet. Through the ringing in his head, Frenchie heard a muffled sob, and thought at first that it was Marty. Was he still alive? He shook his friend's shoulder, but there was no change in those blank eyes. Frenchie heard the sob again and realized that the sound had come involuntarily from his own throat.

He slumped back down in the foxhole. He didn't have time to mourn. A crescendo of fire announced that the SS troops were attacking again. Those bastards were far from done.

Frenchie shouldered his rifle and began firing, not even bothering to aim, shouting in anger each time that he pulled the trigger. The empty brass cartridges spun away, and he slapped in another stripper clip.

The sergeant was going from man to man. He touched Frenchie's shoulder and shouted into his ear, "Pick your targets! Kill these motherfuckers." Then the sergeant moved on.

Again and again, the Germans came at them. Frenchie did what the sergeant had told him and aimed carefully. Once or twice, the enemy soldier he was shooting at seemed to go down, but he couldn't be absolutely sure. If he killed any Krauts, Frenchie didn't feel bad about it.

Without heavy weapons, and relying on rifle fire alone, neither side was able to definitively overwhelm the other. The battle for the bridgehead at Dornot had become a brutal war of attrition—rifle against rifle and soldier against soldier.

Finally, as the September daylight faded, the Germans pulled back to lick their wounds. So far, they had not been able to dislodge the stubborn American force from their foxholes. The Jerries did not retreat, however, but kept up a steady harassing fire.

In the relative lull that followed, Frenchie reached down and closed Marty's eyes. He couldn't believe that Marty was dead. Sure, they had been in some tight spots before, and they had seen plenty of other guys buy it, one way or another. But that had always been something that happened to the other guy.

They'd felt like they had a charmed existence. Until now.

As the twilight deepened, Frenchie went away in his head for a while. He wasn't even sure where his mind went, but it wasn't in this muddy foxhole, that was for sure.

When he came back, he was close enough to the sergeant to overhear him on the radio. "Permission to withdraw, sir. We can't hold this position if the Krauts hit us again." The sergeant waited a beat, as if listening to a response. He had the phone pressed to his right ear and a finger stuck in his left ear. "Negative? But sir—" Another pause. "I understand, sir."

The sergeant hung up, caught Frenchie's eye, and shook his head.

Once again, the sergeant went from foxhole to foxhole, passing the word. "We're to hold this position no matter what," he said, echoing what his commanding officer, safe on the other side of the river, had ordered him.

"Easy for them to say," somebody muttered in disgust. "Hard for us to do."

"Shut it," the sergeant snapped.

Frenchie slid deeper into the muddy foxhole. He had been in the fighting since June. He knew that the sergeant was telling him that they might die here. He thought of Marty's sightless eyes and the lieutenant's exploding face. He started shaking, partly from being cold and wet, and partly from fear. The order to hold this position was akin to a death sentence. His belly clenched, and he thought that he was going to be sick, although he hadn't eaten anything since morning. Sick with fear, he thought. *Malade de peur*.

It promised to be a long night.

CHAPTER EIGHT

NOBODY GOT MUCH SLEEP. A cold rain began to fall after midnight, filling the belly of the foxholes with muddy water. Those who did nod off slept fitfully, half expecting SS commandos to slip in under cover of darkness and knife the sentries. Frenchie faded in and out of consciousness, waking every time that he started to shiver too much.

In the morning, what remained of the American force awoke wet, stiff, and hungry. Frenchie's breakfast consisted of a few swigs from his canteen. The water tasted muddy and metallic. He was pretty sure that he'd have traded his left nut just then for a hot cup of coffee and a doughnut.

The Germans let them know that they were still there by shooting at anyone who stuck his head out of a foxhole. If you had to relieve yourself, you did it right there in the foxhole.

Several of the men wounded in yesterday's fight were really suffering, but doing their best to hang in there. The medic dosed up the worst of the wounded with the morphine that he had left, crawling from foxhole to foxhole to avoid the German fire. It was the best that he could do for the wounded. Medical assistance from the other side of the river was out of the question.

Frenchie blinked, groggy with exhaustion and looking around for Marty. A fresh wave of grief washed over him when he saw his buddy's still form. *Marty's gone.*

Nearby, the sergeant was on the radio again. When he clicked off, he explained to the soldiers that headquarters finally radioed orders to withdraw. The sergeant didn't look happy about it. They were giving up on the bridgehead at Dornot. Resistance was too organized. There were still the two German-held forts from the old Siegfried line to contended with, and the Army had found more luck establishing a crossing at Metz, just to the north.

"Back to the boats," Sarge shouted.

That was one order they were glad to get. But retreat wasn't so simple. They had a lot of wounded, and they needed help back to the river. Several had to be carried out on stretchers, which took a while, considering that the men cried out in pain with each jolt or misstep on the slippery, uneven ground.

"Nobody gets left behind," Sarge growled. "If they're still breathing, they come with us."

Some of the wounded had not survived the night, however, and were left where they lay, foxholes serving as shallow graves. Frenchie gave Marty one last look and left him behind.

At first, as they trudged toward the river, it seemed as if the Germans might let them go, albeit like dogs with their tails between their legs. The enemy held their fire, except for a couple of stray shots just to let them know they were there.

But it was only a feint. As soon as the Americans were all out of their foxholes, exposed on the plain sloping down toward the river, the SS troops opened fire. Thankfully, they didn't seem to have machine guns, or maybe they were just using the retreating Americans for rifle practice.

The GIs had no choice but to make a run for it. The boats were maybe 300 feet away, and Frenchie joined the others in a dash for the river. He started to pass a soldier hobbling forward with a leg wound, thought better of it, and turned back. He threw the soldier's arm across his shoulders and the two of them hot-footed it toward the boats, bullets singing around them.

"Goddamn Krauts," the man muttered. "I owe you one, buddy."

He helped the wounded soldier tumble into one of the rubber rafts that was being pushed out into the current, then slid over the side himself.

He grabbed a paddle and started digging into the water. He knew the drill by now, having made the trip from the opposite direction just yesterday. That seemed like an eternity ago.

Now that it seemed as if the retreating Americans might actually make it back across the river, the Germans finally opened up with machine guns. White-hot tracers flashed across the surface of the river. Bursts of fire hit the flimsy boats, ripping them apart. Those who were not killed outright found themselves flailing in the water.

Swimming when burdened down by a rifle, helmet, boots, and gear was out of the question. One by one, the men who went into the water were dragged down by the current. Over the sound of the firing, Frenchie could hear the desperate pleas of the drowning men before they went under.

His own boat was still intact, but who knew for how long. Bullets danced across the surface of the water like raindrops. Frenchie paddled frantically for the far shore, which seemed so close, and yet impossibly distant.

He felt somebody nudge him.

"Hey, buddy, take this," said the soldier whom Frenchie had helped reach the river. The man held out a five-gallon metal jerry can that had once held drinking water. "It'll float."

"What about you?"

"I'm not gonna make it in the shape I'm in, buddy." The soldier grimaced, and Frenchie could see that that man had been hit again. "Like I said, I owe you one."

Frenchie didn't have time to argue, because in the next instant, a burst of machine gun fire hit the raft. The thing came apart instantly, rubber strips flying everywhere. He felt something hit his thigh. Then the brown water bubbled up all around him. He dropped the paddle and clutched at the jerry can for dear life.

The next thing he knew, he was in the cold river, being dragged down by the weight of his boots and wet clothes. *Hang on to the can*, he told himself. The jerry can had just enough buoyancy to keep him afloat.

However, the Germans were not done with them. Having sunk all the boats, they now strafed the surface of the river, picking off survivors. Frenchie realized he made too much of a target, trying to crawl on top of that jerry can like it was his own personal raft. He changed tactics and slipped down into the water next to the can, still gripping it for dear life but trying not to expose more than his head.

He was pretty sure, though, that it wasn't going to be enough. Bullets still hissed down into the water. He took a big gulp of air and went under, keeping one hand wrapped through the handle of the jerry can, which had just enough buoyancy to keep him from sinking.

When he tried to open his eyes, he couldn't see a thing except murky water. A line of bubbles exploded nearby, then another. Bullets. Too close. He held his breath until his lungs burned, trying not to panic. He tried to tell himself that it was just like being a kid at the beach.

Finally, when every molecule of his body was screaming for oxygen, he came up for air. Immediately, he saw that the current had carried him quickly downstream, away from where the boats had gone down. Nobody was shooting at him anymore. Debris covered the water, but he couldn't see any other survivors.

He hung onto the can with both hands now and let himself drift. The current was strong; he could feel it tug at his legs, wanting to pull him down. He realized that his thigh hurt intensely. He must have been hit, but he couldn't worry about that right now. He had to get even farther away from those SS soldiers, and then he had to get to shore.

He had a problem, though. He felt himself settling lower into the water, even when he tried to hug the jerry can closer. Trying to get a better grip on the can, he soon understood what was going on. Several holes puckered the can. If he hadn't gone underwater, he was pretty sure those bullets would have hit him. He tried to cover the holes with his hands and then to shift how the can sat in the water, but it wasn't going to work. Slowly but surely, the can was losing its buoyancy as it filled with water.

Swimming for shore wasn't an option, at least not yet. He wanted to get as far from those Germans as possible. Even then, he wasn't sure how well his leg would work when it came time to kick for shore. His waterlogged uniform and boots felt like concrete weighing him down. It was going to take a lot of effort to keep the current from pulling him down. He decided that he had no choice for now but to hold on.

The passing shoreline on both sides looked uniformly featureless and uninviting, with steep banks covered in brambles and underbrush. The good news was that there didn't seem to be any German soldiers lining those shores.

Minute by minute, the jerry can settled lower into the water. He passed a point where a large stream emptied out into the Moselle and was momentarily caught in a swirl of current. He kept hoping that his feet would touch bottom at some point, but no such luck. While it wasn't navigable by ships, the Moselle was just deep enough to drown him.

Up ahead, a stone bridge came into sight. His heart sank—he was pretty sure that if the Americans held a bridge, they wouldn't have tried to cross at Dornot. Did that mean the Germans held the bridge? He'd be in trouble if they spotted him. But he couldn't see anybody on the bridge. What did that mean?

Private Frenchie Tremblay had not been privy to the fact that the bridge at Ville sur Moselle was not an ideal military crossing. He could not have known that the bridge had to some extent escaped detection because it was narrow and the road leading to it was not suitable for large numbers of vehicles. But with few other options, the bridge had become invaluable.

Ideally, military planners had pushed for securing a bridgehead that could then be spanned by a temporary pontoon bridge. That's just what had been attempted at Dornot. In the end, the effort to establish an American foothold at Dornot had been a failure. While that fight had raged, American forces attempted other crossings with more success. Like Frenchie with his jerry can, the Germans couldn't stop up all the holes.

It had been Frenchie's bad luck to be part of the action to secure what turned out to be a well-defended area along the Moselle. One that was defended by die-hard SS troops, to boot.

The price paid was high. Between the ambush and then the disastrous retreat, the butcher's bill was nearly one thousand young men killed or wounded. U.S. forces lost fifty-five killed in action, ninety missing in action (mostly drowned and their bodies never recovered), four hundred sixty-seven wounded in battle, and more than three hundred incapacitated by non-battle injuries that ranged from sickness brought on by the damp to near-drownings. German losses were maybe a couple of dozen troops. The generals explained it all away as a feint to distract German forces while successful crossings were made elsewhere. Then again, maybe Marty Pulaski had been right all along, and it really had been one big SNAFU. One thing for sure, nobody was going to go out of their way to remember the Battle of Dornot because it had been a defeat. In this war, only the victories would be remembered.

But at the moment, Frenchie was still just trying to stay alive. He was worried about any Germans that might be hanging around that bridge looming in front of him. Had he gone from the frying pan into the fire? He thought about floating past the bridge and avoiding any trouble, but by now, the jerry can was so full of water that had flowed in through the bullet holes that it started to pull him down, rather than keep him afloat.

Reluctantly, he let go of the can and watched it sink into the brown water. Hoping not to follow its example, he started to swim for shore, using an awkward stroke that favored his hurt leg. The shore seemed to grow closer, if just barely. He struggled to swim in the boots and waterlogged uniform. He tried to get a gulp of air and swallowed the dirty river water instead. Gasping and sputtering, he swam even harder. It was going to take every last ounce of energy to reach the shore.

CHAPTER NINE

WATCHING the retreating flotilla on the river, SS *Hauptmann* Hans Lange ordered his men to continue firing. Bullets churned the surface like raindrops, unleashing a storm of carnage among the boats. His men had a good supply of ammunition, but it wasn't endless. The MG-42 churned through another belt, raking the river relentlessly.

Beside him, a sergeant remarked, "They are retreating, sir."

"Do you think I give a damn? Shoot them! Shoot them all! It's fewer soldiers we will have to fight later."

Reports were coming in of the Americans forming bridgeheads at Metz and nearby Arnaville. One place where they would not be coming across was Dornot. "What are your orders, Herr Oberst?"

"Hold our position," he said.

Hands on hips, *Hauptmann* Lange stared out at the butchery on the river, finally satisfied. *Hauptmann* was equivalent to the Allied rank of captain. Normally, there would be at least a major or *Oberst* in charge of the unit, but the war had taken its toll. Besides, Lange had more than proven his capabilities. He felt confident that his force had not only thwarted the American unit, but destroyed it.

The machine gun fire strafing the river had shredded the retreating boats. Mortar rounds threw gouts of water, adding to the deadly stew. The screams of dying men carried clearly to him across the water.

Finally, he gave the order, "Cease fire!"

From the river now, there was only silence.

All in all, the Americans had been foolish to make their attack here against a well-fortified position. To throw troops against an actual fortress—ringed with razor-sharp concertina wire, no less—seemed beyond foolhardy. What could they hope to accomplish against fortified troops without artillery or air support?

Lange suspected that the Americans were so used to victory by now that they believed themselves to be invincible. His well-trained men had proved them wrong today.

Two soldiers approached, pushing a bedraggled

soldier in front of them, his arms held high in a gesture of surrender. Lange raised his eyebrows. His men had captured an American. A very waterlogged American, from the looks of him.

"*Herr Hauptmann*, we have found a prisoner," one of the soldiers said.

"I am sorry to say, you swam the wrong way," the *Hauptmann* said in German. "You have a terrible sense of direction."

The *Hauptmann's* mildly humorous comment brought chuckles from the soldiers within earshot. The American soldier stared at him, uncomprehending. He had a beefy build and a round face with almond-shaped eyes that hinted at some Slavic ancestry. Polish? Russian? It was hard to say. Most of the Americans that he had come across were mongrels of one sort or another.

"What do you want us to do with him, *Herr Hauptmann*?" one of the soldiers asked. He was grinning. "We could make him swim back."

"Shoot him," Lange said. The Oberst had heard rumors that SS soldiers captured by the Americans did not make it to the rear. He would return the favor. Besides, he had few enough men as it was and did not want to detail anyone to guarding a single captured American. "No prisoners."

The soldier's grin vanished. "Yes, sir."

The soldier shoved the American between the

shoulder blades, pushing him deeper into the nearby field. The American knew what was coming, but to his credit, he did not complain. The machine gun fired, and the prisoner slumped to the ground, dead.

With the Americans thrown back across the river, the SS troops secured their position for the night. He expected no further trouble, and the Americans didn't prove him wrong. Aside from a false alarm involving a herd of cows, it proved to be a quiet night. In the morning, they woke to gray skies and dense, low-hanging clouds. Lange was reassured that once again, they would not have to worry about Allied air attacks.

Having repelled the attempt to force a bridgehead at Dornot, the commander of the SS troops on the east bank of the Moselle faced something of a quandary. He could stay in place in order to stop any additional incursions, or he could move on, perhaps enabling him to halt another attempt at a crossing downstream. Surely, not even the Americans would be bold or stubborn enough to attempt a crossing in the same spot. Orders were a long time in coming. Whatever was left of the command structure had apparently forgotten about him and his unit. Left in limbo, Lange and his men waited, guns aimed toward the river for a follow-up assault that never came. There weren't enough American soldiers left to launch a new attack.

Finally, new orders arrived. Lange called his officers and sergeants together. "We are moving out," he said. "Gather the men. We will leave a small force here in the forts, but the Americans aren't going to attack here again, not when there are easier crossings downstream."

"Where are we going, sir?"

Lange stabbed a finger at the map spread across the hood of a Kübelwagen. "We go here. A town called Ville sur Moselle."

Lange and his men had been ordered to the south of their current position. This town had an intact bridge across the Moselle that must be secured before the American forces could use it as a crossing point. Lange's orders to destroy the bridge were simple enough.

The bridge was not far. By boat, it was no more than a voyage of half an hour. But Lange and his men had no small boats and would have to take the road instead. The problem was that the road did not run parallel to the river. The region's ubiquitous hills meant that Lange and his men would have to move west, away from the river, before turning east again toward the town and its bridge.

With any luck, they would be there by nightfall. Maybe tomorrow morning, depending upon what they ran into on the road.

They moved out and Lange soon realized that he

had not counted on was the fact that there were only a few narrow roads through this hilly region, and many retreating German troops using those roads. What at first was a trickle of troops soon become a flood by midafternoon. Lange found himself hopelessly bogged down as they encountered broken Wehrmacht forces plodding along the road. He found himself disdainful of their attitude of defeat. Many had no weapons but seemed intent only on staying ahead of the Allied advance.

Lange fought the urge to shoot a few of them as an example, or to force them to clear the road for the SS troops. But Lange was not an oblivious fool. Not all of the Wehrmacht forces were unarmed, many were battle-hardened veterans, and they far outnumbered his own men. He witnessed open hostility toward his SS troops in the looks and sour words they received when trying to muscle their way through the throng on the road. As defeat seemed to be the outcome of the war, many now saw the SS troops as zealots who had gotten them into this mess in the first place.

One of his men started shoving a Wehrmacht soldier whom he thought was going to slow. "Hurry it up!"

The man shoved back. Just a few weeks before, it would have been unthinkable for a Wehrmacht soldier to dare stand up to SS troops. As it turned out, this Wehrmacht soldier was not the only one fed up with the SS. A crowd formed, with more shoving all around and hot words. Lange could see that both his men and the Wehrmacht troops had their fingers on their triggers. He needed to defuse this situation before tempers flared even more.

The situation quickly escalated until Lange waded in and separated them. "We are all Germans here," he shouted. "If anyone wants to fight, take your rifle and march the other way!"

The stream of plodding soldiers gradually resumed, but the dirty looks they were getting from the Wehrmacht troops only increased. There did not seem to be many officers around, and those who were present seemed share the same sentiment toward SS troops as their men. It was likely that most of the other officers were dead. The fighting at the Falaise Gap had taken a heavy toll on the officer corps. Unfortunately, many of those who had been promoted did not have the age or experience to lead effectively. Even Lange himself felt that he was not quite prepared to take on a role that went beyond his *Hauptmann* rank, but he had no choice in the matter.

"I don't like the looks of this, sir," one of the sergeants said, grasping his machine pistol tightly.

"Just keep going, and make sure the men don't cause any trouble," Lange said.

Finally, the Kübelwagen's speed was reduced to a

crawl in first gear due to the press of men on the narrow, muddy road. He had hoped to lead his men to their objective by nightfall, but it was going to take them longer.

Blowing the bridge at Ville sur Moselle would just have to wait until tomorrow.

CHAPTER TEN

FRENCHIE DRAGGED himself up the river bank, panting and gasping. He found himself upon a flat stone that formed a landing where someone might launch a rowboat. Stone steps, worn smooth over time, led up the steep bank. The air smelled faintly of dead fish and dank mud. Frenchie sprawled across the landing stone, letting the water run off him, and figured out what to do next.

He was still alive, or at least, he seemed to be, unless this was some dream from the afterlife and he was actually dead. He'd read a Western story like that once in high school English class, "An Occurrence at Owl Creek Bridge" by Ambrose Bierce. But no, his heart pounded and his lungs ached too much from the effort of swimming for this to be anything but real. Also, he began to shiver. The sky remained low and overcast, almost clinging to the landscape, and the wind had a damp edge.

He was bleeding from his leg. He pushed the fabric aside to reveal an angry red furrow in his thigh. Nothing deep, although it stung like fire. He knew that it was a bullet wound. Now that he was out of the river, blood was pooling in the gouge and running down his thigh, staining his trousers. He'd have to do something about that eventually, but he wasn't bleeding to death.

An image flashed in his head of the fat bullet hole in Marty's helmet. He knew that he'd be having nightmares about that for years to come. His stomach clenched all over again, the thought of his friend's death causing actual physical pain.

"I'm sorry, Marty," he groaned. "I'll write your parents. I promise."

He took stock of the rest of his body. There didn't seem to be any bullet holes, which was a good sign. His wet uniform reeked of muddy water and old sweat.

God, he was thirsty. Who would have thought that he'd be thirsty, after swimming the river?

He sat up and looked around. He seemed to be all alone. The water was smooth and empty. He studied the bridge more closely. It was narrow, arched, and built of stone. Frenchie was no kind of expert, but to him the bridge looked ancient or medieval.

Cautiously, he climbed the steps. He'd lost his helmet and his rifle somewhere in the river. His only weapon was a combat knife, which wouldn't do him much good if he ran into an SS patrol at the top of the steps. He couldn't fight back, and they weren't taking any prisoners.

Reaching the top, he was surprised to see a village come into view. There hadn't been anything near the Dornot bridgehead, so he must have drifted farther than he'd thought. Sure, he was glad that he was still alive, but he was terrified all the same. He had no idea where he was, or what might be waiting for him. From boot camp on, a soldier was part of a unit and rarely alone. For the first time in months, Frenchie was on his own. He had to admit that it was a strange feeling.

The thing to do was to be stealthy. He had to creep up on that village and get the lay of the land. If he was lucky, there would be some Americans there. If there were Germans in the village, he was as good as dead.

He kept off the road that led from the bridge to the village and stayed on the path that was a sort of shortcut from the river. The good thing was that the path passed through some trees and garden plots, so that he had some cover. However, he didn't feel all that stealthy. His wet clothes hung off him, his boots squelched with each step, and he was shivering. His leg stung.

Too late, he heard voices. A couple of boys about twelve years old appeared as if out of nowhere on the path ahead. They both carried cane fishing poles, as if they been headed down to the river to try their luck. The boys caught sight of him and froze. Frenchie stared back. Then the boys dropped their fishing poles and ran, shouting, back toward the village.

So much for the element of surprise, Frenchie thought.

* * *

IT WASN'T long before the boys came running back, followed by a tall man in his early fifties who was either some sort of village official or maybe father to one of the boys, along with a young woman about Frenchie's age. He would have been glad to see him, if the man hadn't been carrying a rifle. If Frenchie had looked closely, he would have seen that the stock was patched with tightly wrapped wire.

Not sure what else to do, Frenchie put his hands up.

"Who the hell are you?" the man demanded in

French, pointing the rifle at him. Frenchie understood him well enough.

"Private Tremblay, United States Army," Frenchie stammered, trying to remember how much you were allowed to tell the enemy if you were captured. He wasn't sure if he was captured or not, but he kept his hands up.

"American?" the old man asked.

"Je suis Americain," Frenchie answered. In French, he explained that there had been a battle upstream, trying to cross the river, and his boat had been sunk.

"We heard the shooting in the distance." The rifle wavered a bit. "You speak French."

"My parents are from Quebec," Frenchie answered.

The young woman stepped forward. When she did so, the man finally lowered the rifle. She looked at his leg. The trousers now sported a bright red stain the size of a dinner plate. He realized that not all of the squelching sound in his boot was caused by water. There was some blood mixed in, too.

"You are hurt," she said.

"Shot," he said. "It's just a scratch, though."

Frenchie stepped forward, but ended up staggering. The young woman caught him, or he'd have fallen flat on his face. The man handed the rifle to one of the boys, then took Frenchie's other arm.

Limping between the two, Frenchie made it back to the village.

* * *

THE VILLAGERS DEBATED about where to take him, and they settled on the older man's kitchen. The house was simple and neat, and the kitchen was not all that different from the one in his parents' house, except for that fact that a framed portrait of Napoleon decorated one wall. Oddly, his parents had similar artwork, except their portrait was of Abraham Lincoln. By now, a few more villagers had shown up, crowding into the kitchen, wondering what was going on. From the expression on their faces, it was clear that he must have looked like a drowned rat. A wounded drowned rat. It turned out that he was the first American soldier that anyone had seen in this part of the country. The only soldiers they had seen were Germans, up until Frenchie had appeared, battered and bleeding. So much for being a conquering hero.

Frenchie quickly learned that the man's name was Pierre, that he was a widower since his wife had passed away three years before, and that he was the mayor of this village, which was called Ville sur Moselle.

"Where are the Germans?" he asked.

Pierre shrugged. "Here, there, everywhere."

That didn't make Frenchie feel any better. "Are there Germans here in the village?"

"*Non*. They are on the run now, thank God. France shall be free again! We have been occupied by the Germans for four years now. Our village was lucky in that it was too small and out of the way for the Germans to take much interest in it. They only passed through now and then, expecting us to lick their boots whenever they did." Pierre seemed to be looking around for a place to spit, but changed his mind and swallowed instead.

"Are you sure that you haven't seen any other Americans?"

Pierre pointed at him. "Just you."

"That means all the rest are all gone," Frenchie said blankly. He had hoped that maybe some others had escaped downstream. "My entire unit. Wiped out by the SS."

"The SS are dogs." Pierre nodded sagely and handed him a tiny glass of liquor poured from a squat brown bottle. Frenchie wasn't sure exactly what it was—brandy maybe—and it burned going down. Almost instantly, he felt the warmth from the alcohol spreading through him. Dry clothes were produced, and Pierre shooed everyone else out while he changed. "Let us have a look at that leg," Pierre said.

The wound looked all right, but it was still bleeding. Pierre called the young woman, whose named was Margot, and the boys back in to help. Pierre sent the boys upstairs for a clean sheet, and Margot cut off a long 2-inch strip from the white, starched sheet to make a bandage. Pierre and Frenchie both studied the wound for a long moment. Frenchie had some experience with tending wounds. As a boy, he had helped his father, a veterinarian. He knew that the wound needed to be cleaned, and short of anything like sulfa powder, Pierre's bottle of liquor would have to do. It was likely that Pierre had treated their own scrapes and hurts in much the same way.

He nodded at Pierre, who shrugged and poured a generous dollop of the liquor into the wound. Frenchie yelped in pain and bolted upright in the chair. Nearby, the two boys were watching, and they winced right along with him. Maybe they were familiar with old Pierre's cure-all for cuts and scrapes. "Crimony, that hurts!"

"That's brandy for you," Pierre said. "Good for the inside, and good for the outside."

The stinging pain took a while to subside, but he knew that Pierre had done the right thing to clean the wound, considering how muddy the river water had been.

Frenchie was beyond being self-conscious as he sat there in the borrowed underwear as Margot carefully wrapped his leg. Blood soaked through, so she wrapped it with another strip. When she was finished, Frenchie tugged on the borrowed trousers. His uniform was already hung near the stove to dry.

He began to shake, but not from cold. Again, he thought of the fight yesterday in the field at Dornot, the Germans ambushing them and then coming at them from three directions. He saw the lieutenant's face exploding all over again, and then the hole in Carl's helmet. His staring eyes. A sob escaped him, and he swiped at his eyes. So much for the tough Americans, he thought.

Pierre shooed the boys out again, telling them to go watch the road for Germans. When they were gone, he patted Frenchie's shoulder once more. "I was in the Great War," he said gently. "There is no shame in how you feel. No one who has not experienced it can truly understand. Not all wounds draw blood, but they are painful all the same. The pain is sharp now, but the edge of the knife grows dull over time."

Frenchie wasn't so sure.

Margot brought him a bowl of soup, which smelled delicious. He pulled his chair closer to the table. His stomach grumbled. He hadn't realized how hungry he was. But when he picked up the spoon, his hand shook too much to carry the soup from the bowl to his mouth. He clenched the spoon helplessly.

Leaning close, Margot put her hand around his

and helped guide the spoon from the bowl to his lips. After a few times, his hand didn't shake so much, and he was able to do it himself. He became aware of how good Margot smelled. This was the closest that he had been to a girl since before joining up, not that Frenchie had a lot of experience in that department, anyhow. He caught the scent of lavender and soap. Margot smelled so good and clear that his head swam all over again. When he met Margot's eyes, she looked away, blushing.

Frenchie devoured the rest of the soup. The ham and beans and chunks of potatoes in a salty broth were delicious. When he was finished, he felt stronger already. He thanked them both profusely.

Pierre shook his head. "It is you we must thank. You Americans are fighting and giving your lives to liberate France. To free all of Europe from the Nazis. There is no way to repay what you are doing."

Frenchie had not thought of it that way before. "I will have to rejoin the Army," he said. "The trouble is, I don't know which way to go."

"You aren't going anywhere yet on that leg," Pierre said. "Another day or two and you should be fine. By then, someone will want to use that bridge. The fighting grows closer each day. The Germans need to retreat across that river. The Americans need to get to Germany. The question is, who will get here first, the Americans or the Germans? If it is the

Germans, we will hide you. If it is the Americans, you can rejoin them. What do you think of that plan, Private Tremblay?"

"Sounds good to me." Frenchie held up the empty bowl. "You wouldn't happen to have any more of that soup would you, *sil vous plait?*"

CHAPTER ELEVEN

COLE MOVED FORWARD CAUTIOUSLY, pausing from time to time to listen, or simply to sniff the air. Cole could actually smell the Germans when they were around. The exhaust from their tanks and vehicles wasn't the same as that from American vehicles. Even their sweat smelled different, from the food they ate.

"Don't tell me about how you can smell the Jerries," muttered Vaccaro, watching him. "Not that I'd be all that surprised if it's true."

"Let's just say I got a good nose for trouble," Cole said. "And you ain't got to be a bloodhound to know that there's Germans around here."

Cole and Vaccaro were on point, walking ahead of the rest of the patrol. In this kind of fluid situation, where the next step might bring them directly into

an enemy crossfire, point was a dangerous position to
be in. They had been put there by Captain Norton.

From far behind them, Norton shouted, "Get a
move on, already! The Germans will be back across
the Rhine and halfway to Berlin before we get to the
end of this road."

Cole nodded, but he moved on only when he was
good and ready.

He couldn't tell where the Germans had gone, and
worried that the enemy might be waiting just up
ahead for the patrol to wander into their sights once
again.

The patrol's brush with the Wehrmacht's rear
guard had left them badly bruised. West was being
carried on a stretcher. Without so much as a Jeep, the
squad was forced to take turns carrying him. It was
exhausting work. Each step jostled the wounded man,
who, mercifully, was drugged with morphine. They
had no choice but to bring him along. With the countryside crawling with Germans, it wasn't safe to send
him to the rear.

The men in Captain Norton's haphazard patrol
were among hundreds of thousands of troops heading
east along a battlefront that stretched across France.
Most of the countryside was in chaos, with firefights
like the one they had just experienced breaking out
wherever opposing forces ran into each other on the

country roads. Having occupied the countryside since 1940, Wehrmacht and SS troops now sold each mile of France leading toward Germany dearly.

In a sense, the troops of both sides were all in a race—a race toward Germany.

The final boundary would be the Rhine River. Wide and deep, the mighty Rhine had kept the Germanic tribes separated from the rest of the world in ancient times. In fact, it was the freezing of the Rhine during a series of unusually cold winters that enabled the Germanic hordes to cross the ice and hasten the fall of the Roman Empire.

Once Allied troops made that crossing, they would be in the Fatherland itself.

But before they could reach the Rhine, first they must ford the Moselle River. This tributary of the Rhine flowed parallel to Germany's great boundary river. The Moselle stretched from north to south, roughly from the Ardennes region to down below the towns of Metz and Aachen. Beyond the Moselle, it was only a hard day's push toward the Rhine. Having fought their way from Normandy, the Allied troops could begin to taste victory. Time and time again, however, the Germans showed that they were far from defeated yet.

The Moselle was a meandering river through what was largely a rural region of France. Because it drained so many farm fields, the dominant color was brown. Soldiers looking for a poetic description couldn't really call it coffee-colored or even the color of chocolate milk. The Moselle was simply muddy, especially in springtime or after the fall rains.

The Moselle was rarely more than a couple of hundred feet across, but the current was swift between the steep banks, and the river was anywhere from eight to ten feet deep in most place. A tank or a Jeep couldn't cross, and there was no way a GI loaded with gear could swim it. No, the Moselle was a river that was deceptively difficult to cross, which made the bridges so important to both the retreating Germans and the advancing Americans.

A few villages, some of them not quite cities, dotted the banks of the Moselle. The larger villages had grown up around bridge crossings. Many of these villages had existed for hundreds of years and had their beginnings in ferries that crossed the river.

These bridges were strategically a tricky question for the Germans and Allies alike. The Allies did not want to see the Germans retreat or escape, but couldn't blow the bridges if they hoped to follow. The last German across might blow the bridge, but even that action was not without risks. Blowing the bridge too soon would leave their brothers in arms stranded and at the mercy of the Allies. Waiting too long would mean an open road for Allied troops advancing toward the Rhine.

Crossing a river was one of most difficult challenges that an army could face. The open nature of a water crossing exposed troops to enemy fire. These difficulties weren't new to Allied or Axis troops. For example, Union troops crossing the Rappahannock River at the battle of Fredericksburg had been picked off by Confederate sharpshooters and bombarded by enemy artillery on their way to storm Marye's Heights. It had been a perfect gauntlet of fire.

But the patrol moving toward the Moselle had more immediate concerns, such as how to avoid an ambush around the next bend.

The green kid from Norton's patrol moved up beside Cole. "Sorry I was such a coward back there," the kid said. His voice held an edge of despair. Cole could almost taste the kid's sense of shame. Just a short time ago, he had been cowering behind the wrecked hulk of the tank, hands over his ears, curled into a ball. "I don't know what happened to me. I guess I lost my nerve when I heard the shooting."

Cole spat. He looked sideways at the kid, whose new uniform marked him as a greenhorn. The thumb of his right hand was bandaged, which indicated that he had suffered "M-1 Thumb" by having his thumb caught in the action of the rifle as it snapped shut.

Replacement troops tended to get killed so fast in

the vicious fighting across Normandy, that veteran troops didn't bother to learn their names. Cole didn't bother to ask this one's name. In fact, he didn't say anything at all, but kept his eyes on the road ahead.

"Anyhow, it won't happen again. Thanks for saving my bacon."

Finally, Cole said, "You ain't no coward. Gettin' shot at don't come natural to most."

"Better get used to it, kid," Vaccaro said. "In case you haven't noticed, there's a war on."

"You don't never get used to it," Cole said. "But you get so you can handle the fear."

"If you say so."

"You got to put a rope around your fear and lead it around like a dog. Jest don't let it lead *you* around."

The kid nodded. "That's quite an accent you have. Where you from?"

"No place that you'd want to be from, that's for damn sure," Cole said. "Now fall back behind City Boy there, kid. You want a good ten yards between everybody on a road like this, so a burst from a machine gun don't kill us all."

Although Cole wasn't more than twenty-four, he felt vastly older than any nineteen or twenty-year-old greenhorn. Some might even say that Cole had been born with an old soul.

"My name is Bill, by the way," the kid said. "Bill Laurel."

"Don't know and don't care," Cole replied. "If'n you don't shut up and pay attention, you ain't gonna be around long enough for me to worry none about your name, and that's a fact."

They trudged on in silence, pressing deeper into what was likely German-held territory, the tension so thick that they could have spread it on sliced bread.

A road sign appeared. Though pockmarked by bullets, the sign was freshly painted with letters in crisp black paint. Cole shook his head. One thing about the Germans, which the French did not like to admit, was that they had been very efficient about maintaining the French roads, which were in much better shape than they had been in 1940 before the occupation. The same could be said for every public service, from electricity to telephones to water and sewer lines.

On the other hand, the Germans also oversaw "improvements," such as shipping out the Jewish people, seizing artwork, and stripping the Catholic churches of their old silver chalices or anything else of value. Hitler's "improvements" had even extended to a plan to raze French symbols such as the Cathedral of Notre Dame, but that had promised to be more effort than it was worth. Fortunately for the French, Hitler had been distracted by other projects, such as the invasion of the Soviet Union.

Cole looked at the sign, but the words meant

nothing to him. Even if the sign had been in English, the fact of the matter was that Cole could not read, although he took pains to hide his illiteracy from just about everyone. His upbringing in the mountains had taught Cole to read the sky or a set of tracks, but words remained a mystery to him. Vaccaro was one of the only people who knew his secret.

Twenty feet behind Cole, the kid read the sign aloud. "Ville sur Moselle," he said. "I'm pretty sure that means 'Village on the Moselle'."

"Village on the Moselle," Cole said. "I reckon that means we are headin' for the river. At least Captain Numbnuts back there has us going in the right direction. I was worried we was gonna end up in Italy by mistake."

"Careful," Vaccaro said quietly. "You're in enough hot water as it is with him. For a guy who doesn't say much, you sure know to say the wrong thing. Better make nice and lay low if you ever want your rifle back."

"Captain Norton don't worry me none," Cole said. "Captains and lieutenants ain't worth a cup of spit in this army."

"Yeah, but that captain is in command right now and he doesn't seem to like you very much, which means he doesn't like me either, by association," Vaccaro said. "We're stuck with Captain Norton. It's not like we ever so much as see a colonel or general. They're all back at HQ, where it's safe."

"A general out here?" Cole snorted. "Wouldn't that be somethin'. But to hell with officers. I'm a heap more worried about Germans, and that there might be some around the next bend in the road."

CHAPTER TWELVE

"LET'S GET A MOVE ON," Captain Norton said, once they gone another mile without running into trouble. "I want to be at the river by nightfall. We don't need to be wandering around in the dark with the country-side full of Jerries."

Cole muttered, "That's the first thing he's said that makes any sense."

"Don't let him hear you, for God's sake. He'll take away that grease gun and make you lug that stretcher instead." Vaccaro nodded at the two men lugging West's stretcher. So far, it was two greenhorns who had gotten that task. Norton was keeping Cole and Vaccaro on point.

They walked a couple more miles on what felt like borrowed time, wondering at any moment what they might encounter. The rain had stopped, but the skies hadn't cleared. Low gray clouds clung to the shoulders of the hills like a damp wool sweater. The air smelled cool and crisp, but with a tang of decay from the wet earth and turning leaves. Around the next bend in the road was the village itself, Ville sur Moselle.

Cole and Vacarro, along with Sergeant Woodbine and the new kid, advanced into the village. The rest of Norton's squad took cover along both sides of the road.

"You think there are any Germans?" the kid asked. "I've never done this before."

"Got to learn sometime, kid."

"If there's any Germans, we're gonna find out right quick," Cole said.

The place looked sleepy enough. Unlike many French villages, this one had escaped any bombing. It helped that the village was overhung with trees growing on the surrounding hills. Ville sur Moselle would be difficult to see from the air. A narrow road passed between ancient stone buildings, following the gentle incline toward the river. No people were in sight, but a cat crossed the street, nonchalantly pausing to rub against a pot of flowers growing beside a doorway.

For all that Cole knew, there might be a squad of Jerries set up on the second floor of one of the buildings, ready to open fire. He held up a fist, signaling for the others to halt. Cole stood silently, listening and waiting. If this was a trap here, it was perfectly concealed. The Germans were tricky. Sometimes they let you advance just long enough to let your guard now. However, Cole couldn't sense anything waiting for them.

"What do you reckon?" he whispered to Vaccaro.

"I reckon that we ought to send the kid in first, just in case. Go on, kid."

"If you say so," the kid said, and started to leave cover.

"Shut up, Vaccaro," Cole said. "Kid, you stay put and cover me."

He took a step forward.

Vaccaro and the greenie kept behind the corner of a building, covering him.

Cole was still making his way forward, wary of a German ambush, when a young woman stepped out of a door and almost ran into him. She gave a cry of dismay and stepped back, clearly shocked and surprised. He could see the puzzled look on her face. This deep into France, there hadn't been many Americans yet.

Cole put a finger to his lips, encouraging her not to scream. They didn't need that kind of attention just yet. Her pretty mouth froze in an O, but no sound emerged. He kept the grease gun raised, not quite pointing at her, but ready all the same just in case this was some kind of German trick.

Right behind the young woman there appeared a young man, wearing what appeared to be part of an American uniform, but with faded blue trousers tucked into the tall rubber boots that French farmers favored. He walked with a pronounced limp. When he saw the soldiers, his face broke into a big smile.

"It's about time somebody else got here," he said.

"You're American?"

"Eleventh Infantry," he said, "At least, I'm what's left of it. We got chewed up by the SS trying to cross the river north of here. I went into the water and washed up at this place."

"You seen any Germans?"

The soldier frowned. "Not yet. But with that bridge here, you can be sure that we'll see some soon. They'll need to cross somewhere if they want to get back to the Fatherland."

The soldier then turned and said something to the young woman in French. The upturned tone at the end of his sentence made it sound as if he had asked her a question.

The woman shook her head. "*Non*," she replied. She added a few more sentences in French.

"You speak French?" Cole asked. "You right sure you're an American?"

"Sure, I'm sure. I know French, is all. They guys in my old unit called me Frenchie."

"Frenchie, huh?" Cole looked dubiously at the windows overlooking the street. For all he knew, they were full of Germans and this was some sort of elaborate trap. "All right then, Frenchie, how about you tell me who delivered the Gettysburg address."

"Seriously?"

Cole hefted the grease gun. "I done asked you a question."

"Abraham Lincoln."

"All right." Cole lowered the weapon. "What were you jabberin' to that girl about?"

"I said that we didn't have anything to worry about, now that the army was here."

"We ain't exactly an *army*," Cole said. "Just a squad made up of loose ends. Which means we have plenty to worry about if the Jerries show up in force. Ask her if she has seen any Germans around here."

"Like I said—"

Cole pointed the grease gun at him. "Go on and ask her."

"Hey, take it easy, buddy."

"I said, ask her about the Germans."

Frenchie turned to the young woman and posed the question in French. He translated for Cole. "Uh, she said that Germans used to come through here all the time, but that there aren't any around right now."

Cole nodded. Maybe he was just getting paranoid. If the woman or this Frenchie character had been lying, she would have stolen a glance at where the Germans were hidden with their machine gun or sniper. Instead, she had kept her eyes fixed on Cole and Vaccaro.

Feeling more relaxed, Cole took the opportunity to get a better look at her. The woman was about his age or a little younger, tall, and pretty in that dark French way. Her hair was tucked under a kerchief as if she had been in the middle of doing chores or about to run errands. She wore a dress and canary yellow sweater against the chill.

Cole didn't let his guard down entirely. The woman seemed genuinely surprised to find the Americans on her doorstep. At the same time, she did not seem overly apprehensive. Cole doubted that she was any sort of collaborator. They had met their share among the French.

During four years of occupation, some locals had built ties—whether romantic or entrepreneurial—that made them less than enthusiastic about the arrival of Allied forces. The newsreels always made the French seem jubilant, but there were often a few at the back of the crowd who weren't jumping for joy because they had made a bad choice in casting their lot with the Germans. With the arrival of the Allies, they knew there would be a reckoning.

More villagers became apparent. An old man emerged and stared, leaning on his cane. Someone started shouting and other villagers appeared on the street to witness the arrival of the Americans. There didn't seem to be any young men, but more importantly, there didn't seem to be any Germans.

A boy of about twelve with the same dark hair and pale complexion as the woman came out and ran toward her. She was too young to be his mother; Cole decided that they must be brother and sister. The boy hadn't gotten his full growth yet, but it was clear from his big feet and hands that he was going to be tall like his sister.

"Les Américains?" the boy asked, excitement clear on his face.

"Oui," the woman answered. She grabbed the boy around the shoulders and tousled his hair, but he squirmed out of her grasp, clearly embarrassed by this show of affection in front of the soldiers. Finally, the woman's face relaxed. *"Les Américains sont arrivés."*

Certain now that they faced no danger of a German ambush, Cole signaled for the rest of the patrol to move in. The dry, stone fountain in the village square became the assembly point.

"It's about goddamn time," Captain Norton said. "You'd been gone so long, I was expecting a postcard. I thought the Germans had you running scared."

Beside him, Cole felt Vaccaro tense up, but all

that Cole said was, "Just makin' sure, sir. Didn't want you to walk into an ambush."

The captain stared at Frenchie. "Who the hell are you?"

Frenchie went through his story, while the captain listened, stone-faced. "Why didn't you make any attempt to rejoin your unit?"

"Like I said, sir, my unit was wiped out. And I was wounded."

"Sergeant, place this man under arrest. He's a deserter."

"But sir—

Norton put his hand to his pistol, and Frenchie fell silent, allowing himself to be led away by Sergeant Woodbine.

"Looks like you did find something useful," Norton said, eyeing the French woman up and down. She was looking with concern after Frenchie, seeming to sense that something was wrong. "What's your name, honey? *Appelez-vous?*"

"*Je m'appelle Margot.*"

"See there?" Norton turned to them with a smug look of satisfaction. "All you've got to do is ask."

The sergeant approached. "What are your orders, sir?"

"Spread out and keep your eyes open!" Captain Norton shouted. He himself didn't seem to plan on moving far from the French woman, whom he was still awkwardly trying to make conversation with, but with little success. He patted the sniper rifle. "I'll pick off any Germans coming up the road."

Norton returned his attention to the young woman, but Sergeant Woodbine wasn't through yet. He cleared his throat. "Sir, with all due respect, we need to secure this town."

"Duly noted, Sergeant," Captain Norton said dismissively. "First, you and the men see if you can find anything to eat. Or any wine. I'll stay here and see what I can find out from Mademoiselle Margot."

The soldiers spread out through the village, although there wasn't much to see beyond the main street that led toward the bridge.

Cole and Vaccaro walked down to take a look. The Moselle ran swift, deep, and brown after the heavy rain. Cole had once swam a small river to get the drop on a German sniper, but the Moselle looked far more challenging to swim. He didn't much like water, anyhow, having almost drowned once while trapping beaver in a mountain stream running high with snowmelt.

The river here was narrow and the stone bridge was ancient, dating to the reign of Louis IV. In keeping with the needs of the time period in which it was built, the span was scarcely wide enough for a wagon. Something big as a panzer was not getting across. For starters, it wouldn't have fit, and the sheer weight of all that armor might have brought down the entire structure. But the bridge was more than adequate for soldiers on foot, Jeeps or Kübelwagen. A Chrysler truck might just squeeze over.

Considering the fighting that had raged all around it, it seemed almost miraculous that the village had escaped unscathed. The village and the bridge were largely hidden by the hills that ran down to them and the surrounding dense forest, effectively hiding Ville sur Moselle from the air. The Luftwaffe and then Allied planes had taken turns bombing several of the river crossings, but so far, Ville sur Moselle had been spared by the war. With the arrival of American troops, however, the war had finally come to this isolated village.

Cole looked at Vaccaro. "City Boy, how long do you think it will take them Germans to find this bridge right here?" Cole ran the last two words together, pronouncing them *rye-cheer*.

"They've got the same maps we do," Vaccaro said. "The Jerries are on the run, so they ought to be ahead of us, but maybe they took a wrong turn somewhere and we got a head start on them. It won't be long until they get here. Everybody's got the same idea. Get to the Moselle and find a way across."

"Well, here we are," Cole said.

"Here we are," Vaccaro agreed. He looked back up the road they had just come down. "Now what?"

"We ought to secure the village, that's what. Like the sergeant said. At least he knows what he's doing. We're gonna have company right soon."

The two men started back toward where Captain Norton stood in the modest village square. He still had Cole's rifle slung over one shoulder. Cole did not feel very reassured holding the grease gun. The weapon had no range, and if Germans suddenly appeared on the road into town, he wouldn't be of much use until the Jerries were on top of them.

By now, many of the villagers had retreated into their homes, most of which had thick stone walls. These soldiers weren't Germans, but young men with guns made civilians nervous. Margot was one of the few villagers left, mostly because she was stuck in the village square being chatted up by Captain Norton. Her brother had wandered off somewhere. As the other villagers drifted away, she was the only civilian in sight.

Looking around at the peaceful village, Cole felt less and less relaxed. He sensed a pervasive feeling in the air that something was about to happen. One did not need to be as attenuated as Cole to sense it. The air felt a lot like things did just before a bad thunderstorm. The air fairly crackled.

That's when they heard the sound of a vehicle approaching.

CHAPTER THIRTEEN

Lucky for the GIs in the village, the approaching vehicle turned out to be a Jeep. This one was moving fast. Even so, a Jeep was no race car. With its modest engine, lack of suspension, and the rough roads, a Jeep couldn't do more than forty or fifty miles per hour, but this one managed to be flying like a bat out of hell. Norton's squad caught a glimpse of United States uniforms and relaxed enough not to start shooting.

The Jeep skidded to a stop in the village square, coming so close to Captain Norton and the French woman that they were forced to jump out of the way.

"What the hell?" Captain Norton demanded. He looked more than a little hot under the collar. He started purposefully toward the Jeep, clearly with an ass-chewing in mind.

The passenger in the Jeep stood up. He wasn't really a tall man, but the extra height provided by the vehicle made him tower over everyone. He put his hands on his hips and scowled at the ragtag soldiers staring at him in surprise. He wore a tailored uniform with a tunic coat that belted at the waist, polished boots, and a new helmet. On the helmet was a single silver star, matching the star on his collar.

Catching a glimpse of those stars, Captain Norton came to a halt as if thunderstruck.

Watching from nearby, Cole's first thought was that he had never seen an actual general up close before. His second thought was that the son of a bitch must be lost. What was a general doing way out here?

Cole didn't think much of officers, and this one looked like he'd stepped right out of headquarters. It stood to reason that a general would be at least three times as useless as a captain. Still, he had to give this general points for reducing Captain Norton to a slack-jawed idiot.

Margot used the opportunity to slip away. She headed back toward the house that she had stepped out of a short while ago, but not before stopping to look around for her brother, who was nowhere in sight.

"Sir," Norton finally stammered, and then he managed to salute.

"Are these your men? What the hell are they doing standing around? We need to get them deployed. And I mean now, goddammit! There's a German unit coming up the road right behind me. Now—"

Before the general could finish berating Captain Norton, the French boy reappeared, shouting as he ran full-tilt down the main street.

The boy's words needed no translation. The Germans had arrived.

Just up the road, a Kübelwagen with a mounted machine gun came into sight. The vehicle moved slowly, followed closely by several dozen Wehrmacht troops.

They were no more than two hundred feet away. Upon spotting one another, the soldiers on both sides seemed to freeze.

Except for Cole, who grabbed the French boy and shoved him down behind the general's Jeep.

It was the Germans, however, who reacted first and opened fire. Someone in the Kübelwagen shouted an order, and seconds later, the soldier standing behind the machine gun started shooting.

Cole stuck the grease gun around a tire of the Jeep and squeezed off a burst, but it was hard to shoot with any accuracy at this range. He wished that he had his rifle in his hands.

He looked up and saw Norton fumbling with the

Springfield rifle, finally getting it to his shoulder and shooting back. He seemed to take forever to work the bolt before he got off another shot. The German kept firing that machine gun, further proof that Norton couldn't hit a damn thing. With the scope on that rifle, Norton ought to have been able to drop that machine gunner.

Another burst from the MP-42 ripped the air apart. Bullets strafed the square, catching Captain Norton and the fresh-faced kid out in the open. Both of them went down and didn't get back up.

The general had never climbed off the Jeep but now he had the good sense to dive between the seats for cover. An engine block did a tolerable job of stopping gunfire, even when it came from "Hitler's Buzzsaw."

Without any defense set up, the sudden German attack caused pandemonium among the Americans. Dodging rounds from the MG-42, GIs scattered, diving for cover. Some went down an did not get back up. A sharp voice could be heard above the shooting, cutting through the din: "I want superior fire on that car, goddammit! Target that gunner!"

The general had extricated himself from between the seat of the Jeep. Having made himself heard, Tolliver set the example by firing his Browning handgun at the Germans, although he was too far away to do any good.

A couple of shots from the American side struck the front of the German vehicle but didn't do any harm. Unlike a Jeep, the air-cooled Kübelwagen had no radiator, and the engine was in the back. Such a concept was alien to the Americans. They would have been incredulous to learn that in a few years a similar vehicle—the immensely popular Volkswagen Beetle —would reach American shores, built on the chassis of the wartime Kübelwagen.

The general's orders to return fire were easier to hear than to obey, what with the German machine gun still chattering at them. More German troops moved up, working their way into the village and using whatever shelter was offered by the buildings. They moved efficiently, like men who had done this before—and no doubt they had taken more than one French village in similar fashion.

The Germans also appeared to outnumber the American defenders, and at the moment, they had the element of surprise and firepower on their side.

Unless something happened, the Americans would soon be wiped out or forced to surrender, and the crucial bridge over the Moselle River would fall into German hands.

Cole felt the squad falling apart around him. He fired at the Germans, although they were too far away for the grease gun to have a telling effect. He really wished that he had his rifle. With the Springfield, he could have easily picked off the German machine gunner who was chewing them up from the back of that Kübelwagen.

He glanced over at Captain Norton's body. The dead officer's body lay splayed out on the paving stones in an unnatural position, surrounded by blood. He had been killed in the first burst from the German attack. Nearby lay the green kid who had been so concerned about being seen as a coward. Maybe that had meant he was a split second too slow in getting behind cover.

Cole felt bad about the dead kid. Given a little more time, he would have made a good soldier. What was his name? Bill something? Didn't make a damn bit of difference now.

On the other hand, he didn't feel so bad that Norton was dead. The man had been an incompetent officer and a nuisance. He wasn't going to thank the Germans for killing him, though. Norton had been a horse's ass, but at least they'd been on the same team.

He could see his own Springfield rifle still slung across Norton's shoulder.

He needed to get his hands on that rifle if they were going to have a chance to take out the German machine gunner.

The question was, could he get from the Jeep to the dead captain without getting mowed down?

He might have a chance when the German

stopped to reload. The MG-42 chewed through belts awfully fast.

He ejected the magazine and inserted another.

"Stay down," Cole told Frenchie, who didn't even have a weapon, and pushed him down against the stone pavers of the courtyard for emphasis.

Briefly, the machine gun stopped chewing up the square. The German gun crew would need a few moments to either feed in a new belt or put in a new barrel to replace the one that had become superheated.

Now or never. Cole ran from behind the Jeep, keeping low, and fired the grease gun in the general direction of the German Kübelwagen and the advancing Jerries. He doubted that he would hit anything, but if those fat .45 caliber rounds made them keep their heads down, all the better.

Reaching Norton's body, he tossed away the grease gun. Cole tugged at the rifle to free it, but the sling was pinned under the body and soaked through with blood. Cole reached for his knife, a razor-sharp custom Bowie knife forged from Damascus steel, and sliced through the canvas sling.

The rifle was back in his hands. He felt its familiar heft. Damned if it wasn't like a part of him.

But this was no time for a family reunion.

Cole sprawled behind Norton's body, using it for over. He put the rifle to his shoulder. Through the telescopic sight, the Kübelwagen sprang much closer. The rifle was zeroed in for roughly that distance.

The German soldier behind the machine gun had recharged the weapon and began firing, the muzzle flashes so close that they seemed to be stabbing into Cole's eyes. The muzzle swung in his direction and Cole heard bullets strike the flagstones and walk toward him. Bullets screamed off the flagstones. He heard a round chunk into Norton's body at his feet.

Cole put the crosshairs on the German and squeezed the trigger.

The man went down and the machine gun fell silent.

He worked the bolt. Through the scope, he looked for another target to acquire. One disadvantage of the telescopic sight was that it narrowed his field of view. That was why it helped to have a spotter keep an eye on the big picture and call out targets. Picking them out with the rifle scope took too long.

He saw a pair of Jerries peeking from around the corner of a building and squeezed off a couple of shots. He thought that he hit one, and raised a puff of powdered stone close to the other. The man reappeared, and Cole took two more shots. The second one did the trick, and the German slumped to the street.

The Springfield's clip held five founds. Five shots, but too many damn targets. The spare clips that

Captain Norton had taken from him were still in the dead captain's cartridge belt. Cole would have to waste precious seconds retrieving them while the Germans continued to press the attack.

He heard a voice say, "Right hand, soldier."

He held out his hand and felt a fresh clip slapped into it. He pressed the clip into the chamber and reloaded.

"Three o'clock, about three feet up behind that yellow building," the voice instructed.

He swiveled the rifle in that direction and acquired the target, zeroing in on a German who was keeping up a steady fire. Cole squeezed the trigger and the German went down.

His eye left the scope long enough to catch a glimpse of his spotter. To his surprise, it was the general. He had retrieved Cole's discarded grease gun and squeezed off a burst.

"They're trying to get back on the machine gun," the general said.

Cole pivoted until the Kübelwagen was back in sight, then put the crosshairs on a German who had climbed up behind the machine gun. He went down in a spray of blood.

With a buzzing noise like a supercharged wasp, a bullet went by too close for comfort, making his whole body thrum involuntarily, as if he had just touched a live wire. Every soldier hated that sound.

More rounds zipped past, underscoring the fact that he and the general were too exposed.

"Go!" the general gave him a shove. "Get to the Jeep. I'll cover you."

Cole ran as the general opened up with the grease gun. He jumped behind the safety of the Jeep with Tolliver on his heels. The French boy was still there and had curled into a ball, trying to make himself as small as possible. At least the boy had some sense.

Using the hood of the Jeep for support, Cole began to pick off the targets that Tolliver acquired for him.

He turned his attention back to the Kübelwagen. The driver was dead or wounded, but he glimpsed an officer getting behind the wheel. Cole put a bullet through the windshield, knocking off the officer's hat and peppering him with glass. Before Cole could fire again, the officer ducked down and hit the gas, slewing the Kübelwagen around.

The retreating vehicle was a sign that the tide had turned. The Americans kept up a withering fire. Although they were outnumbered by the Germans, the Americans had a slight advantage in that they were more spread out, whereas the Germans had to attack down the narrow street. The houses sat right against the other, offering sparse cover other than the doorways and a couple of trees.

Also, it helped that the Americans had Cole.

General Tolliver passed him another clip. He put the sights on a soldier who was advancing at a trot and dropped him. Two soldiers edging their weapons around a corner went down next.

"At the far end of the street, there's a guy advancing with a Panzerfaust," Tolliver said. "It's a long way off, but see what you can do."

Cole practically screwed his eye to the rifle scope. He spotted the soldier running forward with a Panzerfaust. Though meant to defeat tanks, it would be just the weapon to clear the square of defenders.

Cole wasn't about to let him get that close. He held high and squeezed the trigger. The German threw up both hands and crumpled, dragged down by the weight of the Panzerfaust.

Beside him, Tolliver whistled.

But the Germans weren't about to give up just yet. They had their own ace up their sleeve. The Kübelwagen had withdrawn to the far end of town. The officer stood and gestured at a soldier, who came forward and rested his rifle across the hood of the vehicle. Through the binoculars, Tolliver caught a glimpse of a German sniper, with a telescopic sight on top of his rifle. It was too far to say where he was aiming, but it was no stretch of the imagination to think that he was targeting his American counterpart.

"Down!" Tolliver grabbed Cole by the shoulder

and pulled him behind the front of the Jeep. A split second later, a bullet carved a shiny groove in the hood of the vehicle, just where Cole had been positioning his rifle.

"Sniper," the general said. "He's set up behind that vehicle."

Cole slid behind a tire, hoping to return fire. But by then, the Kübelwagen and the sniper were backing down the road and out of sight. For now, the German attack was over.

CHAPTER FOURTEEN

IN THE WAKE of the attack, a silence descended over the village. The chill autumn air, the old stone buildings, and even the distant rough hills seemed to be holding their breath, watching and waiting for something to happen next. Indifferent, the Moselle River flowed silently between its steep banks, gurgling around the stone pillars of the ancient bridge.

Although the town's streets were quiet and empty, Cole was sure that there were many eyes upon them from behind the closed doors in the surrounding houses with their thick, stone walls. The people of the town had the good sense to make themselves scarce once the shooting started.

Cole reached up and ripped the tape off the front of his helmet. With Captain Norton dead, Cole didn't need to cover the Confederate flag on the front of his helmet. He would wear that flag with pride, goddammit. He balled up the strips of tape and tossed them in the general direction of Captain Norton's body.

Then he spent a moment looking over the rifle. It seemed none the worse for wear, although he wouldn't mind getting a fresh coat of oil on her. Cole was fanatical about cleaning and oiling his rifle. He noticed a couple of fresh hash marks carved into the stock. Were those supposed to represent the Germans that Norton had killed? Cole shook his head in disgust. The only enemy soldiers that Norton had shot were in his imagination. Besides, Norton must have known that being captured by the enemy with a sniper rifle with hash marks on it—showing that you celebrated your kills—was a surefire way to make sure that you never made it to the rear.

Now that the shooting was over, he and the general straightened up from where they had been sheltering behind the Jeep. Tolliver gave the Jeep a quick inspection, whistling at the bullet holes peppering the vehicle. There didn't seem to be any fluids leaking, however, so the bullets hadn't hit any of the Jeep's vital organs.

General Tolliver clapped Cole on the shoulder. "That was some fine shooting, son. What did you say your name was?"

"Cole, sir."

"Cole, huh. Sounds familiar. Haven't I heard your name around?"

"Maybe so, sir. I really couldn't say."

Vaccaro overhead the general and said, "Sir, that newspaper reporter Ernie Pyle wrote an article about Cole. That reporter made Cole out to be the best shot in the whole damn Army. If you think that you've heard of him, I'll bet that's why."

"Is that so?" The general gave Cole a long look. "What was that captain doing with your rifle? If I'm not mistaken, you were carrying a grease gun. Seems like the wrong weapon for you."

"It's a long story, sir. But if it's all the same to you, I believe I'll hang on to this here rifle."

"You do that, Cole."

"Thank you, sir."

* * *

GENERAL TOLLIVER LOOKED around at the village square. His hands were shaking, so he grabbed the door frame on the Jeep so that no one would see the tremors. He could scarcely believe that he had just been in his first battle. It was odd, but at the time he hadn't been scared. He had grabbed a weapon and started firing at the enemy without giving it much thought. The fear only seemed to come to him now, along with those shaky hands.

He looked around for his driver, who seemed to have survived. He would have felt awfully bad if he had not, considering that Tolliver had dragged him into this mess. A few other men weren't so lucky, including the captain who had been leading these men. Where did that leave him?

In command, he realized. Tolliver would gladly have deferred to some lieutenant with combat experience, but there were no other officers. Whatever happened next was up to him, he realized. He could see the men milling about, some of them looking dazed after the firefight, wondering what to do next.

He took a deep breath to calm himself. The last thing he wanted was for the men to see him looking scared. They didn't know that he was a bean counter back at HQ. He wasn't about to tell them. Keeping quiet about his background wasn't a matter of pride, but a simple understanding that he had to instill some confidence in these soldiers. Someone had to take charge if these men were to have any chance of holding this town. Hell, someone had to take charge if they were just going to *survive* against a superior force of Germans. He was a general, and by God, he planned to act like one.

Tolliver waved the sergeant over. "Sergeant, tell the men to gather round."

"Yes, sir." Woodbine hesitated. "Uh, sir, what should I do about the deserter?"

"What deserter?"

Woodbine gave Frenchie a nudge forward. Frenchie favored his wounded leg, grimacing slightly as he walked.

Woodbine said, "When we got here, this private was already in the village. He said his unit was mostly wiped out by the SS just north of here, at some place called Dornot. Captain Norton ordered him arrested as a deserter."

Tolliver put his hands on his hips and got a good look at Frenchie. "You were at Dornot?"

"Yes, sir. The Germans got most of my unit when we were coming back across the river. They really tore us to pieces. I drifted down the river and ended up here."

"All right, Private. I heard about Dornot back at HQ. How's that leg?"

"I got lucky, sir. Bullet went right through."

The general nodded. "You go on and see if you can find yourself a rifle. We'll need you when the Germans come back."

"I'm not under arrest, sir?"

"For what? Sounds to me, son, like you were surviving, not deserting. Anyhow, would you rather be under arrest or would you rather keep fighting Germans?"

Frenchie grinned. "I'd rather fight Germans, sir!"

"There you go, then. Sergeant, let's get these men together now."

* * *

SERGEANT WOODBINE GAVE the order to assemble, although it wasn't really necessary—most of the men were within earshot of the general, smoking cigarettes and wondering what to do next.

Once the men had gathered, Tolliver took a moment looking them over. If he liked what he saw, it didn't register on his face. As a matter of fact, the longer he studied them, the more that his expression seemed to indicate that Tolliver had taken a big slug of prune juice or bitten into a sour apple.

Cole couldn't blame him. Only about twenty men had survived the German assault on Ville sur Moselle. They included Cole and Vaccaro, Frenchie, the general's young driver, and the remaining men from Captain Norton's original patrol, including Sergeant Woodbine.

Woodbine seemed solid, but some of those other guys were green, a fact made obvious from their new uniforms, and also from the fact that some of them had hunkered down and hidden during the German assault, rather than shooting back. They didn't get it yet that the enemy would still kill you, whether or not you shot back. Sergeant

Woodbine had done the best he could to get all of the men to return fire, but he couldn't be everywhere at once.

While the general inspected the troops, such as they were, Cole kept his eyes on the road coming into town. He knew for damn sure that the Germans weren't done. The general noticed Cole looking, and he looked, too. He seemed to know as well as Cole did that the Jerries would be back—and soon.

The general cleared his throat. "You men did good," he said. "You held your own and then some. But I've got to tell you, the Jerries aren't done with us. And chances are that they're gonna hit us even harder. Last time, they stumbled into us, but we can count on a more coordinated attack. They need this bridge. We need this bridge too, goddammit, and we're not letting them have it. Not if I can help it."

The general paused, although it wasn't clear if he expected an actual response. "By the way, my name is General Tolliver. I was supposed to link up with the Third Army to serve as an observer for General Eisenhower to check on the supply situation, but somehow that didn't happen. I suppose a lot of you men were also supposed to be somewhere else. But here we are.

"I can damn sure promise you that I am not going to report back to the Supreme Commander of Allied Forces in Europe that I lost an opportunity to secure and hold a bridge over the Moselle River. So, what you and I are going to do is hold this bridge."

General Tolliver put his hands on his hips and continued to survey the soldiers, and then the village beyond. He spoke the next words quietly, as if talking to himself. "It's not much, but we just might be able to hold until this weather clears or we link up with another unit." He corrected himself with the words that came next. "Might? To hell with *might*. We have to hold, and by God, we *will*."

Again, General Tolliver paused and looked around at their faces. He had gotten their attention, that was for sure.

Sergeant Woodbine shifted from foot to foot, looked around, and responded for the group by saying, "Yes, sir!"

The general went on. "When the Jerries hit us again, they'll come from the same direction," he said, waving a hand at the road beyond the village. "I'd say the hills are too steep here for them to try and circle the village. We have the river at our back. There's no need to worry about Germans coming at us from that direction unless there's a German unit that got here before us. In that case, they could be on the other side of the river and come back across the bridge. Has anyone seen evidence of that? Cole?"

"No, sir," Cole said.

"Thank God for that much. Germans on one side

of us is enough. All right, the plan is that we are going to hold here until we get some reinforcements," the general said. "From here on out, this is our very own Alamo. Got it? Sergeant, I want to know what we've got in the way of ammunition."

"Yes, sir."

Tolliver stepped down from the Jeep, signaling that his speech was over. He looked at his driver and then at the Jeep. "Private Smith, this thing is shot to pieces, but see if you can get it to run. We'll keep it in reserve in case we need to haul ass somewhere or get a message out. Right now, our communications network consists of those four wheels."

"Not much gas in it, sir," the driver pointed out.

"It will be enough. It will have to be."

Sergeant Woodbine was back with his report. It had not taken him long to circulate among the men because there weren't many defenders. "We have the Browning, sir, and a box and a half of ammo, which is enough to hold off maybe one more attack." Woodbine was referring to the .30 caliber Browning M-1919 mounted on the back of the Jeep. "It looks as if the Germans left behind a Panzerfaust. Might come in handy if any armor shows up."

"Let's hope to God that doesn't happen," Tolliver said. The thought filled them all with dread. "How are we set for rifle rounds?"

"Most of the men had the standard issue of M-1 rounds, but they've shot some of that."

Being green troops, these soldiers generally carried 96 rounds in stripper clips of eight rounds each. Veterans of the fighting in Normandy had learned the hard way to stuff their pockets with extra ammo and always carried as much as they could.

Not long ago, Cole had nearly run out of ammunition for his Springfield near the Falaise Gap fighting, just as he was confronting a particularly deadly German sniper. That mistake had nearly cost him his life when he went up against that German. He did not plan on running low on ammo again. Not if he could help it. Besides the clips he had taken back from Captain Norton's cartridge belt, he had more ammunition in his haversack.

Cole had grown up in the mountains where one bullet or shotgun shell might be all you needed to bring home supper. The experience had taught him the value of a single bullet, because if he missed, like as not he and his brothers and sisters would go hungry. The thing was, deer and rabbits didn't shoot back. The Jerries did. Cole patted his pockets one more time just to reassure himself that the ammo was there.

"We have what we have. We've just got to make every shot count," Tolliver said. The general pointed at Cole. "Cole, considering that you are the best goddamn shot I have seen, I want you up high on one of these buildings. You will be our eyes. If you see the Germans coming at us, start shooting the sons of bitches. That's all the warning that we'll need."

"Yes, sir. If it's all right, sir, I want to take Vaccaro here with me. I'll need a spotter. He can be on the binoculars while I'm on the rifle, just like you were, sir."

"Very well." The general pointed to two more men. "You two start clearing these bodies. Find a cellar to put them into for now."

"What about the Germans, sir?"

"What about them? They can feed the crows, for all I care."

"Yes, sir."

Tolliver issued more orders, singling out two more men. "You and you, get up there where the village starts and keep an eye out. Pick up that Panzerfaust they dropped while you're at it."

"Now, sir?"

"Now, goddammit! The rest of you, stay close for disposition and if you're not doing anything else, keep your eyes on the road for those Jerries. Understood? Now, you all know what to do. Let's get it in gear, people."

"Yes, sir!"

As the two men detailed to remove the bodies moved off, one of them muttered something about

Captain Norton not being much of a loss. He'd made the mistake of saying it just loud enough for the general to overhear him. It was the wrong thing to say.

With a shout, the general froze the man in his tracks. "Soldier! I did not know Captain Norton from a hole in the ground, but I will not abide that kind of talk! Every man who died here was a hero, as far as I'm concerned, whether he was an officer or enlisted. Have I made myself clear?"

The soldier snapped to attention. "Yes, sir!"

Sergeant Woodbine stepped forward and gave the soldier a shove in the direction of the bodies to be clear away. "You heard the general. Captain Norton died for his country. Let's show him respect."

"He did indeed die for his country and we honor him for it, just as we honor these other brave men," General Tolliver said. His chastising of the soldier had gotten everyone's attention. He realized that he had an opportunity here to say something more. He needed to galvanize these men who were not yet a cohesive unit and get them to work together. "But let me tell you men something else. It's an honor to die for your country, but it's a whole lot better to make the other son of a bitch die for his country instead. That's what we are going to do from here on out. And we are going to do it together. You may not know the man standing next to you, but by God, you are going to fight for one another. We are all Americans here, and that's the enemy out there. Now, get to work, goddammit!"

Tolliver hoped it was enough, because they would need more than bullets to stop the Germans. They would need determination.

THEIR ORDERS RECEIVED, Cole and Vaccaro started up the street.

"So, that's a general?" Vaccaro said.

"Ain't what I expected," Cole said.

"What did you expect?"

"I expected a prick like Captain Norton, but this old man's got hisself a backbone. Let's just see if he can keep us from getting wiped out by the Krauts."

"What would you say are the odds of that?"

"Right now, I'd say it's down to a coin toss."

They looked around for a good place to set up their sniper hide. The village was too small to have any towering structures. None of the buildings was over three stories. Even the village chapel was a squat affair. In this case, however, it wasn't height that mattered but a clear view of the road into the village —and any Germans coming down it.

This meant that they had their pick of houses. Neither one of them particularly looked forward to barging into one of the houses and trying to explain to the frightened residents what they were up to.

"Should have brought Frenchie with us," Vaccaro said.

"I got an idea," Cole said.

He started toward the house into which the French girl had fled. She had interacted with the soldiers enough that she might let them in without a fuss.

Vaccaro saw what he was up to and grinned. "Good choice. I wouldn't mind seeing that girl again."

"This ain't a social call," he said, and was about to pound his fist against the door, when the door opened.

Clearly, the girl had been watching the activity on the street and had seen them walk up.

Cole looked past her into the house. His first concern was whether or not she was alone. He caught a glimpse of the boy who had come running to warn them about the Germans. The boy stood just behind her, wide-eyed at the sight of the American GI at their door. Cole didn't see anyone else.

The village row house was neat and modest by French standards, although compared to the shack hammered together out of scrap wood and tin that Cole had grown up in back at Gashey's Creek, it was palatial. The door opened into a narrow hallway, which was decorated with an ornate mirror and a table on which sat a vase of fall flowers. The sight of the bright flowers was incongruous compared to the war-torn countryside.

"*Entrez vous*," she said, and stepped aside.

Cole and Vaccaro went in, with Vaccaro grinning stupidly at the girl. Cole gave him a shove. "C'mon, City Boy. Gawk on your own time."

Cole pointed at the stairs with his rifle. It was hard to know what the girl thought he was asking, but she stood back and gestured for him to go ahead.

The stairs were narrow, and Cole kept the rifle pointed upwards, just in case there were any surprises. Vaccaro was right behind him. He heard a creak on the stairs below and he spun around, but it was only the boy, trying to follow them. The girl tugged him away and scolded him.

"Kids," Vaccaro muttered. "She looks too young for him to be her brat. I'll bet it's her little brother."

"Do them a favor and tell them to get in the cellar, if they've got one."

"*Hidey-vous,*" Vaccaro said in his best Brooklyn-accented faux French. He pointed downward. The walls of the house were thick, but not thick enough if the Germans started throwing anything serious at them. "*La cave.*"

Vaccaro spoke French with a thick Brooklyn accent, but the girl seemed to get it. She also pointed at the floor. "*La cave,*" she said, nodding.

"That's right, honey," Vaccaro said. "*La cave. Oui.*"

She ushered the boy out. They heard the sound of a door opening and closing, and they were alone in the house.

"How do you know them French words?" Cole asked. He was impressed, in spite of himself.

"Where do these people hide their calvados and other booze? *Dans la cave.* Don't you pay attention to anything?"

"Shut up, Vaccaro. Let's go shoot us some Germans."

CHAPTER FIFTEEN

COLE WAS sure that the Germans wouldn't take long to reorganize and attack. One thing about the Germans was that they were relentless once they set their minds to something. When they did attack, he wanted to be in position.

They had reached the top of the stairs and he checked one bedroom, and then the other. Both had good views of the village square, and if they leaned out far enough, they could see the road leading into town. Cole opened the window and eased his rifle out. Vaccaro took up position in the room's other window and peered out with his binoculars, which gave him a much wider field of view than Cole had through the telescopic sight.

Cole swept his scope over the village to get the lay of the land. Under Tolliver's directions, Sergeant

Woodbine had placed men at the edge of the village to serve as skirmishers and set up a defensive line at the village square. Vaccaro could see the men arrayed below, using whatever they could for cover. Here and there lay the bodies of Germans killed in the previous fight. General Tolliver had not wanted to bother moving the dead Jerries, but the sight of the gory, bullet-riddled bodies was not reassuring to the living. Cole wasn't a general, but the problem was clear— there just weren't enough men to properly defend the village from a concerted attack.

"I got movement," Vaccaro announced.

Cole screwed his eye against the telescopic sight. "Where they at?"

"Watch the street," Vaccaro said. "Here they come."

Cole saw a German soldier running at a crouch, heading toward the outskirts of the village. He got the rifle moving, leading him a little. It wasn't much different from targeting a running deer.

He squeezed the trigger. Down went the enemy soldier.

Cole worked the bolt of the Springfield, ejecting the spent shell and inserting another round of .30/06 into the chamber. He looked around for another target, but the Germans must have seen their comrade fall. No one came running in behind him.

Were the Jerries probing rather than making a full-fledged attack?

"Talk to me, City Boy."

"There's nothin' to see. They're all spread out now. Sneaky Kraut bastards."

In the village below, the American defenders had also spotted the Germans and started to fire. The Browning let loose with a five-second burst. Whether or not he hit anything, Cole couldn't tell because of his limited field of view, but it was certainly giving the Germans pause. Last time, the Jerries had stumbled into the village. This time around, they were being far more cautious. The problem was that the Browning only had enough ammo for a handful of bursts like that.

Cole spotted a German creeping forward, again on the right side. Definitely probing the American defenses. Aiming his rifle, Cole put a stop to that. He could see a couple more Germans trying to edge their way along the left-hand side of the village street. Again, the Browning cut loose and sent them retreating.

This was shaping up to be a classic German attack. Advance on one flank, advance on the other, and then straight up the middle.

The defending Americans only had one machine gun, and no heavy weapons, but Cole was proving to be their ace in the hole. The Germans would be better off skipping the flanking movements and storming the town in a rush. He wouldn't be able to get them all if they switched tactics. At this rate, Cole was going to pick them off one by one.

Vaccaro started to say, "There's another one—"

He didn't get to finish. A bullet punched through the window. Glass shattered, followed by the sound of Vaccaro hitting the floor.

Cole ducked below his own window, glad of the thick stone walls. He was sure that had not been some stray shot. Someone must have glimpsed Vaccaro in the window because he was more exposed. Considering that the Germans were still a good distance away, hitting the target had taken some skill. The shot hadn't come from any of the troops that Cole could see below.

Sniper, he thought.

He would worry about the sniper later. He had more immediate concerns, such as whether or not Vaccaro was still alive.

Cole belly-crawled to where Vaccaro rolled around in the broken glass from the window. "I'm OK, I'm OK," he said. "At least, I think I'm OK."

Cole checked him for blood but could see no wounds.

"Yep, I reckon you're in one piece. That was a close one, though."

Keeping low, Cole looked up at the broken pane.

It was just about where Vaccaro had been positioned, glassing the road into town. By all rights, he should have been dead. The window glass deflected the bullet's trajectory just enough that it must have struck Vaccaro's helmet with a glancing blow.

"We got us a sniper," he said.

"More like, a sniper got us."

"Stay put. I got me an idea."

Keeping below the window, Cole crawled over to a side table, where the girl had left a hand-held mirror. He had seen it when he first entered the room. It was an inexpensive mirror with a wooden handle and frame, but it would do just fine. He grabbed it and crawled back to Vaccaro's side, then pressed the mirror into his hand.

"You want me to comb my hair?" Vaccaro wondered.

"Use that mirror to see if you can spot that sniper. Keep your head down while you're at it."

"Thanks for the advice, Hillbilly."

Cole crawled back to his original position but did not yet put the rifle out the window. He did not want to make himself a target just yet, but lay crouched beneath the window. He nodded at Vaccaro.

Staying on the floor, Vaccaro raised the mirror above the window sill, angling it so that he could see out. The odds of seeing the sniper, who must be some distance away, were not good. But Vaccaro might catch a glimpse of *something*.

They were not disappointed. Seconds after Vaccaro raised the mirror, another bullet ripped the mirror from his grip. The mirror exploded into silvery shards.

"Holy shit!"

"Did you see him?" Cole asked quietly.

"I saw him, all right. Just beyond the town, in that cluster of buildings along the road. The white house. Window on the right."

"Yeah?" Cole had a good memory for landscapes. He had studied the view from the window earlier. He set a picture of the house Vaccaro had described in his mind's eye.

"Pretty sure I saw a muzzle flash."

"You sure or are you just pretty sure?" If Vaccaro was wrong, and the sniper was in another location altogether, Cole had an even chance of getting his head blown off as soon as he raised it above the window sill.

"Goddammit, Cole. Pretty sure. In case you didn't notice, that son of a bitch shot the mirror out of my hand before I could get a good look."

"Take your helmet off and stick it up there to see if he takes the bait, why don't you."

Muttering, Vaccaro took off his helmet. "Ready?"

"Mmm."

"Now!"

Vaccaro lifted his helmet, inviting a bullet. At the same time, Cole rolled to his knees and balanced the rifle across the window sill. The view sprang closer through the rifle scope. He saw the distant white house, just where he had pictured it. The distance was greater than he had thought. He had to admit that the German was a good shot to hit anything from so far away.

If the German sniper was good, Cole felt confident that he was an even better shot. He took just a second to acquire the second-floor window, then fired. Then he ducked back down. Nobody had tried to shoot Vaccaro's helmet. He reckoned that it was a fifty-fifty chance that he had shot the sniper or that the man had been too wily to take the bait in the first place.

"Get him?" Vaccaro asked.

"Maybe, maybe not. If he was there, I got him. But it's time to move."

"You got that right."

One of the basic tenets of sniper craft was that you didn't stay in one place for too long. Not if you wanted to live to fight another day. For a sniper, survival depended upon being stealthy. It meant staying hidden. Part of what made a sniper so terrifying and effective—not to mention hated—was the ability to strike seemingly out of nowhere. A sniper's chances of being discovered increased exponentially each time that he took a shot.

Cole didn't know if he'd hit the German sniper or not. But for now, after a close call, being able to walk out of the room alive seemed like enough of a victory. He took one glance back into the room. The room was no longer neat and tidy. Empty brass casings from the Springfield lay on the floor, along with the shattered remnants of the window glass and mirror. One of the glass panes of the window was entirely shot out. That was war for you—it always made a mess.

They descended the stairs to find the house empty. Wisely, the French girl had indeed fled along with the boy. Hopefully, they were down in the cellar. Bullets didn't care who was a civilian, and who was not.

"I got a bad feelin' about this, City Boy. That German sniper was a little too good. What are we up against?"

"Best we can hope to do it get him next time."

But there was no time to set up a second sniper hide. Instead, he and Vaccaro joined in the fight taking place for Ville sur Moselle. Now that the Germans had probed their defenses, things were about to get hot. They took up positions behind the fountain in the town square. It was clear from the dirt and debris in the fountain basin that it had not flowed in years, but the stone fountain provided good cover from enemy fire. Also, from the fountain they had a clear view right down the street.

"Here they come!"

The second attack was concerted and savage, but the Germans were driven back again by the small American force. The Germans kept attacking by twos and threes, and the defenders picked them off easily or pinned them down before they could advance deeper into town. If the Germans had rushed them all at once, the outcome might have been different.

"Pick your targets," General Tolliver shouted, moving from group to group. "Aim and fire. Make each shot count."

Cole shook his head, watching the general run for the next knot of defenders. It was a wonder the damn fool hadn't been killed. He had to admit that General Tolliver knew how to place his limited forces to effectively defend the town. Also, he had managed to inspire even the greenest troops with both his words and his actions. The man didn't seem to be afraid of anything.

Cole thought that maybe, just maybe, they still had a chance to hold the town and that bridge.

The Jerries were stubborn, but they weren't stupid. Once it became clear that they weren't going to be able to take the town, the attack ground to a halt. The Germans laid down a final fusillade of covering fire so that their comrades pinned down in the village could make their escape. Cole and the others were only too happy to let them go. A few more bodies lay in the street, but they wore German uniforms.

"There they go," Vaccaro said. "I got to admit that I love to see the Germans run off like that with their tails between their legs."

Cole said nothing, watching through the scope for any sign of the sniper they had encountered earlier. Given the layout of the village and the high ground surrounding it, a sniper was worrisome. From relative safety, he could pick off the defenders one by one. The only thing that would be worse was if the Germans called up a panzer. They wouldn't have a prayer against a tank unless someone got really lucky with the captured Panzerfaust.

From the village square, Cole could still see the house in the distance where the sniper had set up shop. Upstairs, he could see the window that he had fired into earlier, and it still appeared empty as the eye socket of a skull. Had he gotten lucky and taken out the German?

Like the mountain folk back home liked to say, *boil up a pot of beans and a pot of luck, and see which one fills your belly.* In other words, wishful thinking wouldn't do him any good.

His mouth tasted like gunpowder and dust. He spat. Beyond the scattered houses, somewhere in the cover of the woods, the Germans had withdrawn to lick their wounds for now. But the Germans needed to get through this town and take that bridge—and soon—before the weather cleared and the Allied planes returned and picked off the Germans.

As for the bridge, the Germans would cross it and then destroy it in order to slow the Allied advance. The Americans needed to keep that from happening so that another route remained open for their own forces to cross the Moselle.

"This ain't over yet," Cole said.

CHAPTER SIXTEEN

A COUPLE of the defenders had suffered minor wounds in the skirmish against the Germans. One man was shot in the arm, while another had been shot through the calf. Both men were lucky in that the rounds had not hit any bones or tendons. They could still fight, once they were patched up. The worst-off among the wounded was still West, whom they had carried into town. The poor man was really suffering and wouldn't last much longer without hospital care. A fever had set in and West drifted in and out of coherence.

Nothing much could be done for West or the other wounded, other than making them as comfortable as possible. Unfortunately, their cobbled-together unit lacked a medic or much in the way of medical supplies. For the pain, both men were taking liberal swings from a bottle of French brandy.

As it turned out, Frenchie was showing himself to be a man of many talents. Not only did he speak the *lingua franca*, but he had also helped his father back home bandage injuries and treat the sick. Never mind the fact that the patients were four-legged because his father was a country veterinarian.

"A horse doctor, I guess you'd say," Frenchie explained, slipping a man's shirt off his shoulder so that he could examine the flesh wound. He dusted the soldier's wounded arm with sulfa powder and then wrapped it tight with gauze. "Also a dog, cat, and dairy cow doctor."

He worked deftly, like someone who had done this many times before. Cole was impressed. "You're a damn sight better than some of the Army doctors I seen. You get out of this mess, you ought to become a medic. They could use you."

"The funny thing is that I never wanted to be a medic. I thought that I could do more good as a soldier. Guess I was wrong about that."

"The Army needs all kinds of soldiers, Frenchie. You're sort of a fighting medic."

The wounded soldier winced as Frenchie pulled the bandage tight. Finished, he patted the man's good shoulder. He also pried the brandy away from him. "Keep it up and you'll hurt worse from that booze,"

Frenchie said. "Calvados is potent stuff. You've had enough."

General Tolliver hurried past with the sergeant, taking stock of the situation. They had posted a couple of lookouts. Tolliver knew as well as anyone that the Germans would be back sooner rather than later for another bite of the apple. They were not done yet. Two lookouts had been posted to give them as much warning as possible when the next attack came.

"How are we set for ammunition?" the general asked.

Sergeant Woodbine had already checked with the men. "They've got thirty or forty rounds each. The Browning has maybe one belt left."

Tolliver swore. Somehow, he still managed to look crisp in his uniform. The glinting star on his collar and on his helmet looked conspicuously bright. "We can hold off maybe one more concerted attack. That's if they don't throw everything at us at once, which is what they should have done, instead of coming at us piecemeal."

"Agreed, sir. The Jerries are not always willing to change tactics. They're stubborn that way."

The general stood with his hands on his hips in the middle of the square. He looked around the town, taking stock. He seemed to be thinking things over.

Cole looked toward the distant house where the

German sniper had been located, then back at the general. He wished that the general would do his thinking someplace less exposed.

He walked over to the general. A timid man would have sidled over, but Cole didn't sidle well.

"General, if you keep standin' there with all them stars some Kraut sniper is gonna shoot your ass." He added, "Sir."

General Tolliver glared at him. "Soldier, I might point out that you have a Confederate flag painted smack dab on your helmet. Not only is that against regulations as recognizing a former hostile enemy of the United States but it makes a damn good target in itself."

"Ain't nobody killed me yet, sir, so it's good luck, I reckon."

The general continued to glare at him. "I'll tell you what's lucky, Cole. It's the fact that my people fought for the Confederacy. Otherwise, I'd make you take that goddamn helmet off."

"Yes, sir."

While it was true that they were both Southerners, the general was from Virginia, where the oldest families were descended from English cavaliers and still held onto some pretense of being aristocracy. They had owned slaves to till the rich cropland. Cole's own Scotch-Irish people had settled the Appalachian Mountains, where life was hard and luck ran thin as the growing soil. You couldn't get much farther from the Virginia gentry than that.

General Tolliver stalked off, shaking his head and muttering something about dumb peckerwoods. Cole noticed, though, that when Tolliver stopped, he had managed to put the tall fountain between himself and the German position.

Once Tolliver was safely out of earshot Vaccaro said, "Hillbilly, you ought to know better than to go giving orders to a general."

"That general has got some sand," Cole said, a grudging note of admiration in his voice. "But if he gets hisself killed, then the Krauts are gonna come through this town like shit through a goose and take that bridge. The next in command is Sergeant Woodbine, and he seems like a good man, but he ain't gonna hold that bridge."

"You got that right."

It soon became clear that the Americans were not entirely on their own in this fight. Five of the village men presented themselves to General Tolliver, offering to join the Americans. None of them was a day under fifty and their hair was mostly gray—if they still had any. Two appeared to be shopkeepers, soft in the middle and a bit stooped. They all carried weapons that could hardly be called adequate. Two were armed with ancient single-shot rifles that had possibly been used in the Franco-Prussian War. The other three carried battered shotguns that might be useful against hawks and foxes. The German occupiers had confiscated most handguns and any modern weapons, but had let the French keep their hunting shotguns. The antique rifles must not have been worth the Germans' attention.

The would-be defenders' designated spokesman was named Pierre, who was also the mayor. This was the same man who had helped to rescue Frenchie. He was tall and gaunt, with dark, earnest eyes sunken into his head. In fact, he bore a vague resemblance to Abraham Lincoln. His hands gripping the battered shotgun looked large and strong. In his prime ten or twenty years ago, he must have been a formidable fellow. He wore a tweed cap and a worn corduroy coat. He didn't speak any English, but Frenchie helped translate.

"He says they can help us fight," Frenchie explained.

Ordinarily, Allied forces turned down such volunteers because they lacked training or weapons. If anything, the French volunteers tended to get in the way. The exception would be offers of help from the local Resistance, members of whom had shown themselves to be vicious fighters. General Tolliver, however, was in a difficult position. There were a lot more Germans about to come at them, and not many defenders.

"All right," he said, reluctantly. "Sergeant, get these men into position."

As they marched closer to Germany, Allied forces had been warned about divided loyalties in the towns and countryside. This did not seem to be the case in Ville sur Moselle. The sight of Pierre and the other men joining the fight seemed to galvanize the towns-people. Slowly, they emerged from their houses and cellars, bearing gifts that all soldiers appreciated: food and liquor. They pressed everything from sausages to fresh bread to pies on the soldiers, along with bottles of wine and brandy.

"Thanks for the bread," Cole said to an older villager, pronouncing the word as if it had two syllables.

Vaccaro shook his head. "It's bread, not *bray-ed*, you dumb hillbilly."

"Be nice or I ain't gonna share."

Judging by the fact that the food was simple and sparse, the occupation must have been hard on the townspeople. Still, their generosity was welcome and meant that the soldiers would get some relief from their K rations.

Margot's brother, Marcus, came running up to Cole, clutching the empty rifle cartridges in his hand. His friend, Simon, tagged along. The boy tried to give the brass casings to Cole, who only grinned and said, "You hang onto those, kid."

Smiling, the boy put them in his pockets and ran off. Cole shook his head. Back when he was a young 'un, he used to do the same thing with his pa's shells. He used to put them under his thin pillow at night because he liked the smell of the gunpowder.

"Get yourselves something to eat," the general announced, accepting some hard-boiled eggs himself. "Then we need to make this village Kraut-proof."

Given the hills surrounding the town, the Germans had just one way to come at Ville sur Moselle, which was to attack straight up the main street in order to reach the bridge.

General Tolliver wasted no time preparing for the next German attack. His plan was to barricade the street. A couple of old wagons and carts were produced to anchor the barricade. Working in twos and threes while the lookouts kept watch, the soldiers added whatever they could pick up and carry to the barricade. Crates, an old door, a section of wrought iron fence, and a wooden bench were soon wedged among the wagons. The soldiers began to carry yet more items out of the houses: upholstered chairs and sofas, mattresses, kitchen tables. Some of the French housewives protested, but Pierre put a stop to that with a few words here and there, some of them spoken sharply.

"What's he saying?" Vaccaro asked Frenchie.

"He told them to stop complaining and start

carrying out their furniture, unless they wanted the Nazis back."

"Can't argue with that."

Apparently, Pierre was a man of some authority in town because several of the people did, in fact, begin to help the soldiers by bringing out whatever they could find by way of building materials.

The barricade grew quickly as a result. The old crates and lumber were interspersed here and there with the bright purple upholstery of a sofa or a velvet-covered armchair. None of it would stop a panzer for a second, should one appear, but the barricade would slow down troops advancing on foot.

Cole and Vaccaro joined in. They were lugging an enormous workbench with another soldier when his head suddenly exploded in a spray of blood and brains. The gruesome sight was quickly followed by the distant crack of a rifle. Some of the townspeople screamed and ran for shelter. He and Vaccaro dropped the workbench and dove for cover.

The German sniper that Cole had feared earlier was now at work.

CHAPTER SEVENTEEN

"SNIPER!" someone shouted.

The warning wasn't really needed, considering that the crack of the rifle shot from beyond the village spoke for itself.

One of the men from Captain Norton's squad was down in the square, a pool of blood already spreading out from beneath him. The man had died instantly. Cole scrambled for the fountain, Vaccaro close on his heels. A third man pressed himself against the stone, panting for breath. Cole was surprised to see that it was the general.

"You reckon this is the start of another attack?" Vaccaro wondered.

"No, they'll need time to regroup," Tolliver said. He added with a bitter note, "The Jerries are just doing this to harass us."

Cole said nothing, but watched the surrounding hills with his pale eyes.

Another shot rang out. A woman screamed, and Cole turned in time to see a puff of stone dust drifting away from the wall of a house. Margot had been carrying a pile of clean sheets and towels for the makeshift aid station that had been set up in her house. Margot stood there as if pinned to the wall, her eyes wide with terror.

"Someone get her indoors!" Tolliver shouted.

No sooner had the words had even left his mouth, then Frenchie came running out of the house, grabbed Margot by the arm, and pulled her inside. A couple of towels fell off the pile she'd been carrying and fluttered to the pavement.

Another bullet smacked into the stone where she had stood only an instant before.

Cole turned back to the woods. Low hills rose just beyond the village, which sat in a kind of hollow bowl beside the river. All that the sniper would have to do is get up in those hills, into one of those trees, and he could pick off the defenders.

Which was just what he was doing.

The problem was that it was almost impossible to determine where the shots originated. Cole couldn't see the muzzle flash—the day was gloomy, but not gloomy enough. The noise of the rifle echoed and bounced off the low hills, giving no indication of where the sniper was hidden.

As Cole's eyes searched and his ears strained for any clue, the sniper fired again. Someone screamed from one of the houses. The screaming went on and on, and he could envision someone standing over a dead body in horror. Someone must have been peeking out a window, and the German noticed. That sniper was good; he'd give him that much. But it rankled Cole that he was shooting at civilians.

Cole fired the rifle at the hills. He didn't even have a target. He ducked down, and an instant later a bullet smacked into the fountain. The sound of the rifle shot rolled and echoed toward them.

"What the hell?" Vaccaro said. "He knows we're here now."

"Now that we got his attention, he's not going to shoot at the people in town."

The general spoke up. "This is your department, son. We can't let a sniper pin us down until the next attack. We need to prepare."

"Yes, sir."

"I like your plan. He doesn't know that you're shooting at nothing. Shoot back and give the son of a bitch something to worry about. I'm going to make a run for it."

Cole grinned crookedly. "I reckon it's your funeral, sir."

Tolliver shook his head. "That's not the best way to put it, Private."

"Ain't no good way to say it, sir." Cole turned to Vaccaro. "City Boy, here's what we're gonna do. I'm gonna shoot. When that Jerry shoots at me, you shoot back. Get down low on the side of the fountain, like you were there waiting for him and I was just the bait."

"What am I shooting at?" Vaccaro asked. "I can't see him."

"Just aim for that hill yonder. I reckon even *you* can hit that. Like the general said, he don't know if we figured out where he's at or not, so he'll keep his head down for a while." Cole turned to the general. "Ready, sir?"

Tolliver nodded, got in position to run, looking like a sprinter.

Cole stuck his head above the rim of the fountain long enough to get off a shot, then ducked down. The general was already running for the solid walls of the aid station. From the hills, he heard the sound of a rifle shot and then a bullet smacked the fountain. From the ground beside the base of the fountain, Vaccaro fired.

The German didn't shoot back.

"Maybe you got him," Cole said.

"If I did, that would be the luckiest damn shot of the war."

"Yeah, well. Like the general said, you done gave that Jerry somethin' to worry about. If he's smart, he's gonna move."

They had just executed the classic sniper trick of bait and switch. Lure the enemy into firing at a target, and then have a second sniper take the shot when the enemy had revealed himself. The German would recognize the tactic. For his part, it stood to reason that the Americans must have a target. Right about now, he would be wondering how the Americans had somehow spotted him.

The hills had fallen silent. One of the first rules of surviving as a sniper was to keep moving. Even after one shot, it was wise to think that your position was now on its way to being compromised. The enemy could zero in on where you were hidden. The best option was to move with stealth to a new sniper hide. Cole supposed this was exactly what the German was doing. After all, he had plenty of woods and hills to choose from. And then he could start shooting up the village all over again.

Cole kept low behind the fountain and rubbed at a gouge in the smooth curve of the lip that hadn't been there ten minutes ago. Those Mauser bullets could do some damage. His stomach rumbled, and he realized he was hungry. And thirsty. He took a swig from his canteen, the water tasting metallic. He gulped it down. The hunger would just have to wait.

In fact, he liked being a little hungry because it kept him sharp.

"Maybe I could get in behind him," Cole said. "It would only take me, what, a few hours to sneak out of the village and up on one of those ridges, and then work down toward him."

Vaccaro snorted. "You could do that if you had a few hours, but it's going to be dark soon. He'll be long gone by then. Besides, you're just as likely to run into half the German army in the meantime."

"Half the German army?" Cole snorted. "You think that's what's out there trying to take this village?"

"To hell if I know," Vaccaro said, annoyed at Cole's mocking tone. "Feels like it, anyway. So, what are you going to do?"

"You mean, what are *we* gonna do? We are gonna stay right here and shoot at the bastard from time to time."

"Shoot at what? We can't see him. We have no idea where he's at."

"Don't matter," Cole said. "He don't know that we don't know where he's at. Not for certain he don't. As long as he keeps focused on us and worries about us shooting back at him, he won't bother to shoot up the rest of the village."

"In other words, we're the bait. Sitting ducks."

"You got it. We can move once it gets dark. Just try not to get shot in the meantime, City Boy."

* * *

OVER IN THE makeshift aid station, Frenchie was trying to calm down Margot. She had nearly been a victim of the German sniper, whose bullet had barely missed her. As that realization settled in, Margot began shaking badly. This was a normal reaction to almost getting shot. She was a brave woman, but her nerves were already stretched thin by the day's events. Margot and her small village had found themselves thrust into war.

Frenchie had poured her a glass of water, but her hands were shaking so badly that she couldn't bring it to her lips. She put the glass down in frustration.

"Here, let me help you," he said gently in French.

Margot took the glass once again in her trembling hands. Frenchie put his hands over hers and helped guide the glass to her lips. Margot smiled.

"Thank you," she said.

"See? Just like you helped me when I first got out of that river. I was weak as a baby, but you fixed me right up."

Margot smiled shyly in reply.

At that moment, General Tolliver came barreling through the door. He was panting; the last time that

Frenchie had seen him, he'd been taking cover behind the village fountain with Cole and Vaccaro. The general must have sprinted over from there. Frenchie started to get to his feet, but the general waved him down. It took him several moments to catch his breath.

"Not as young as I used to be," Tolliver said. "She OK?"

"She's pretty shaken up, sir."

Tolliver nodded, then seemed to finally notice that Frenchie was on his knees beside her chair, helping her hold a glass. A faint smile crossed the general's face. "You seem to be taking good care of her, soldier."

"Yes, sir."

"If there's any fighting that needs to be done, though, I don't want you skulking in here with this young lady. I know you're the next thing we've got to a medic, but when those Jerries hit us again we're going to need bullets, not bandages. There just aren't enough of us. You report to Sergeant Woodbine when the time comes."

"Yes, sir."

Tolliver nodded. "Now, is there a back door to this place, and where does it go? That sniper has the front covered and I need to make sure that we are ready to defend this village, which I can't do hunkered down in here."

Frenchie asked Margot that question, and she pointed and explained that it opened into the alley.

That was all that Tolliver needed to hear. Seconds later, he was out the back door.

"That sniper could shoot anyone in the village!" Margot said. "I must make sure that Marcus stays inside."

She had started to get up, but Frenchie held her gently by the elbow before she could run out the door. "Your brother will be fine," he reassured her, speaking French. "He wouldn't want you to get shot, either, while looking for him. If he takes after his big sister at all, he has plenty of sense."

"How can we stop the sniper?" Margot wondered.

"That's the problem with snipers. They are pretty hard to deal with. But we have a couple snipers of our own. Especially that guy Cole. Let's let him deal with that German."

"Cole? I know the man you mean. He has the look of a killer." Margot held up her right hand, which trembled like a leaf in a storm. She exclaimed, "Look at it shake!"

"Being shot at has a tendency to do that to a person. Believe me, I know," Frenchie said. "I've got an idea. This might help."

Along with some meager supplies for bandages and a pot of soup, one of the townspeople had provided a bottle of rough red wine. Frenchie poured her a small glass full, and helped Margot steady the glass that she raised to her lips. Her fingers felt warm and soft to the touch, milky white. And so clean! He was a little embarrassed about his own hands, which were rough as sandpaper and stained with gun oil and grime, no matter how hard he scrubbed them. He was glad, at least, that his swim in the river had washed the stink off him. Any sort of shower or clean clothes were out of the question in the combat conditions he had been living in.

She drank down the wine in one long swallow.

"Better?" he asked.

Margot nodded.

"Sugar or alcohol always help the jitters." He held up the bottle. "More?"

"*Non*," she said. "We have work to do."

Their work consisted of caring for the wounded. So far, they had been able to patch the wounded right back up with the exception of Private West, the soldier who had been carried into the village after the skirmish on the road to Ville sur Moselle. He was badly hurt beyond anything Frenchie or Margot could do for him. He felt cold to the touch no matter how many blankets they covered him with, and he had slipped into unconsciousness. Perhaps that was a blessing. He had lost a lot of blood and the only real hope for his survival would be a bag of plasma and possibly a surgeon. For that, though, they would have to link up with the advancing Allied forces. Right now, a German unit stood between them and any kind of help, so getting the man to a field hospital was not an option.

Their other job was to make ready for more casualties. There were bound to be more wounded once the Germans hit them again. This was why Margot had been carrying in towels and old sheets when the sniper had gotten his crosshairs on her.

"How long do we have?" she asked.

"The attack could come at any moment," he said. He nodded at the sheets. "We had better start making bandages."

With the general gone out the back door, it was just him and Margot working quietly, side by side. This close, he noticed how good she smelled. Like clean laundry and vanilla. He stopped working for a moment and just sat watching her. Margot must have felt his eyes on her, because a red flush crept across her face.

He would gladly have spent all day here, working alongside Margot. Frenchie hoped that the Germans took their time getting around to the next attack.

CHAPTER EIGHTEEN

BACK OUTSIDE, glad of the fresh air away from the hospital smells, General Tolliver made his way down the main village street, mentally going over the preparations for the defense of the town. Fortunately, the German sniper seemed to be done for the moment, which made him wonder what the Jerries were up to next. It was the quiet before the storm. When the Germans returned, the defenders had damn well be ready.

Think, he urged himself. *What am I forgetting?*

He reviewed a mental checklist: ammo, medical supplies, barricades, posting sentries. He hadn't gotten to be a general, even one who commanded a desk, without sweating the details.

Tolliver came upon the kid who had been the driver for his Jeep. Private Smith was now a sentry, his rifle pointed toward the road that the Germans would come down.

He felt like he owed it to this kid to keep him alive. Hell, he owed it to all of them.

"Keep your eyes open, son," he said to the soldier. He noticed how the young man's shoulders were hunched down into the collar of his jacket. The day was damp and chill here in this hollow by the river. He chided himself for not remembering that the men would be cold and hungry. There was so much to think about. He would see if the village women would make coffee and maybe sandwiches.

"I'll have someone come by later with some food and maybe some coffee," he said.

"Yes, sir," the young soldier said.

Tolliver moved on. He decided that when you took away the life or death consequences, the defense of the town was simply another logistical problem to be solved. It wasn't all that different from his usual problems with supply and demand. He reviewed his mental checklist until it was like a broken record in his mind. Was there enough ammunition? Were the defenses adequate? Did he have enough men?

Nonetheless, Tolliver realized that he was a long way from signing requisition forms and reviewing inventories. The defense of the village wasn't a problem to be solved with a dull pencil, but with a sharp stick.

He hadn't asked for this situation and he had no illusions about his abilities or experience. Tolliver knew he was out of his element. Until today, he had only heard fighting from a distance. But he was in command now, the only officer and a general at that, so there was no question of anyone else taking over. He couldn't ask whether or not he was up to the task because the task had landed in his lap. He could not pass the buck. People would live and die according to what he did here today.

The thought made him nauseous. Why in hell had he ever thought it was a good idea to take that Jeep ride?

Not for the first time since arriving at this village, Tolliver wondered about his Civil War ancestor. Is this how he had felt on the eve of battle? And then, tamping down his uncertainties, the Confederate Tolliver had led his men into Union guns at Gettysburg and finally in that cornfield outside Richmond, with fatal results. With all due respect to his ancestor, he hoped to do better than that.

He had placed men as sentries and lookouts so that they could give warning of the German approach. Also, he'd had the townspeople help to build that barricade across the road at the edge of town. Basically, they had piled together carts and sections of wooden fencing and even furniture. The result was hardly formidable—it looked more like the makings of an estate auction of cast-off possessions than a defensive line. But anything to slow down the German assault was a good start.

Tolliver had ordered a second, smaller line of defense to be created a couple of hundred feet deeper into the town. Truth be told, if the defenders were forced to this second barricade, then they would be in serious trouble.

Ammunition would be a problem. The defenders had already fought off two German attacks and there was no hope of resupply. How were the men set?

He tracked down Sergeant Woodbine, who was smoking a cigarette near the dry fountain in the center of the village square. Nearby stood the sniper, Cole, the one with the pale eyes. He was watching the road, alert as a wolf. In Tolliver's experience, most enlisted men were in the Army because they had to be. They were maybe drafted, or doing their part for the war because everybody else was. They were soldiers by necessity.

But Cole was different. All you had to do was look in those eyes to know that the man was more like a gunfighter than a soldier. The pale eyes glanced at Tolliver as he walked up, seeming to go right through him, then flicked back to the road.

Tolliver nodded at him, deciding that Cole needed no words of encouragement. He approached Sergeant Woodbine.

"Sergeant, any change in our ammunition situation?" Tolliver asked.

Woodbine exhaled a stream of smoke before he answered, thinking it over. "There's maybe enough for one last fight. Most of the men have thirty or forty rounds each, and the villagers that have a shotgun or an old hunting rifle only have a handful of shells apiece—if those old guns don't blow up in their faces, that is."

"Doesn't sound like much," Tolliver said.

"Like I said, sir, there's enough ammo for maybe one good fight. After that, we'll be down to bayonets and rocks."

Tolliver realized that he had spent most of the war signing off on requisition forms for things like cases of ammunition, without really thinking about what a single bullet could mean. It had all seemed so mundane and routine in his bean counter's mode. Hypothetical. Not anymore.

"Spread the word that they need to make every shot count," Tolliver said.

Woodbine took another drag on his cigarette. The expression on his face seemed to indicate that the men already knew that, but all he said was, "Yes, sir."

Cole spoke up. "We got company," he drawled, shifting his rifle to his shoulder.

Tolliver looked toward the road. To his surprise,

there seemed to be a delegation of Germans approaching in a Kübelwagen. He counted three men —a driver, an officer riding next to him, and a soldier in the back. They displayed a white flag prominently. Was it a flag of truce or a flag of surrender? Worse yet, was it a trick?

"What the hell do they want?" the general wondered out loud. Based on the intensity of their attack on the town, these were hardened German veterans. They hadn't come to give up.

"They ain't coming to surrender, sir," Cole said quietly, as if reading Tolliver's mind, his rifle aimed at the Germans. "They're sniffing around to see what we got planned for them."

"Sounds about right." Tolliver agreed that getting a glimpse of the town's defenses was the clever thing to do, although it rankled that the Germans might be thinking that they were pulling a fast one.

Cole said, "You want, I can shoot them."

"Hell no, don't do that," Tolliver said quickly. Cole's matter of fact tone was a little disturbing. It wouldn't be right to shoot the enemy waving a white flag, even if he suspected that was a ruse. "Woodbine, Cole, with me. Let's go see what these bastards want."

They walked down to the edge of the village, passing the two barricades. The Germans had stopped there, waiting for them, engine running. The

Kübelwagen's motor made a puttering sound with a wheezy whine mixed in, so very different from the bobcat growl of a Jeep's motor. Tolliver wondered what the protocol was here, and realized that he didn't have a white flag of his own, so he dug into his pocket and took out a handkerchief, waving it over his head a couple of times so that there would be no confusion about their intent. In response, the Germans waggled their white flag, which he saw was a rag tied to a stick, and switched off the Kübelwagen.

The driver stayed behind the wheel, but the other two Germans got out. One was an officer, tall and spare, with piercing blue eyes in a face tan from the summertime battles across Normandy. The eyes seemed very bright in the gloom, taking Tolliver's measure at a glance. Tolliver squared his shoulders in response. Clearly, this officer was a combat veteran, which made Tolliver wary. Was it possible that the German officer might sense that Tolliver himself had never commanded more than a desk?

The other German was about six feet tall and solidly built. He carried a rifle with a telescopic sight and had a look about him, Tolliver realized, that was much like Cole's. Another killer. This German radi- ated a threatening aura. He had no doubt that this was the sniper who had been shooting up the village just a short time ago. Tolliver felt the urge to draw his

Browning and settle the enemy sniper's hash, but they were operating under a flag of truce.

Out of the corner of his eye, he noted how Cole had moved away from him and Sergeant Woodbine, keeping his rifle to his shoulder with the muzzle pointed slightly down, but ready to aim and fire at a moment's notice.

The general approached the German officer and nodded.

"Thank you for meeting us," the German said in heavily accented English. He spoke slowly, but his meaning was clear enough. "I am Generalmajor Unterbrink."

"General Tolliver."

"Two generals? Fighting over a tiny village? Whatever is the war coming to." Unterbrink gave him a small smile as if he knew something amusing that Tolliver did not. Tolliver disliked him instantly. Unterbrink acted like one of those stuck-up bastards who didn't think you were good enough to join his country club.

"Are you here to surrender?" Tolliver asked.

Unterbrink seemed surprised. "Surrender? Actually, I hoped to ask *you* to surrender, General."

"That's not an option."

Unterbrink absorbed the news without emotion. "I understand. In fact, I did not expect that you would surrender. Perhaps we can come to a reasonable accommodation. You are outnumbered. Your men don't need to die. My men don't need to die. They would like very much simply to return home. All that we seek is to cross the river. Stand aside and let us pass."

"You know I can't do that," Tolliver finally said, although he was sorely tempted. The German general made it all sound so reasonable, like a gentlemen's agreement. But Tolliver wasn't falling for it. He could not simply stand aside and let the Germans cross that bridge. "Did you really think we'd let you march through here, or did you just want to get a good look at our defenses?"

Unterbrink gave that small smile again. "Your defenses? Such a thought never crossed my mind." The German looked around. "Surely, by defenses you don't mean that pile of furniture in the street?"

For a moment, no one spoke. The two snipers had locked eyes and seemed to be sizing each other up, as if daring the other man to make a move. Tolliver had no doubt that at a signal from him or Unterbrink, that the two snipers would start shooting. Despite the temperature, he felt a trickle of sweat run down between his shoulder blades. This was like a standoff at the OK Corral.

"Are we done here?" Tolliver asked.

Unterbrink nodded. "Good luck to you, General."

He turned and climbed into the Kübelwagen, not

giving the Americans so much as a second look. The German sniper backed toward the vehicle and slid onto the seat, keeping his eye on Cole the whole time, his weapon at the ready. The engine cranked over, prompting more high-pitched chattering from the German motor, and then the driver backed up and drove away.

The three Americans watched them go, waiting until they were out of sight, and then Cole and Woodbine turned to look at Tolliver.

"Goddamn Krauts," he said. The encounter had literally left a sour taste in his mouth, and he patted his pockets for a pack of cigarettes. Unterbrink had gotten an eyeful, all right, taking in the makeshift barricade and the fact that the defense consisted of a handful of soldiers and geriatric villagers. "I want everything buttoned up all over again, Sergeant. Those Krauts will be back, and next time they won't be waving a white flag."

"Should've let Cole shoot them, sir."

The general thought that maybe Woodbine was right, but there was no helping that now. "When they come back, Cole can do all the shooting he wants."

Both Cole and Woodbine grinned at that. "Yes, sir."

CHAPTER NINETEEN

DARKNESS HAD FALLEN WITHOUT INCIDENT, and night brought a respite because it seemed unlikely that the Germans would launch a nighttime attack. An uneasy quiet settled over Ville sur Moselle. The river made its ancient gurgle at their backs, while now and then through the trees they could hear the Germans laughing or talking because some trick of the way that sound carried in the river valley made the enemy seem much closer.

Still, General Tolliver was worried about the Germans trying some funny business under cover of darkness. Short of a full attack, there remained the threat of a commando team infiltrating the town.

Sentries were posted, augmented by villagers with dogs who would start barking if their keen ears or noses detected trouble of the Teutonic kind. Those not keeping watch either slept or found something to eat. The villagers kept their lights off or huddled around dim candles. After their experience with the German sniper earlier, they knew that any light that shone was likely to get someone shot at.

Pierre and two of the villagers who had pitched in to help the Americans sat drinking in his kitchen. They should have gone out to help the sentries, but Pierre had opened a jug of wine, and one glass had led to another. Gustave was a shop-keeper, soft in the middle and with thin, sloped shoulders, but he had a fierce spirit. Short and stout, their friend August resembled an old wooden keg. The three men had known one another all their lives.

"We know this territory better than anyone," Pierre said, waving his glass for emphasis. The glass was squat and thick, missing a tiny chip from the rim. No long-stemmed crystal wine glasses here. The red wine itself was rough and unrefined. French men drank wine the way that Americans drank beer—without much fuss or fanfare. "We should slip into the woods and spy on the Germans."

"Or shoot at them," his friend, Gustave, added.

"Yes, why not!" Pierre said. "The three of us will go at first light, and then return to let the Americans know what we saw."

"The Germans will never see us," August said. He

slapped down his glass and snapped his thick fingers. "We shall be silent as smoke!"

"And if we shoot a few Germans along the way, so much the better," Gustave said, and reached for the bottle to refill their glasses. Already, the wine in the jug was quite diminished.

Their boastful plan was just the kind that men hatched after a few glasses of wine late at night, and that was usually quickly forgotten in the morning, or remembered with a laugh and a rueful shake of the head. A trio of middle-aged men drinking late at night and boasting about their heroics was harmless enough, so long as they never left the kitchen.

Had they been fighting the Germans these last few months just like the American soldiers had been, they would not have boasted so lightly. Either that, or they would have guzzled a lot more wine.

Pierre did not pay much attention to his youngest son coming and going in the kitchen. Simon was twelve years old, and very excited about the battle being fought over town. He was too young to understand the real violence taking place, or what was at stake for the villagers. He was amazed and impressed that his father and his friends were now soldiers, helping the Americans. He paused to look at the rifles and the shotgun, leaning in the corner. The weapons smelled strongly of gun oil, which males of any age find to be an intoxicating scent.

Sneaking into the woods to spy on the Germans sounded like a real adventure. He immediately thought of how he and his friend, Marcus, could be heroes if they went along.

"Papa, take me with you! Marcus and I can help! We can crawl through the bushes right up to the Germans and no one will see us."

His father laughed and ruffled his hair. "I know you and Marcus are brave boys," he said. "But we need you here to help protect the town while we are gone."

"Please, papa!"

"This is not a business for boys," Pierre said with finality, and Simon hung his head, knowing better than to argue with his father in front of his friends. Papa seemed to be in a good mood now, but when he was drinking, Simon knew that his father could quickly lose his temper. Even that wasn't so awful. Despite his boasting about killing Germans, his father was a gentle man. He had never raised a hand to Simon, not even to spank him when he had, from time to time, more than deserved it. However, his father wouldn't think twice about giving him more chores to do.

Leaving the men in the kitchen, Simon slipped out of the house and down the street to where Marcus lived with his sister, Margot. It was a journey he had made hundreds of times day and night, but now the familiar town felt so different and even dangerous. It was a town under siege. Here and there in the darkness, he spotted the hulking figures of the American soldiers. Not until he had nearly run into him did Simon finally see the skinny American sniper standing in the shadows, keeping watch, his cut-glass eyes tracking the boy. Simon shuddered and gave him a wide berth.

It was late, but Marcus was always up for an adventure. The door was open—no one locked their doors in the village, even with strangers lurking in the night. Simon slipped inside the house. The downstairs had been cleared to make way to the wounded, but everything seemed quiet at the moment. Margot must already be asleep. Quickly, Simon went up the stairs and found Marcus at his bedroom window, watching the comings and goings as best he could. With so much excitement, the boy couldn't sleep.

"I saw you coming," Marcus said. "You didn't even see that sniper hiding there by Madame Diver's house. I saw you jump when you came across him!"

"He's a good one to stay away from," Simon said.

Quickly, he told Marcus about what his father and the other men planned to do in the morning.

"We must go with them!"

"Papa said no," Simon said.

"Then we will follow them without them knowing," Marcus said. "Once we are in the woods, we can show ourselves. They won't have any choice but to let us stay with them."

A thought came to Simon. "Where is your sister? We can't let her find out."

"She was downstairs, helping the wounded, but she might be asleep by now. It's late."

The boys had no real weapons, but they felt that they couldn't go into the woods without some means of defense. Simon had brought along his slingshot. It was a homemade affair with the bands cut from an old bicycle inner tube. He planned to load his pockets with small, smooth stones.

"If I get close enough to a German and hit them just so—"

"You'll knock him out!" Marcus was enthusiastic about the slingshot. He did not own one himself, or any other likely weapon. He went into the kitchen and debated taking a carving knife, but surely Margot would notice that it was missing. He settled on his pocketknife. The blade wasn't any longer than his little finger, but it was better than nothing.

As far as the boys were concerned, they were ready to take on the Germany army. Too excited to sleep, they settled down to wait for morning, when they would slip into the woods behind old Pierre and his friends.

CHAPTER TWENTY

OVER THE CENTURIES, French farmers had learned a thing or two about surviving marauding armies that stripped their farms bare. It didn't matter whether the soldiers were German, French, or even American —a hungry soldier meant disaster all the same to a peasant.

It wasn't uncommon for the French farmers to hide some of their potatoes and dried corn in deep holes, for example, to be dug out after the soldiers had passed, leaving just enough stored in their barns and root cellars so that the passing troops would be satisfied.

The farmers had learned that it paid to set a few pigs loose as well. Foraging on acorns or on wormy windfall apples in abandoned orchards, the pigs grew fat without any effort from the farmers and far from the reaches of passing troops. It was easy enough to hunt up a pig in the woods when one needed meat. Over the years, some of the hogs had grown half-wild and developed long hair and even tusks.

Moving through the misty, fog-shrouded hills surrounding the Moselle, a patrol from General Unterbrink's unit had the good fortune to come across a group of these feral hogs. The shy hogs scattered, but not before one of the soldiers got off a shot. They carried their prize back to camp with them, the pig slung upside down from a stick balanced on the shoulders of two of the men. The sight of the men carrying their prize into camp was as ancient as time itself.

Luckily, the soldier had the good sense to shoot one of the smaller, more tender pigs—one that weighed no more than fifty pounds. Good eating.

"Where's Hauer?" one of the men called, setting down his burden with a grunt near the campfire built to keep off the chill. "Didn't he used to be a butcher?"

"Roast pork tonight, eh? I'll see if I can find him."

The Germans had not always been soldiers, and some of their skills from civilian life were useful from time to time. Such was the case with Hauer, who really had been a butcher. In no time at all, with help from the other soldiers, he had the pig strung up by one of its hind legs.

"You have to bleed it," he explained, and with one swipe of his knife, he cut a gash in the throat of the pig. The animal had not been dead long, and blood gushed out to soak the ground. Instead of a Wehrmacht-issued blade, Hauer carried a simple sheath knife with a wooden handle. The knife was well-used with a blade worn thin and smooth from much sharpening. It was a tradesman's knife rather than a soldier's, but wickedly sharp.

He wiped the blade and returned it to the sheath, then considered what to do next. Normally, a butcher dipped the carcass into scalding water and then scraped off the loosened hair. However, they didn't have a tub big enough or any way to heat the water quickly.

Ancient hunters hadn't had those items either, so Hauer settled on the more traditional method of burning the hair off. He made a torch by wrapping a strip of canvas around a branch and pouring kerosene over it. He recruited a couple of other men to help him scrape away the scorched hair. They wrinkled their noses at the disgusting smell of burning hair. The smell brought to mind images of blackened tanks and charred corpses. One man couldn't take the stink in his nostrils and passed off his knife to another.

"Not so bad," Hauer announced, inspecting their work so far. He brushed the torch across a few spots they had missed, leaving behind smooth pigskin.

Then Hauer had them wash down the carcass with clean water. He stood back to admire their work. The pig now looked naked as a newborn babe. He used an ax to cut off the head.

Next, the former butcher in him went to work. Taking his sharp knife, he slit the pig's belly from the anus to the throat and dumped the guts in a warm pile that steamed in the cool fall air. Done properly, there was no smell but that of the warm blood.

The communal butchering was something that the farm boys were used to, as well as the hunters among them, but others found the parting out of the pig disconcerting. The headless, pale-skinned carcass looked vaguely human. In twentieth-century German cities, not everyone was familiar with where their meat came from. Several men suddenly hurried off to other duties, real or imagined, or remembered equipment that needed maintaining.

Using the ax, Hauer chopped the ribs away from the backbone, working down one side at a time. It was hard going, though, and Hauer handed off the ax to another man and directed the chopping with blood-caked fingers. Once the last rib was cut away, he now had two sides of meat.

He saw no point in doing up cuts of meat for the display case or to hang to entice customers as he might have done in his old shop. Using the ax, he cut off a nice rack of ribs for General Unterbrink's cook. The rest of the pig went over their campfire.

"Make sure it cooks through," Hauer said, but that was the extent of his advice. He was a butcher by trade, not a chef. He left the cooking to a couple of older, heavyset men, who tended the cooking meat and the fire lovingly.

Even those who had been queasy at the sight of the butchering process couldn't ignore the delicious smell of roasting meat. By and large, the soldiers were well-fed with no shortage of rations. However, tinned ham did not compare to the juicy, fresh meat roasting on the spit before them. One by one, the men drifted back to the fire and admired the sizzling and popping of the fat.

For a little while, as they joked around the fire and passed a bottle, it was almost possible to forget the war. Tomorrow, they might very well be dead. Who knew or cared? They had taught themselves not to think too far into the future. Today, at least, they were still alive, they were still German soldiers, and they were going to eat very well indeed.

Like the others, Hauer looked on approvingly as the meat sizzled and dripped into the fire. He turned to the soldiers who had brought in the pig. "Tomorrow, let's go back into the woods and see if we can find another," he said.

CHAPTER TWENTY-ONE

IN THE MORNING, the soldier who had shot the wild pig organized a hunting party to see if they could get another. Hauer volunteered to go along with the soldier, whose name was Schneider, mainly out of curiosity. While he was a good shot with a rifle, he'd never been much of a hunter. He thought that he might learn something that would be useful to him as a sniper.

"Old Unterbrink wants to organize an attack on the village but he's waiting on ammunition," Hauer said. "There are a couple of supply trucks just to the north that he's waiting for."

"Supply trucks?" one of the men asked, incredulous. Most supply vehicles had been destroyed in the battle at the Falaise Gap or its aftermath. "How is that possible?"

"Somebody hid them, and with the Allied planes grounded by this weather, they think they can get them to us."

"Let's find another pig and cook it for lunch, before Unterbrink gets his ammo and we attack the village again."

"Nothing like a good meal before you get killed," said one of the older soldiers, and the group of men laughed.

Even Hauer had to smile. He had to admit that being in the woods, hunting for wild pigs, was a nice interlude from the war. The hilly terrain was isolated and empty. Fog kept the Allied planes away. The odds of them encountering any American troops in these hills was almost nil. They would be down in the village, preparing for the inevitable German attack. Schneider was right; their roasted pig might very well be the last meal for some of the Germans if the Americans put up a good fight

The group of hunters was relaxed, smoking cigarettes, and joking. It probably wasn't the best approach to hunting, but then again, the pigs were only half wild. Maybe they only needed to be half quiet?

After a while, Schneider hushed them. "We are near where I shot the pig yesterday," he said. "Hauer, get your rifle ready, in case I miss. You're the crack shot here."

They moved forward stealthily. The forest pigs, or perhaps deer, had worn a path through the woods and they followed it easily enough. The damp leaves underfoot barely made a sound and the light that filtered down through the tree limbs was pale and wispy, with a bit of fog mixed in. Hauer had the uneasy sense that someone could be hiding in the brush just a few feet away and he would never know. A dank, feral smell clung to the forest floor and Hauer guessed that the pigs were the source of that.

They were being so quiet that the other group moving through the woods never heard the soldiers. The Germans passed around a bend in the trail to a place where it widened and came face to face with a group of French civilians.

There were three of them, and they froze in surprise at the sight of the Germans. The men were armed with old rifles and a shotgun—one slung over a man's shoulder with a length of rope—but they didn't have them at the ready. One of the men started to slip a rifle off his shoulder but stopped when Schneider leveled an MP-40 machine-gun pistol at him and shouted, *"Nein!"*

The Frenchmen were bunched up, and Schneider could have killed them all with a two-second burst.

Hauer had wondered why Schneider had brought along a *Schmeisser* to a pig hunt, but now he was glad that he had. His own rifle was slung over his shoulder.

He hated to admit it, but the Frenchman might have been quicker to get his weapon into play.

Now, it didn't matter. With the Frenchmen covered by Schneider, Hauer walked up and took their guns away. The weapons were so old that they were practically antiques better suited to being hung over a fireplace for decoration than for actual use.

"They must be French Resistance," Schneider said, glaring at the men. "Let's take them back to Unterbrink and see what they know."

"It's a long way back to camp, and we haven't got our pig yet," Hauer said. "Let's just find out what they know and then tell the general."

Hauer looked the Frenchmen over doubtfully. Most of the Resistance fighters they had encountered were young men and women in their prime. Young enough to have fight and spirit. Young enough to be dangerous. These men were much older, even a bit gray and grizzled. One of them was quite tall and thin, while the other two were of average height and a little heavyset, breathing heavily from their hike in the woods. Resistance? Hauer didn't think so. By now most of the Resistance was well-armed thanks to the Allies. These men carried antiques.

"Who are you?" Hauer asked.

The tall one took a step forward, seemingly oblivious of Schneider's machine pistol pointed at him. He shook a fist at Hauer. "We are French patriots!" he shouted. The man spoke German, which wasn't surprising, considering their proximity to the border and the years of occupation.

"What are you doing in these woods?"

"We came to observe your movements," the man said boldly.

"So, you are with the *Machi*?" Hauer asked, using the slang term for the Resistance.

"No," the tall man said. "We are from the village."

Then it dawned on Hauer. "You are from Ville sur Moselle?"

"Yes."

"Then you may prove useful to us. How many Americans are in the village?"

The tall man shook his head. "I will tell you nothing! I can see from your rifle that you are one of the soldiers that has been shooting up the village. Why would I talk to you?"

"The Americans sent you to spy on us?"

"We are not spies. We are patriots," the older man insisted.

"Communists," Hauer said, hissing the word. Most of the French Resistance fighters were communists who didn't much like German fascism ... or American democracy, for that matter. "Backstabbers in the night."

"Take them back to Unterbrink," Schneider suggested again. He seemed to be getting anxious about what to do with the Frenchmen. "He will want to talk to them."

"Yes, you said that before."

"What else would we do with them?"

"Why bother Unterbrink? Let us get this over with and get on with our hunt. Shoot the fat one there and see if the others will talk."

Schneider glanced at him, gauging if he was serious about shooting the Frenchman out of hand. One look at Hauer's face told him what he needed to know.

Hauer gave his comrade a nod, and the silence of the woods was shattered as Schneider hit the man with a burst from the MP-40. Hauer couldn't be sure, but in the silence that followed, he thought he heard a frightened cry in the bushes to their left. The Frenchman writhed on the ground in his death throes, and then lay still.

Hauer turned to the spokesman, who hadn't so much as moved an inch. He was staring at his comrade's body. "Well?" he asked.

The tall man clamped his lips up tight. Hauer nodded at Schneider, who shot the other man. Smoke and the smell of gunpowder now hung heavily in the stillness of the clearing.

Hauer looked at the Frenchman. "How many Americans in the village?" he asked again.

"I will tell you nothing!" the surviving Frenchman

blurted out, raising his arms and closing his eyes. His voice quavered with emotion. "You have killed my friends. Go ahead and shoot me. We die as patriots. *Vive la France*."

Schneider fired the machine pistol and the tall villager crumpled to the forest floor.

Hauer turned to Schneider. "Cover me," he said. "I think there may be more of these bastards hiding over there."

Hauer walked toward the bushes where he had heard the noise, his own rifle at the ready. The scoped rifle wasn't a close-quarters weapon, but at this range all that he would need to do was point and shoot. He could have had Schneider hose down the bushes with the machine pistol, but he did not sense a threat.

Still, he approached the tangles of underbrush carefully. Every soldier had a sixth sense about these things, and he could sense that someone was down in those bushes, holding his breath. "Come out of there," he said in German, then ordered in French, "*Viens*."

He poked the rifle barrel among the branches and pushed them aside.

A boyish face was revealed. Then another. Hauer poked the rifle barrel at the two boys, and they popped up, their hands held high.

Behind him, Schneider laughed. "You have caught a couple of rabbits, Hauer!"

Hauer guessed that, like the men, these boys must have come from the village. He marched the boys into the narrow clearing. Seeing the dead men on the ground, the boys went pale. A choked sob escaped from one of the boys.

The taller of the two boys, who had a shock of dark hair, held a sharpened stick. It wasn't quite a spear, but more like a pointed walking stick. Hauer snatched it from the boy's hand and tossed it away into the trees. The second boy, the smaller one, had a slingshot in his pocket. Hauer pulled it out, more curious than anything. He used to have one much like it when he was a boy.

Weaponless, the two boys stood there, staring at Hauer. The smaller boy began to sniffle and whimper.

Hauer kept his rifle pointed at the boys.

"*Machi?*" he asked.

The boys shook their heads vigorously.

Hauer sighed and said in German, "So tell me, how many Americans are down in the village?"

Both boys stared at him, uncomprehending. Leaning down to the boys' level and speaking in a low voice, Hauer tried again in his limited French. "*Ami? Un, deux, trois ... trente ... cent?*"

Hauer poked the muzzle of his rifle at the smaller boy.

The taller boy blurted out, *"Vingt."*

Hauer straightened up and nodded with satisfaction at the boys. They had just confirmed that there were twenty Americans defending the village. Hauer had no reason to think that the boy was lying. The number coincided with the troops he had seen when conducting sniper operations against the village the previous day. This was real intelligence that General Unterbrink could use, no matter that the information about the village's defenses had come from these mere boys.

"You can shoot them now, Schneider," Hauer said.

"Hauer?" Schneider asked, a note of disbelief in his voice. "What do you mean? They are boys."

"Boys grow up to be soldiers," he said, turning away. He started back toward the dead villagers. "You want to shoot them now or fight them later?"

For his part, Schneider tightened his grip on the machine pistol, but he hesitated before pulling the trigger. The boys stared at him, knowing what was coming next. Both of them started to cry and tremble.

Schneider saw that Hauer was several meters away, his attention focused on going through the pockets of the dead villagers. In a hoarse whisper, Schneider said urgently to the boys: "Run. *Aller!*" To emphasize his point, he jerked his chin at the forest beyond.

The boys understand at once and ran like the wind. Schneider waited until they had gotten a few meters away, and then fired into the ground behind them. They boys ran even faster and were at the point of being swallowed up by the underbrush.

Then a shot rang out, making Schneider flinch, and then another. Both boys fell into the tangled brush and did not move again.

When Schneider turned back, he saw that Hauer stood there with his rifle, working the bolt action.

"Those damn boys, they almost got away," Schneider said. He couldn't bring himself to admit to Hauer that he had let them escape. "They—"

Hauer straightened up. "You let them go," he said. "I was watching, you know. You are too soft, Schneider. Maybe I ought to shoot you as well."

Schneider kept his finger on the trigger of the machine pistol. "They were just boys, Hauer."

"What's done is done," the sniper said, turning away. "We may as well go back. If there were any pigs, that shooting scared them off."

After a moment, when he was sure Hauer wasn't going to change his mind and shoot him, Schneider took his finger away from the trigger.

Hauer followed the trail back to their encampment, noticing that Schneider would not talk to him or make eye contact. *To hell with him,* Hauer thought. Some men just didn't have the stomach to do what was necessary. That had never been Hauer's problem.

Thanks to the boy, at least now they had an idea

of how many American soldiers held the village. He knew from the parlay that he had taken part in with General Unterbrink that one of the defenders was a general. Another was a sniper. If old Unterbrink got his ammo, then with any luck those two would both be dead soon, along with the rest of the Amis. Unterbrink could then lead his force across the Moselle using the bridge in town and they would all be that much closer to Germany.

The only real disappointment, Hauer reflected, was that they hadn't gotten another pig.

CHAPTER TWENTY-TWO

COLE WAS CLEANING his rifle inside the storefront that the Americans had taken over when Frenchie came looking for him. He had Margot with him. Thanks to his language skills, Frenchie and Margot had managed to hit it off.

Good for him, Cole thought, looking the French girl over. He knew that it didn't take much to spark a romance in these times, when you didn't know if you would still be here from one day to the next. *Got to take some happiness where you can in this world.*

Briefly, he thought of Jolie Molyneux, the young French woman and Resistance fighter who had been his squad's guide in Normandy. Jolie had caused some tension between Cole and Lieutenant Mulholland. The young woman had been badly wounded by a

German sniper and the last that Cole had heard, she was still recovering.

Frenchie and Margot might be enjoying one another's company, but there was nothing happy about Margot's expression at the moment. Worry lines creased her face.

"What's the problem?" Cole asked, setting his rifle aside.

"It's her brother," Frenchie said. "He's missing."

"Missing?" When Cole was growing up, he had sometimes disappeared into the woods for two or three days at a time. Nobody had much wondered where he'd gone. Anyhow, most of the time he had taken off to avoid his old man when he was on a bender. "I reckon he'll turn up."

"Look around you, Cole. We're in a village surrounded by the Germans. Where would the kid go? His name is Marcus, by the way," Frenchie said. "Besides, Margot was talking with one of her brother's friends. This kid said that Marcus and his best friend, Simon, were planning on following Pierre into the woods. Remember Pierre?"

"That tall, skinny French fella?"

"That's the one. He's actually the mayor. Pierre and two of his buddies decided to reconnoiter and see what the Germans were up to."

"That ain't the smartest thing I've heard today."

"It gets worse. It turns out that Simon is Pierre's

son. The apple doesn't fall far from the tree and all that. Simon and Marcus may have followed Pierre into the woods."

Cole picked up the rifle again, put a drop of oil in the chamber, depressed the trigger, and slid the bolt home. The action worked smooth as silk. Even in the dull light, the rifle gleamed. Despite the mud and rough conditions, Cole probably had the cleanest rifle in France. Balancing the rifle across his knees, he asked, "What's this got to do with me?"

"Margot was hoping—I was hoping—that you could take a look for her brother."

"In the woods?"

"Yeah, I guess so."

"In case you ain't noticed, Frenchie, the woods around here has got Germans in it."

"Why do you think Margot is worried?"

"You could go look for him yourself," Cole pointed out.

"Yeah, but you're the next best thing to Daniel Boone that we've got."

When Cole didn't respond, Frenchie snorted and started to walk away. "Hey, forget I even asked. I'll go find the kid myself."

As Frenchie started to walk away, Cole said, "Hang on now. Don't get your panties in a wad. I'll go take a look for the kid."

"Thanks, Cole. I knew you would. You want me to come with you?"

"Hell, no. I reckon you'd make enough noise to let the whole German army know we were traipsing around those woods. What you can do is make sure that General Tolliver doesn't know I'm out looking for some kid when I ought to be helping get ready for the attack. What's that word you used? If he comes looking for me, tell him that I'm *reconnoitering*."

Frenchie and the girl left, but Cole wasn't alone for long. He was just reassembling his rifle after cleaning it when the sergeant appeared. He was smoking a cigarette, cupping it in his palm to hide the bright ember. Outwardly, Woodbine appear calm enough, but his chain-smoking habit betrayed his nerves.

"Cole, I was looking for you. The old man thinks that the Germans will hit not long after first light. You and Vaccaro need to be up high so that you can take out as many of the enemy as you can when they come up that road."

"You ain't got to tell me twice, Woodbine."

The sergeant nodded. "I'm just passing the word. Tolliver wants everyone in position."

"Good thing we've got him," Cole said.

Woodbine furtively crushed out the cigarette butt. "I guess you haven't heard the rumors, then."

"What are you talking about?"

"According to Tolliver's driver, the general is nothing but a bean counter back at HQ. He works in supply. He's never even been in the field."

Cole snorted. He was genuinely surprised. "Don't that beat all."

"Anyhow, you didn't hear it from me," Woodbine said, and moved off into the darkness.

JUST BEFORE DAWN, Cole slipped into the woods on his mission to find the French girl's kid brother. Cole hoped that the Germans took their time launching their attack. With any luck, he would find this kid and be back before the attack started.

It felt good to be alone for a change. He hadn't even dragged Vaccaro along because if the Germans attacked this morning, General Tolliver would need every man he could get to defend the town.

The general would not be happy if he found Cole missing. Cole hoped that Frenchie would hold up his end of the bargain and run interference for him. With any luck, Cole would find these kids quickly and drag them back. Cole traveled light, armed only with the Springfield, his Bowie knife, and a couple of hand grenades for good measure.

The knife was not regulation issue, but had been sent to him by an old friend back home, who had

hammered it into shape in his backyard forge. That
had been one of the few times that Cole had ever
received anything from stateside. The other exception had been a brief letter informing him that his
younger brother had joined up and was fighting in the
Pacific. He'd gotten Vaccaro to read the letter and
then tell him what was in it, claiming that he'd been
afraid it was bad news from home.

Cole walked east, watching the sky turn pink
where the clouds did not quite touch the horizon.
The birds were starting to wake up. He could
hear the staccato chatter of gunfire, but it was far
to the west on the other side of the Moselle and
didn't concern him. He took a deep breath and
smelled the damp loam, a wisp of wood smoke
from some distant fire, and the musky odor of
some animal that shared the forest path. He
could almost have been in the mountains back
home.

The woods at dawn always had been one of his
favorite places. Memories of home and the mountains came flooding back. What he wasn't keen on
was the fact that the woods might be crawling with
Germans.

The terrain surrounding Ville sur Moselle was
steep and rugged. The village itself was nestled in the
cleft between large hills that ran down toward the
river before leveling off. This terrain forced the

Germans to follow the road into the village in order to reach the bridge.

Pierre and the other villagers would have been familiar with the landscape. They must have spent a lifetime walking and hunting in these hills. To Pierre, it must have seemed like child's play to get into the hills above the Germans, spy on them, and report back to the American defenders. Those dumb Frenchmen probably thought they'd be heroes for doing it.

Trouble was, the Germans might get the same idea to conduct some reconnaissance in the woods. The French villagers—much less the boys—would have been ill-equipped to deal with any German patrols.

Cole could guess where Pierre and the others had gone into the woods. A well-worn game trail disappeared into the trees, likely where the deer and wild pigs came down to sample the villagers' gardens. He bent down and examined a bare patch of mud. It had rained yesterday, but not overnight, so that gave him some time frame for when someone had passed through here. The rain would have washed out any fresh tracks. He saw hoof prints—belonging to pigs rather than deer—and a couple sets of boot prints that were several hours old. Definitely not prints made by German or American boots, which he was more than a little familiar with, so chances were good that he was seeing Pierre's footprints. One of the prints was smaller. Could it be the boy's?

He walked deeper into the woods, feeling the gloom and the trees press in around him. The sound of birds was reassuring, though. They wouldn't be chirping away if anyone prowled these woods. When the woods fell silent, that was when he needed to worry.

The ground rose quickly as he followed the trail, reminding him of the familiar mountains back home. He found himself getting out of breath. *Got to cut out them cigarettes,* he thought. He'd been cutting back, but he would be better off giving them up altogether. It didn't help that their rations included cigarettes, as if the Army was encouraging them to smoke.

Focusing on the trail before him, he looked for any other indications of footprints. The pigs had followed this trail and made a mess of it. Here and there, he noticed how the leaves did not quite hide the impression of a footprint in the trail or where a twig lay snapped in two by a boot. People had passed this was, as well as game. Most eyes would have passed over it, but Cole was an experienced tracker and hunter by nature. He could not read words on the page, but he could read these natural signs as plainly as others read a newspaper.

What he saw was that two groups had passed through within the last few hours. The first group was made up of bigger and heavier individuals. It looked like three men, which fit the description that Frenchie had passed along from Margot. The members of the second group—just two, from the looks of it—were smaller and lighter. A couple of boys, more than likely. He'd bet the farm that one of them was Margot's brother.

Cole moved on cautiously. The last thing he wanted to do was surprise the French villagers who might be on the trail ahead. They might think that he was a German and open fire. Considering that the tracks on the trail had been made yesterday, the likelihood of running into the French villagers seemed slim. But stranger things had happened. Worse yet was the possibility of encountering a German patrol sent to probe the American position. Cole didn't relish the thought of being seriously outnumbered, or worse yet, caught in the middle between the Germans and French.

Moving along the trail, he crossed the face of the hill above Ville sur Moselle and the river. There were still enough leaves on the trees that the view of the village below was obscured. In the winter it would be a different story. An enemy sniper could sit up here and pick off the American defenders one by one, so long as he was a really good shot.

Cole grimaced, thinking about that. The German sniper whom he had tangled with yesterday had been that good. More than just good, if truth be told. That German was a crack shot. Cole wasn't in any hurry to face him again.

He came around a bend in the trail and froze. The trail widened here and looked as if this was where pigs or deer foraged or bedded down. But what caught his immediate attention were the three bodies spread across the clearing.

From their civilian clothing, he immediately recognized the dead men as villagers. They'd gone looking for Germans. It sure as hell looked as if they'd found them.

"Goddammit," he muttered.

Cole wasn't eager to get back to the village and tell anyone that he'd found these men. Not like this. The question was, what had become of Margot's brother and his friend? Maybe there was a chance that they had survived.

He stood and looked around the site, hoping for some clue as to the boys' fate. He was just thinking that perhaps they had escaped, after all, when he spotted their small bodies several yards into the woods. *Not them, too*, he thought.

Before he could investigate, Cole heard a groan and realized that one of the men in the clearing was still alive. Approaching, he recognized Pierre from the village. Cole's stomach tightened when he saw the shape that the man was in. Pierre was badly wounded, his abdomen covered in blood.

He knew from his experience as a hunter that a gut-shot animal could live for hours. Even for days. That was why a hunter practiced enough to be a good shot, and if he didn't kill an animal right away, he tracked it down to finish the job. A good hunter didn't want an animal to suffer. Pierre had been left to die a slow and painful death.

Pierre barely had strength to lift his head, but Cole gave him a drink from his canteen. He took a gulp or two, and Cole half expected the water to come leaking out. Once Pierre had the drink, he began to mutter, trying to tell Cole something.

"What?" he asked, moving his ear closer to Pierre's lips.

"Le sniper," he said, barely audible. *"Le sniper."*

What was Pierre trying to say? Cole was confused at first, but then it began to make sense. Pierre was telling him that a German sniper had done this. He could only guess, but he had a pretty good idea that it was the same sniper who had accompanied the German general into town yesterday. It wouldn't have been unusual for a sniper to also be scouting these woods. That particular German had looked just about right for this sort of job.

Cole nodded back at Pierre that he understood.

Pierre gasped in pain. The poor bastard was really

suffering, and there was no hope for him. Not with his guts lying on the forest floor.

Cole debated what to do. He lacked any means to help Pierre. The man had lost too much blood. He was a dead man, for sure. Trying to move him would only put the man in a state of pointless agony. But Cole wasn't about to abandon him to a painful, lingering death in the woods.

Cole touched Pierre's head gently, turning away his line of sight. The gesture was not all that different from what he might have used on a wounded deer that he had tracked down. Pierre breathed a sigh of relief, as if he knew what was coming and welcomed it.

Cole took a step slightly behind Pierre so that the Frenchman couldn't see what he was doing, raised his rifle, and shot him behind the ear. The sound of the lone shot seemed brutally loud and echoed through the woods and hills.

He guessed from the caked blood on Pierre's clothes that the poor bastard had been out here overnight. Hard as it had been to do, killing Pierre was an act of mercy. The Germans who had massacred the villagers and the two boys would be long gone. With any luck, though, they had heard the gunshot. Cole was sending them a message. It meant, *I'm comin' for you.*

CHAPTER TWENTY-THREE

IT DIDN'T SEEM right to leave the bodies of the dead villagers scattered across the clearing, so Cole arranged them side by side. He didn't have a shovel, so there was no hope of burying them. The Germans hadn't bothered to take their weapons, so Cole laid them beside the men, like ancient warriors sent to the afterlife with their spears and swords. He picked up the old firearms and sniffed at them, getting a whiff of gun oil but no smell of burned powder. The villagers had never even had a chance to use their weapons.

Cole wasn't much for church-going religion, but he believed in God. You didn't put a man to rest without a prayer. He took off his helmet and mumbled the Lord's Prayer over the dead. He said the final words more clearly, feeling their power resonate within him:

"For thine is the kingdom, the power, the glory forever. Amen."

Then he committed the dead villagers to the woods and the forest creatures. By springtime, only scattered bones would remain. In some ways, he thought that this was better than going into a hole in the ground.

Moving down the trail toward the German position, all of Cole's senses felt on hyper alert. His eyes sprang to each branch moving in the wind, each flicker of a bird through the trees. He was supposed to be a soldier, but he had murder in his heart.

When he had gone looking for Margot's brother, he had not also gone looking for a fight. His plan had been to take a look in the woods and then get back to help in the defense of the village. But plans had changed. He was bringing the fight to the Germans. Anyhow, when hadn't he ever been ready for a fight?

He hadn't gone more than a quarter of a mile through the woods when he heard the Germans. Their low, guttural voices in the valley below carried up to him on the ridge. He could smell meat cooking —fresh pork, most likely, over an open fire. Goddam, but that smelled delicious. He'd had to make do that morning with canned rations. In spite of the scene back at the clearing, his stomach rumbled. There wasn't a man alive who could smell roasting meat and not be hungry.

He stopped long enough to mount the rifle so that he could use the scope to spot the Germans through the trees. However, all that he saw were leaves and gray bark. They were still too far away and screened from Cole's view by the surrounding woods.

He continued along the trail, cushioned by the damp leaves. The animals had made such a smooth path that his boots moved silently. He kept his rifle ready. This close to the Germans, he might run into a sentry at any point. After all, the Germans were familiar with the trail, as evidenced by the massacre of the villagers. Chances were good that they would have posted a guard.

The trail led over the hill to the village, but the narrow path was not a practical route for launching an attack with a force that included a Kübelwagen mounting a machine gun. The winding path was better suited to wild pigs or possibly for use by a handful of men, not an entire squad. Yesterday, when the German sniper had peppered the village, he had likely used the trail to use the heights to his advantage. The Germans would make their main attack using the road leading toward the village and river crossing. But Cole became concerned that a handful of Germans could use the trail to get inside the village and surprise the defenders. He would need some insurance against that.

Up ahead, Cole's alert eyes caught movement. A German sentry. Just as he had figured. The man was well-hidden by his blue-gray uniform, which blended into the shadows of the autumn woods. Cole had only managed to get so close because of his natural ability to move silently through the woods. Cole froze, hoping that he hadn't been seen.

The German was leaning against a tree, intent on lighting a cigarette. A machine pistol hung across the man's front, within easy reach. If so much as a twig snapped, the man could cut Cole in two with single burst. The question was, had he already spotted Cole and was pretending not to notice? Maybe he didn't want to give Cole a reason to shoot *him*.

In fact, Cole itched to shoot him, but he wasn't ready yet to let the Germans know he was there. The gunshot that had ended Pierre's suffering had been far enough from the German camp. Now, Cole must be on their doorstep.

The man was too far away for Cole to get at him with his knife and Cole did not want to alert the Jerries with a rifle shot. Before the German could look up, Cole had retreated back up the trail.

Out of the sentry's line of sight, Cole weighed his options. He was sure that he was close to the German camp, which meant that there were lots of the enemy in the vicinity, and just one of him. The smart thing to do would be to get the hell out of there. But Cole wasn't always good at doing the smart thing. What he wanted to do was inflict some pain on these Jerries for what they had done to those French kids back in the woods. Also, if the Germans hoped to use the trail as a back door into the village, then Cole planned to close it.

One of the best ways to even the odds and multiply his numbers was to make a trap. Setting traps was one of Cole's specialties. Trapping had kept food on the table back in Gashey's Creek, and it had helped him stay alive on more than one occasion here in France.

When he made a run for it down this trail, it would help to have something up his sleeve to slow down the enemy that would surely be coming after him.

He needed something quick to build and deadly. But what?

Cole thought about the things he carried. Twine. A knife. Grenades.

He could easily lash his knife to a sapling and set a trap that would whip the knife into a Jerry coming up the trail after him. But he didn't want to give up his knife, which had been hand-made for him by an old craftsman back home.

That left the two grenades. He took one out and

set it beside the trail. Using his knife, he cut a leafy branch and set it across the trail. Then he tied the twine to a small tree and stretched it across the trail, using the leafy branch to disguise it. The other end of the string he tied to a grenade.

Now came the tricky part. Made him sweat a little, to tell the truth, because if he didn't get it right he'd be leaving parts of himself scattered around the woods. He depressed the lever and pulled the pin, then wedged the grenade into a tangle of tree roots and then added a flat rock on top for good measure. Gingerly, he eased his hand off the lever to make sure that the rock and tree roots kept the grenade wedged in place. He wasn't quite happy with the pressure on the lever, so he moved the rock around a bit.

Finished, he stepped back and breathed again. Someone running down the trail would step over the leafy branch, hit the tripwire, and yank the grenade free. One man moving fast might get out of the kill zone in time, but anyone running behind him wouldn't be so lucky.

His trap set, Cole slipped off the trail into the woods. He wanted to get closer to the German camp without taking a chance of being spotted by the sentry on the trail.

The trees were dense and enough vegetation clung to the underbrush that he was hidden quickly. Moving quietly off the trail, however, was more problematic. Luckily for Cole, the damp leaves favored him and he moved stealthily downhill toward the German camp.

Near the bottom of the hill he crossed a stream, most likely a tributary that flowed into the Moselle. Though narrow, the stream ran deep and was swollen by the recent rain. Cole wasn't in any hurry to cross the muddy, roiling stream. He didn't much like water, having once become entangled in a beaver trap and nearly drowning in a deep mountain creek. The woods began to thin out on the other side of the stream, and he found himself looking at the German camp, no more than a couple of hundred feet away. Using the game trail, Cole had taken the long way around across the hill and come in behind the Germans.

These were the men who had attacked the village. He could see the road leading straight toward Ville sur Moselle and the bridge. The village couldn't have been more than half a mile away. The German force sat astride the road like a bottle stopper—no one in, no one out.

He could see a mix of different uniforms and equipment. Clearly, this unit was cobbled together, much like his own. The only mechanized vehicles were a couple of mud-splattered Kübelwagen. He did a quick count and came up with at least fifty Jerries. Veteran Wehrmacht troops. Hard fighters, as proven by their attack on the village, and ruthless. If they attacked the village en masse or split up to come at the village from two directions, the defenders were going to be in trouble.

Studying the Germans, Cole realized that he didn't have much of a plan. He might have bitten off more here than he could chew. He reckoned that things would get hot as soon as he jammed a stick into that hornet's nest.

Belly to the ground, he studied the Germans through the scope. One of the things about being a sniper that appealed to Cole was that his trade required intense focus. The world was a big place, as Cole had discovered in the Army. He had crossed an ocean, trained in England for the D Day landing, and now here he was in France. Before that, all that he had known were the mountains. Vast as the mountains were, they constituted just one corner of that big ol' world. A telescopic sight simplified matters. Seeing the battlefield reduced to a circle of magnified view reassured him. That little circle was all that a sniper had to worry about.

You saw the enemy in that circle, you shot him. Simple as that.

But today, he reckoned his job wasn't quite that easy. Larger forces were at play, such as the impending attack on the village. Nobody watched his blindside. Cole was on his own. And his mind kept

going back to the scene of that massacre in the
woods. The splattered blood from those kids on the
forest leaves. The memory brought angry bile to his
own throat.

Somebody had to pay for that. Considering the
number of targets arrayed below, maybe a whole lot
of somebodies.

As he watched, a single German military truck
drove up. He recognized it as an Opel Blitz, which
was somewhat smaller than the U.S. Army's GMC
Deuce and a half. He worried that the truck might be
carrying reinforcements. That was the last thing he
needed. No troops came spilling out, however. Just a
couple of guys who had been up front in the cab.
Curious, Cole waited to see what the deal was with
the truck.

The Germans began unloading the truck. If the
truck didn't carry reinforcements, he saw that it
contained the next worst thing. Ammo. If the Jerries
were low on ammunition, this explained why they
hadn't already attacked the village yet today. Now
that they had resupplied, Cole was sure that they
would hit the village before nightfall. Maybe even at
any minute.

Directing the unloading was a tall German officer.
Cole picked him up through the scope and saw hair
graying at the temples. He recognized him as the
same the general who had carried the flag of truce

into the village. He wished that Tolliver would have let him shoot the smug son of a bitch. Cole watched the general shouting and pointing. One thing for sure: when the old man barked, the other Jerries jumped.

Cole thought about taking him out here and now. German units relied more heavily on officers to make many of the decisions. Even the lowliest American GI was more used to thinking for himself. Maybe that was just part of being an American. When it came to the Germans, the trick was to cut off the head of the snake.

He was just lining up the reticle when a soldier went running up to the officer. Something urgent, it looked like. The officer walked off and was soon out of sight behind the truck.

Silently, Cole cursed. He had lost his chance. Another few seconds, and the officer would have been as good as dead. The good news was that he had no shortage of other targets. He could take his pick. It's just that they weren't generals.

Cole thought about his position. In front of him was spread the German camp. Easy pickings. Directly in front of him was the roiling stream and behind him, the hill that he had descended from the trail on the ridge. The thought of someone taking the high ground above and behind him made him uneasy. He was somewhat reassured by the fact that they'd have to be part Cherokee to make it down through the woods to get the jump on him without making any noise. Just this once, he wished that he'd brought Vaccaro along to cover his ass.

But like his pa always said, "You go wish in one hand and shit in the other, boy, and see which one fills up first." If his pa was in a good mood, he had followed up that bit of wisdom with a snort. If he'd been drinking, he usually gave Cole's ear a sharp slap with a hand hard as a hickory board. Just thinking about the old man now made Cole's head ring.

Ain't no sense now in wishin'. His plan was to move around once the shooting started. With any luck, the Germans might think there was more than one soldier hidden in the trees. Cole found a suitable log and got set up behind it. About twenty feet away, he could see a large, moss-covered boulder that would make a good sniper hide. Beyond that was another log.

Once things got too hot, his plan was to high-tail it out of there, back up the ridge. He'd be most of the way down the trail to Ville sur Moselle by the time the Germans got up the nerve to head into the woods.

The scope helped him get up close and personal with the Germans. They were still busy unloading the truck, scurrying around the camp. The tall officer hadn't come back into sight, which was too bad, but you couldn't have everything.

Cole picked out a soldier leaning against the truck, having a smoke while he watched the others works. He put the crosshairs on the German and pulled the trigger.

The man slumped over. Cole worked the bolt and picked out another Jerry holding a wooden box of ammo. He had frozen at the sound of Cole's rifle. Cole shot him.

It was shaping up to be a turkey shoot. The only problem was that these turkeys would be shooting back any minute now.

Cole lined up his crosshairs on a soldier who had stopped to light a cigarette like he didn't have a care in the world. A machine pistol hung from a strap over the German's shoulder. He squeezed the trigger and the German crumpled to the ground. He ran the bolt and acquired another target. This one looked toward the woods, momentarily frozen by the single rifle shot. Cole took him out.

He fired again, bringing down a third German. But the element of surprise was over. Already, the soldiers had scattered for cover. Bullets began to sing through the trees and dig into the hillside. They hadn't figured out where Cole was hiding yet, but if they thought the suppressing fire was going to make him keep his head down, they were right about that much.

He rolled away from the log and belly-crawled like a salamander toward an old stump several feet away. If he kept moving around, he reckoned he could keep the Germans confused. More bullets chewed up the trees overhead. He was at a steep angle above the German position, which meant that most of them were shooting too high. You had to hold low to hit a target above you. Not that he was going to pause right then and give the Jerries a shooting lesson. He got behind the crumbling stump and rested his rifle over it, then got back on the scope.

His pa used to say that Cole had eyes in the back of his head. That was helpful when your old man was a mean drunk. In the woods, it paid to have that kind of sixth sense. Maybe it had kept his ancestors alive when they were fighting Indians and such. He couldn't have told anyone how he knew there was someone coming down the hill toward his position, but he sure as hell sensed it. A few seconds later, he heard boots shuffling through the leaves.

There had been a German sentry up on the trail. When the German heard the shooting below him, he must have gone to investigate and come at Cole from behind. The German was coming at him from higher up the hill, being none too quiet about it. Cole could hear him, even with all the shooting going on. Sounded like a herd of elephants.

Cole got himself turned around and swung the rifle to face the new threat. He didn't put the scope to his eye yet, but stared into the woods, hoping to detect movement.

He and the German saw each other at just about the same time. The German stopped and put his rifle his shoulder. Cole could practically feel those iron sights on him, hot as a brand. A bullet hit the stump behind him, exploding into a shower of soft splinters. A little to the left, he thought. He was sure that the German sentry wouldn't miss again.

Quickly, he got the German in his sights, hardly bothering to aim. As soon as the crosshairs touched the man's torso, Cole jerked the trigger. It wasn't good technique and it sure as hell wasn't elegant, but the German doubled over, the rifle spilling out of his grip. Gutshot. Cole took more careful aim this time and finished him.

He hoped to hell that was the only German he had to worry about coming at him from the rear. There were plenty enough Germans in front of him. He got turned around again and settled the rifle across the stump once more. Through the scope, he glimpsed the top of a helmet behind some sort of ammo crate. He lined up the sights and fired, ran the bolt, and looked for another target. The action felt silky smooth and the smell of gunpowder in his nose was intoxicating. He could do this all day long.

But the Germans weren't going to let him. Already, bullets chewed up the underbrush around him. He had planned on teaching the Jerries a lesson and exacting a price for that massacre in the woods. But he had lost the element of surprise and the tables had turned. He saw that a couple of Germans were maneuvering that Kübelwagen so that they could rake the woods with the machine gun mounted on the back of it. He wouldn't be able to stay here for long, that was for sure.

The fox had gotten into the hen house. But now the big dogs were coming for him.

CHAPTER TWENTY-FOUR

AT THE FIRST SHOTS, Hauer and the other Germans dove for cover. Already, two men were down, one shot through the neck and the other through the chest. Then a third and fourth fell, both hit in the torso. Each bullet arrived with telling accuracy. The sniper on the hill did not seem to miss. Hauer was sure that the sniper must be an American soldier. This was not the work of some untrained Resistance fighter armed with an ancient rifle.

"Sniper!" someone shouted, although by then, the warning was unnecessary.

To the untrained eye, the bullets seemed to cause pandemonium as soldiers scrambled for cover. However, these were veterans of dozens of similar attacks these last few months. The rifle fire had not disrupted them for very long. The sniper had picked off four men quickly, but now there were few easy targets. The Germans organized themselves and started to shoot back into the woods. But as long as the sniper was operating, they were effectively pinned down.

"Hauer!" shouted Unterbrink. The general was sheltering on the far side of the truck. His voice carried clearly, almost like a snarl.

When he heard his name shouted, Hauer made his way toward the general, keeping his head down. Unterbrink looked annoyed that the enemy sniper had managed to disrupt the unloading of the ammunition and the preparations for the attack on the village. The general wanted to know what the hell was going on. "How many snipers are in those woods?"

"It is just one man, sir," Hauer said.

"Are you sure?"

"Did you notice that pause, and then the shots came from a new location? He is moving around to make us think there is more than one of him."

"*Verdammt nochmal!* I don't care if it is one sniper or one hundred," Unterbrink snapped. "Put a stop to this attack! That is your job, Hauer. He will put us behind schedule. We cannot prepare for the attack if we are pinned down. Now that we have ammunition, we need to attack that village and take it while it is still daylight. For all we know, the sun could show its face tomorrow, and with it those damn Ami planes will return. If that happens, the sniper will be the least of our worries."

"Yes, sir."

Hauer moved off, but he did not immediately return fire. His comrades were already doing that, making it plenty hot for the sniper. He was still shooting at them with telling effect.

The general wanted the Ami sniper taken out, but Hauer had some ideas of his own for how to deal with him. He wondered if this was the same sniper that he had encountered back at the village. He recalled the American's hard stare and felt an involuntary stab of doubt. There had been no posturing on the American sniper's part. The man had been a killer, plain and simple. Hauer had become good at recognizing that quality in other men. Nonetheless, the man had to be something of a fool to attack the German squad, alone and unsupported.

Already, the rest of the unit began laying down a withering fire into the woods. He was sure that the American sniper would slip away. He himself would have done the same. Hauer also had a good idea that the American would fall back to the trail that crossed the ridge and led down to the village. The sniper would follow that trail right back to the Americans, reporting what he had seen. He would warn the Americans and villagers that another attack was coming. Hauer intended to stop him.

His plan was simple. He would move to the right of the sniper and then climb the hill until he reached the trail toward Ville sur Moselle. From there, it would be a simple matter of setting an ambush for the American as he tried to return to the village using that path. No different from hunting a wild pig.

Hauer caressed the hilt of his butcher's knife. With any luck, he might even capture him and teach him a lesson in pain similar to the one he had given the Frenchman. The American wouldn't be so tough once he had been captured and separated from his rifle. Hauer could take his time killing him, then butcher him like a helpless sheep.

And to that end, Hauer had a few tricks up his sleeve.

Dodging the sniper's line of sight, he crept toward General Unterbrink's Kübelwagen. On the retreat back through France toward the fabled West Wall, Hauer had been among those German troops who ransacked French houses to take anything of value. They figured that they were owed something, although the wily French had hidden almost anything of value.

To his delight, though, Hauer had found some old

WWI trench armor in a barn. That war had been fought with one foot in the past and one in the future, with horses and even armor being used alongside airplanes and machine guns.

The armored cuirass or breastplate appeared to be of German manufacture, and the hardened alloy steel was nearly a centimeter thick. An old suit of armor was soft as butter compared to modern steel. The armor hooked over one's shoulders and was secured with straps, so that it protected one's chest and belly. To protect the groin and legs, plates had been riveted so that they articulated much like the sections of a lobster's tail. The wearer essentially donned a steel shell.

Cotton padding on the underside was an attempt to make the armor more comfortable and to help absorb the impact of bullets, but the heavy armor wasn't the sort of thing that one wore on a daily basis. Mostly, such armor had been donned by stationary machine gunners with the notion of turning the gunners into human pillboxes.

Amused at Hauer's discovery, General Unterbrink had let him toss it in the back of the Kübelwagen.

"That's just like you, Hauer," the general said. "Everyone else is worried about stealing a silver candlestick, but you found something of practical use."

"Do you think it could actually stop a bullet, sir?"

As a veteran of the Great War, Unterbrink had some experience with the armor. At least, he had seen it used in the field. Unterbrink examined the armor closely, announcing that the armor was an alloy of hardened steel, which would make it extremely tough. "The curved surface of the armor helps to deflect a bullet, even a rifle round," the general had said. "But it is not foolproof. You see, mainly the armor is useful against shrapnel and pistol rounds. The best defense is to wear the armor and then not get shot in the first place!"

"It will certainly stop a pistol round, sir, and maybe a rifle bullet if it hits at an angle."

"That much is true, Hauer. I saw it save more than one's man life. I can't imagine wearing that around all day, however."

This particular armored cuirass included a sort of cup device that had been welded to the right shoulder, enabling the wearer to mount a rifle. Otherwise, the recoil would cause the stock to slide off the rounded armor.

Hauer had taken off the worst of the rust with a wire brush, and then coated the scrubbed metal with gun oil. Good as new.

Given the weight of the armor, many men would struggle with it. Hauer, however, was powerfully built through the torso and shoulders. Butcher's shoulders.

He agreed with old Unterbrink that the steel would stop shrapnel or a pistol round, or a bayonet stab, and would likely stop bullets from one of the Americans' lighter machine guns.

The question was, would the armor work against a rifle? The Springfield rifles used by the Ami snipers fired a powerful round. As he had suggested to the general, Hauer thought that the effectiveness of the armor would depend on the range and the angle of the bullet. Working in his favor was the fact that many snipers did not bother trying for headshots because it was too easy to miss. They aimed for center mass.

Anyhow, the armor was better than nothing and if he did get shot and the armor worked, the enemy sniper was going to get quite a surprise.

He slipped the armor on over his tunic, then covered it all with a poncho. With any luck, he had just made himself bulletproof.

"Sergeant!" he called, getting the attention of a battle-hardened *Feldwebel* nearby.

"What is it, Hauer? We are a little busy now. Maybe you want to go hunting later, eh? We'll get another pig."

Hauer grinned. "Better yet, why don't I go hunting for that sniper? I am going to move up the hill and get behind him."

The *Feldwebel* gave him a quick nod and spread the word to his men. He had informed the sergeant because the last thing Hauer wanted was to get shot at by his own side.

While the firefight was still taking place, Hauer took off up the hill to the right of where the enemy sniper was positioned. The boys were chewing him up with a steady rate of fire; the Ami wouldn't last long before he had to get out of there if he hoped to survive. Hauer was sure that the sniper intended to harass them rather than go down fighting. There would be time enough for that during the upcoming attack on Ville sur Moselle.

Hauer ran up the hill, laboring under the burden of more than twenty pounds of armor, along with his rifle and extra rounds, not to mention his canteen and other gear. He felt as loaded-down as a peasant's donkey on market day.

He was none too quiet about climbing the wooded hillside, but the shooting below covered up the ruckus that he made. The hill was quite steep and the footing uneven. By the time he reached the trail at the top of the ridge, he was regretting every sausage he had ever eaten and every cigarette he had ever smoked.

Winded, he stood for a few moments with his hands on his knees, catching his breath. Despite the cool temperatures, he was sweating heavily under the iron plating. Briefly, he debated stripping it off, wondering if the armor was only going to be a hindrance, but he decided to keep it on for now. He had already done the hard part in climbing the ridge.

It looked as if he had come out on the trail in the perfect spot to ambush the sniper when he retreated this way. Hauer moved along the relatively flat trail until he found a windfall a short distance off the path. What had once been a mighty oak had blown over in a storm, exposing its tangled roots where they had torn from the ground. Hauer was so used to seeing the result of man-made destruction that it was almost surprising to be reminded that nature still had its own violent forces.

He got behind the downed log, well hidden from anyone coming down the trail. Several weeks before, Hauer had cut a strip of inner tube and stretched it around his helmet like a big rubber band. He took a few minutes now to stuff tips of branches and bits of leaves into the band to break up the outline of his helmet and help him blend into the tangled mass of the windfall.

He set the Mauser in a forked branch to help steady his aim, then took a look through the scope. From here, he had an unimpeded field of fire. The retreating American sniper would walk right into his sights. Just like shooting one of those wild pigs. He regretted that it would be over too quickly. If he had the chance, he would try to wound the sniper, get his rifle away from him, and then finish him with the knife.

Hauer settled down to wait.

CHAPTER TWENTY-FIVE

THINGS WERE STARTING to get too hot for Cole, with bullets chewing up the woods around him. Time to get the hell out of Dodge. But that was easier said than done, with lead flying all around him.

A bullet neatly severed a twig just inches from his head. Cole worried that he had overstayed his welcome, like when you drank up all a man's whiskey and he turned mean at the sight of the empty jug. These Jerries were plenty mean right now.

He had brought along a couple of grenades—next best thing to having Vaccaro with him. One grenade was now serving to booby trap the trail back to the village. He pulled the pin on his remaining grenade and threw it across the stream toward the Germans. He didn't know if he'd come close to anybody and he didn't much care. He needed a diversion.

As soon as the grenade went off, he was on his feet and running up the hillside. The blast created enough confusion for him to get out of what had been a tight spot. Thanks to the cover provided by the underbrush, the Germans hadn't seen him retreat.

Still, bullets snicked by close enough to set is hair on edge, some whining as they ricocheted off trees. That sound always made Cole's spine quiver. Cole kept going uphill until he reached the game trail. Then he turned west and ran along the trail as hard as he could.

Cole didn't know if the Germans would come after him or not, once they figured out that he had stopped shooting. He had seen how they were unloading ammunition and preparing for another go at the village and bridge. Once they had run him off, would they even bother to pursue him? Not if he was lucky, they wouldn't. The last thing Cole wanted or needed was a posse of SS soldiers hot on his trail. They'd be mad as hornets, that was for damn sure.

He would have felt better about the situation if he'd had more ammunition. But all that he had left was the clip in the rifle. Five shots? He had not expected a firefight and had shot up most of the ammo that he had carried with him. If the Germans did come after him, and if they had more than five men, then he'd be in serious trouble. In order to travel light, he didn't have a sidearm. He did have his Bowie knife, but he never put much stock in bringing a knife to a gun fight.

While one part of his mind puzzled out his current situation, another, more primitive part of his mind stayed on hyper alert. It was the hunter in him, something deep and primal that never switched off. Cole thought of that part of him as the critter. Sure, the critter was part of him, but also a separate entity hunkered down there in some cave of his mind, sniffing the air with a grizzled snout, ever watchful. So far, the critter had helped keep him alive.

Now, the critter dragged a claw along Cole's backbone to get his attention. What the critter noticed was that he couldn't hear any birds. His ears still rang from the firefight, but even as he moved deeper into the woods there was utter silence. When he had come through this way earlier, there had been a few forest sounds: bird songs, chattering squirrels, the machine gun staccato of a woodpecker. The quiet meant one thing.

He wasn't alone.

Cole stopped and listened. His hearing remained muffled, but he could hear well enough to know that he wasn't hearing anything. No sounds from the trail behind him, and no sounds ahead.

Just because he couldn't hear someone, didn't mean that they weren't there.

He decided to play it safe and get off the trail, at least for now. Surrounding him was dense woods. Whoever was out here was probably on the trail. The last thing he wanted to do was walk right into a German patrol coming from the direction of Ville sur Moselle.

Cole slipped easily among the trees and underbrush. Fall had thinned out the woods, offering less concealment, but it also made movement through the trees easier. He went up the hill, about a hundred feet into the woods, and moved roughly parallel to the trail. He soon lost visual contact with the trail, but he moved steadily east and used landmarks to navigate: an oak tree up ahead with a big knot on its trunk, and when he came even with that tree, he picked out another landmark far ahead, this time a recent windfall with a fresh, split trunk that created a bright spill of color in the drab forest.

He wasn't exactly Injun quiet—moving through fallen leaves and the litter on the forest floor wearing Army boots wasn't conducive to that—but he was sure that if someone waited on the trail below, they wouldn't hear *him*.

After ten minutes, he had passed the windfall and he hadn't seen anything other than trees or heard anything other than a few distant birds as the forest came back to life. Satisfied, he moved back toward the trail. The going would be a lot faster and he wanted to get back to Ville sur Moselle as soon as possible with a warning that the Germans were about to launch a fresh attack.

Cole stepped onto the trail. Looking east, he thought he recognized the section ahead. A little further on was the trap he had rigged. He would have to watch out for that. Getting blown up by his own trap would be a hell of a thing.

The critter snarled, *behind you*. Cole spun in time to see a man who had been crouched behind the windfall, looking in the opposite direction. The man spotted him and spun around, holding a rifle, and seeking a target. Maybe it hadn't been the critter at all, but just that motion catching his eye. He caught a glimpse of a German *Stahlhelm* and rifle with a scope. Without hesitating, he threw his own rifle to his shoulder, got the sights on the German sniper's torso as the man turned, and squeezed off a shot before the Jerry could fire his own rifle.

Cole had heard more than a few bullets hit bodies, both human and animal. They usually made a wet, raw meat sound when they hit. Nothing pretty about that sound. What he heard now was a metallic *clang* like a bolt tossed into a bucket. It was the oddest damn thing.

He had expected the German to go down. The man only staggered back, as if Cole had punched him instead of shot him.

Tough bastard, Cole thought. But something didn't add up. He put the crosshairs on the German's torso again. By now, the man was moving and the shot wasn't as dead center, but still on target. No time to get fancy. He pulled the trigger.

Again, the German sniper staggered. But he didn't go down.

What the hell?

He had shot the man twice but had failed to take him down. Then he saw the German's rifle coming up.

Run, the critter inside him howled.

Cole turned and high-tailed it down the trail.

He felt like he had a big old X painted between his shoulder blades, but he dodged and weaved as best he could, juking left and right. He would've put a jackrabbit to shame. Behind him, the German fired and Cole actually felt the supersonic crack of the bullet go past his ear. The sound sent fresh shivers down his spine and made his legs feel slightly rubbery. Cole ran until his lungs burned.

The deer and pigs had made a winding trail that prevented a clear line of sight. He went around a bend and wasn't such a target anymore. Cole kept running, in part because he was just plain spooked. How in the hell had the German sniper gotten the drop on him like that?

If Cole had stayed on the trail initially, instead of

slipping off into the woods as a precaution, he would have walked right into the Jerry's sights. The German would have drilled him.

More worrisome was the fact that he had put two shots on the German without apparent effect. What the hell was going on here?

He saw the log ahead where he had set his trap and leaped over it. With any luck, it would slow down or stop the German. He kept going and ran full tilt into the clearing where the massacre had taken place. He caught a glimpse of the bodies and hoped to hell that he wasn't about to join them anytime soon. The sight was also like salt in the wound. He had gone after the Germans intending to exact a pound of flesh, and now here he was running for his life. So much for being an avenging angel.

Behind him, he heard the blast of the grenade. The Jerry had run right through the tripwire. But had the grenade killed the German or merely wounded him? If the Jerry had been moving as fast as Cole, there was a chance that he had actually run through the kill zone by the time that the grenade detonated.

American grenades killed with shrapnel while the German version relied on a deadly shockwave. Close was usually good enough with any grenade, but how lucky was the German? Was he dead?

Cole wanted to make sure.

At the far end of the clearing, Cole fell to one knee and worked a fresh round into the chamber.

A split second later, the German sniper came rushing into the clearing. He was dragging one leg, so the booby trap had done some damage, but he was still on his feet.

With his hammering heart and unsteady stance, Cole didn't trust himself to try for a headshot at a running target. He aimed again at the torso. Cole fired.

The German grunted and spun halfway around from the impact of the bullet, but he didn't go down. His rifle was coming up, up—

Cole didn't stick around to get shot. He plunged into the woods and ran downhill. The German fired and Cole could hear the bullet bouncing among the trees. He rushed pell-mell through the woods, roots trying to trip him, branches snapping at his face and briers snagging at his clothes, but he didn't slow down.

At the bottom of the ridge ran the same stream that had created a moat between him and the German camp. The stream was probably a tributary of the Moselle. The water was muddy from the recent rain and swift moving. Couldn't be more than a couple of feet deep and not more than ten feet wide, but too much to leap across. From the crashing sounds behind him, it was clear that the German was pursuing him—none too gracefully. In the distance, he heard the swell of small arms fire. The attack on the village had already begun. They would need every rifle to defend Ville sur Moselle. Right about now, General Tolliver was likely wondering where the hell Cole was.

Gettin' my ass kicked, Cole thought.

He could still hear the sniper running through the woods behind him. That leg wound, and maybe that last bullet, had slowed him down, but the son of a bitch was still coming.

Turn and fight, said the critter, feeling cornered, eager to bare its teeth.

But Cole wasn't just critter. Another, more calculating part of him existed. He *did* plan to fight, because there really wasn't any other option, but he had just two or three bullets left in the stripper clip. He had already put not one, not two, but three bullets on this guy, but hadn't managed to stop him yet. Cole knew that he'd hit him, but he hadn't put him down—not yet. He needed the German to stand still long enough for Cole to line up the crosshairs on him one more time.

He didn't have time for anything complicated. He pulled a dollar bill out of his pocket and dropped it on the bank of the creek. In the drab gray and brown of the natural world, the paper money stood out sharply.

Then Cole quickly moved back up the hill, in a slightly different direction from the one that he'd come down. By the time that the Jerry reached the creek, Cole was snuggled into the underbrush, a hundred feet away.

He slid the rifle through a fork in a small tree to hold it steady. Worked the bolt. He had one more bullet after this one. Otherwise, he'd be down to his knife. He knew that the German wasn't going to take him prisoner—and Cole wasn't about to let him.

He put his eye to the scope and looked back at the creek. His field of vision was crisscrossed by all sort of twigs and branches. The ones up close looked big and blurry. In fact, his field of view was such a mess that he could barely see the fine black reticule against that backdrop. This was going to be tricky.

Then the German appeared. He wore a poncho, which made it impossible to tell how or why the German was bulletproof. For the first time, Cole got a good look at his face. The heavy, brutal visage reminded him of a foreman on a coal mining crew back home. He had big shoulders and a thick neck. Cole wasn't afraid of anybody, but he sure as hell wouldn't be eager to tangle with him one on one. The German was breathing heavily from the effort of running down through the woods.

Cole tried to get a clear shot, but all he could see was that web of branches. All it would take was one tiny twig to deflect the bullet. The man was looking this way and that. In another second, he'd be moving again and Cole would miss his chance.

The man disappeared from the sight picture. Cole realized that he must have bent over to pick up the money. Next to the helmet on a stick, using a lure of some sort was the oldest trick in the book, but he'd fallen for it. The sniper's head and face reappeared in the scope.

At this range, the bullet would be a little low from where Cole put the crosshairs. He thought about a headshot, and just as quickly, ruled it out. With two bullets left, he didn't want to take that chance.

He aimed at the German's chest, but the target was obscured by the branches of the dense under-brush. He held his breath and waited. For an instant, Cole's crosshairs found the tiniest gap through the branches. He squeezed the trigger.

Cole worked the bolt, then heard a splash as the German went into the water.

One bullet left. He hoped to hell he wouldn't need it. So far, this bastard had been awfully tough to kill.

He couldn't see a goddamn thing through the scope because of the blur of intertwined branches, so he moved his head away from the scope, leaving the rifle pressed to his shoulder. Still nothing. He braced himself for any return fire from the German.

Cole crept forward, slowly untangling himself from the dense brush where he had hidden himself. He moved toward the stream. He hoped to find the German's body in the water. But Cole found no sign of him, except for his helmet where he had lost it among the brush on the river bank. Cole took that as a good omen. Maybe that last shot had finished him off, once and for all. The dollar bill that he'd used as bait was nowhere to be seen.

Keep the change.

He felt let down that there was no body. Cheated, somehow.

The German's rifle must have fallen into the water. He had caught a glimpse earlier of the scoped weapon. Cole suspected that the rifle was a standard-issue Mauser K-98 sniper model. Cole had seen them before. The Germans issued a lot of them, as opposed to the U.S. Army, which had been slow to figure out the value of a sniper. The Germans seemed to have no shortage of good snipers.

The mystery was, how had Cole managed to shoot this son of a bitch, not once, but twice, without stopping him? The German had been big and solid, but he wasn't Superman. Besides, a rifle that would drop a huge buck or a bear instantly was no match for any man.

Fortunately, Cole's final bullet must have done its job.

Stealthily, he began to move downstream, following the bank of the stream. The rushing water masked any nearby sounds, but in the distance he could hear shooting from the direction of the village. Things must be starting to heat up if the Germans had resupplied with all that ammo. He moved more quickly, expecting at any moment to see the German sniper's body hung up on a snag in the rain-swollen stream, but there was no sign of him.

He moved more slowly, sensing that something wasn't right. Had the German's body been swept completely away? Finally, he caught a glimpse of something caught on a branch in the current. Keeping his rifle raised to his shoulder, he approached cautiously. The silhouetted figure moved sluggishly, but Cole thought that maybe the current was causing the movement. As he drew closer, he became convinced that it was not the enemy sniper's body, but a sodden German poncho. Carefully, he leaned out over the water and reached for the poncho. Cole didn't much want to go for a swim. He caught the poncho and pulled.

Under the surface, something weighed down the poncho, but it seemed too light for a body. He tugged harder. The force of the current pulling back nearly dragged him in. With a final grunt of effort, he managed to get the poncho and whatever it held free of the creek and swung it up on the bank.

To his surprise, the poncho was tangled around a chunk of metal. It took him a moment to figure out what he was looking at. This was some sort of armored plating, like maybe a knight would wear. He had never seen such a thing before. All that Cole could do was stare at it.

"Don't that beat all," Cole said.

Then everything fell into place and caused him to chuckle. He felt relieved that the problem hadn't been his shooting, after all. The problem was that he'd been shooting at thick steel plating. The German had armored up.

He examined the armor more closely, truly amazed. He had never seen such a thing as body armor. There were dents, and one of the bullets appeared to have gone all the way through. Maybe he had gotten the son of a bitch, after all. He didn't see any blood, though. Had the German stopped to take off the armor to keep it from pulling him under, or had it simply separated from the body as it tumbled in the current?

He looked out toward the rain-swollen stream, which had enough of a current to sweep a body away. Had he actually killed the German? Cole might never know. He hated to think that the German had escaped with his rifle, but that remained a possibility.

Leaving the sodden poncho and armor on the stream bank, he straightened up and started walking downstream in the direction of the village. He had no doubt that this creek flowed directly into the Moselle and that the village would be nearby.

The firing was stronger and more rapid now from that direction. He reckoned that the Germans had launched another attack.

There had been a lot of Germans compared to the number of defenders. And the Jerries now had no shortage of ammo.

Cole hurried.

CHAPTER TWENTY-SIX

NEARLY BREATHLESS FROM his dash through the woods, Cole reached the outskirts of the village and then plunged through the backyard vegetable gardens and sheds into the single main street, where a sharp fight was taking place between the defenders and the Germans. The number of men engaged was small, but the fighting was as intense as any that Cole had seen since wading ashore four months before. These men had faced each other previously. The two generals had met face to face. This wasn't just war. This was personal.

He saw that the road into the village had become like a raging torrent of steel and fury as the Germans attacked. Cole ran out from the woods to join the defenders in the village. Nobody paid him any attention because all their focus was on the German attack. Cole could see German soldiers, bent low, advancing toward the village. Some fired from the hip at a run, while others paused to throw their Mauser rifles to their shoulders when a target presented itself. The muddy road precluded any dust, but the damp air stank of gunpowder and was filled with smoke, creating a fog through which the soldiers ran, appearing as shapeless dark silhouettes, their muzzle flashes bright against the gloom.

Would the defenders hold? Flip a coin, Cole thought. They were standing on the edge of a knife blade. This fight could go either way.

Not for the first time, Cole felt that they were lucky to have Tolliver in charge rather than that idiot, Captain Norton. Norton would have lost the fight quicker than a hound sucks an egg.

General Tolliver had made a good effort in erecting barricades at the edge of town, using horse carts and hand carts, dining room tables, and even an upholstered chair or two. In effect, he had turned the whole village into a fort. Several defenders hunkered behind the defenses, shooting back at the Germans. Mixed in with the American GIs were a few civilians. Like most men in rural France, they had a tendency to dress in battered old suit coats, and it was a strange sight to see the village men in these coats running to and fro with rifles and shotguns.

While the makeshift barricades provided some

defense against small arms fire, they were no match for the vicious stream of lead from the German MG-42 mounted on the Kübelwagen. Splinters and stuffing from the furniture filled the air like snow. A couple of stick grenades hit the barricade and turned chairs and boxes into kindling. Something in the piled debris caught fire, and flames began to lick at the gloom, sending up a plume of greasy black smoke.

As the flames spread, the defenders began to fall back, running for the sturdy stone houses or to the fallback position that Tolliver had created as a second line of defense. Some didn't make it. As Cole watched, the MG-42 reached out and knocked down two men running away from the crumbling barricade. One wore an Army uniform, and the other man was a civilian. Both lay very still, their bodies twisted at odd angles on the cobblestones, killed instantly by the machine gun.

Cole spotted Vaccaro behind the fountain in the village square, busy with his scoped rifle. He ran for the fountain and slid in next to Vaccaro. Bullets smacked into the decorative stonework, scattering chips of granite, but they were a lot better off behind it than behind one of those makeshift barricades.

"It's about time you showed up, Hillbilly," Vaccaro said, looking up in surprise to see that Cole had returned. "Took you long enough."

"I would have been here sooner, but I ran into some Germans," Cole said.

"Did you find those kids and old Pierre?"

Cole just shook his head. He didn't want to explain about that right now.

"They're dead? What the hell happened?"

"I don't know about the boys, but as for the villagers, that German sniper happened to them, that's what. Let's just say that German sniper was an ornery son of a bitch," he said. "One of the villagers was still alive and he told me what happened."

"He killed them?"

Cole nodded. "It was bad, I got to say."

"But you took him out?"

"He ain't goin' to bother us no more."

"I'm glad to hear that, Hillbilly," Vaccaro replied in his Brooklyn accent, his voice too loud as always. "Truly I am. But there seem to be plenty more Germans where he came from."

"What do you say we even them odds?"

"Sounds like a plan to me."

Vaccaro didn't seem to have any shortage of cartridges for the Springfield, so Cole filled his pockets.

Cole slid his Springfield over the rim of the fountain. No shortage of targets popped into view, but they came and went too quickly. Sighting them through the scope, with its limited field of view, wasn't the easiest thing in the world. The Germans' gray-blue uniforms blended easily into the fug hanging in the air, making them difficult to see.

He couldn't help but think of it as being a lot like shooting squirrels back home. Maybe it was the color of the German uniforms and the way that they blended into the smoke. Just try picking a squirrel out of a backdrop of gray winter woods. Wasn't the easiest thing to do. A squirrel moved in herky-jerky motions, in fits and starts—a lot like the Germans scrambling for cover. With a squirrel, you had to wait for the movement to see him, which was just what Cole did now. He fixed his scope on the fog and waited for the figure of a German soldier to appear. One emerged, pausing to fire his rifle, and Cole lined up the reticule on him and fired. The enemy soldier doubled over and fell. Cole ran the bolt and waited for another target. To his left, he heard Vaccaro fire, then grunt with satisfaction. *Yep, jest like shootin' squirrels.*

Then again, squirrels didn't shoot back. A spray of bullets hit the fountain. The Germans must have spotted them. Cole ducked down, not a moment too soon. A few chips flew up and pattered back down on Cole's helmet as he sheltered below the rim. The twang sound of a ricochet as the slugs hit the stone sent shivers down Cole's spine.

"Son of a bitch!"

Cole glanced over at Vaccaro, who was bleeding from a cut on his cheek where he'd been hit either by a jagged splinter of stone or by a shattered bullet. Vaccaro's fingers searched his own face frantically, trying to determine the damage.

"Jest a scratch," Cole said to reassure him. He didn't add that Vaccaro had been an inch or so from losing an eye. "I seen you cut yourself worse shaving."

"Hurts like a mother fucker," Vaccaro said, grimacing. He wiped at the blood, then ran the bolt of his own Springfield. "Time to return the favor."

Moving in tandem, they both fired over the rim of the fountain. Cole wasn't sure that he'd actually hit anything that time, so he worked the bolt and waited for another target. More Germans slipped through the smoke and fog like ghosts, consternating him. Again, he realized that his rifle was not the ideal weapon for the conditions. He would be better off firing a machine gun into the gloom, in hopes of blindly hitting something. That was just what the other defenders were doing, pouring fire into the haze and smoke.

The German advance wasn't slowing any. Thinking back to how many Germans he had seen preparing to stage the attack, Cole supposed that the defenders were outnumbered two to one. The defensive position gave some advantages, but Cole still didn't like those odds.

He noticed that the fire that had started in the barricade was beginning to spread. Flames and thick smoke billowed from the fire.

"The general had us soak some of the furniture with kerosene," Vaccaro explained, nodding at the leaping flames. "The plan was to set it on fire when he had to fall back. He thought that it would help discourage the Jerries. I've got to say, I think he had the right idea."

Cole had to agree. He could see that as the Germans reached the barricade, which had been abandoned by the defenders, they were not having an easy time of it. The burning barricade prevented them from using it as an anchor point for their own attack. The flames were pushing them back, forcing them to try and find a way around it or push through a section that was not already on fire. This was precious time lost and also left them exposed to the defenders' guns.

Once again, he had to admire the general's strategy. Tolliver knew how to plan a defense.

Looking around, he spotted General Tolliver behind the fallback position, or second line of defense. More furniture and even mattresses had been piled to create a haphazard barrier. Cole could even see what looked like a few bathtubs in the mix. The barrier looked odd, but it did the job.

Tolliver held an M-1 Garand rifle in his left hand,

which was an unusual weapon for a general, but this was an unusual situation. Tolliver was shouting orders, waving at the men to spread out along the line. The problem was that the defenders were spread too thin, even with the help from the villagers. Four or five bodies now lay sprawled in the street between the two lines of defense, testament to the Germans' deadly fire. Each casualty meant a soldier or villager who could not be replaced.

Several of the defenders were wounded, with minor injuries like Vaccaro's. The worst of the wounded had been carried to the makeshift aid center in Margot's house, where they were being tended to by Margot and Frenchie. From time to time, Frenchie raced out of the house to the line of defense, carrying a fresh batch of bandages to patch someone's wounds.

"Dang fool is gonna get hisself killed," Cole muttered. In Cole's mountain twang, the last word came out as *kilt*.

"I hate to tell you this, Cole, but we're all gonna get killed if this keeps up."

The City Boy had a point. Cole could see that the Germans weren't going to be stopped by the flaming barrier. Once they got through, the second line of defense couldn't hold for long after that.

Cole wasn't sure what the general's plan was, once the Germans pushed deeper into the town. Would they fight house to house? Would they be forced to make a last stand at the river in hopes of holding the bridge? Neither one sounded like a good option to Cole.

He concentrated on making each shot with the rifle count. He had fired off a couple more shots when he heard the shouting behind him.

Cole looked up to see Margot in the doorway of her stone house across the square, pointing excitedly toward the river. He didn't know what it meant, but it couldn't be good.

Frenchie came running over to the fountain, sliding behind like it he was going for a home run. "Margot says some of the villagers saw Germans on the bridge. The bastards are attacking from two directions!"

Cole looked, but the bridge itself was out of view. This was not good news, especially when Frenchie added that the German troops wore the black uniforms of the SS. If the defenders faced Germans coming at them from two direction, then they were caught between a rock and a hard place.

"I don't like the sounds of that," Vaccaro said.

"We had best tell Tolliver," Cole said. "If the Germans hit us from the rear, then we're all goners."

CHAPTER TWENTY-SEVEN

COLE TRACKED down Tolliver and informed him of the situation at the bridge.

"Goddammit," the general muttered. He chewed his lower lip. "We can't fight in two directions at once. We're spread too thin as it is. How many Germans, do you figure?"

"Nobody said, sir."

"I don't suppose it matters if it's a squad or an entire brigade," the general said. "Hell, half a dozen Germans is too many."

"They saw black uniforms, sir," Cole added after a moment's hesitation.

"SS." The general shook his head. "Don't it just figure."

The soldiers they were fighting now were regular

Wehrmacht, and they were tough enough. SS troops would be even worse because they were fanatics. Another thought hung in the air. SS troops meant there wouldn't be any possibility of surrender for the American GIs, nor much hope for any of the towns-people getting out of this alive. At this juncture of the war, everyone knew that the SS did not take pris-oners—nor did they expect to be taken prisoner. No, the fight at the bridge would be a fight to the bitter end. A fight to the death.

Tolliver glanced toward the flaming barricade, which had been completely abandoned to the Germans. The remaining defenders were doing what they could to stop the attackers at the fallback position.

Then Tolliver looked up the main street in the direction of the river, just as Cole had done earlier. The bridge was beyond their line of sight, but that was hardly reassuring. The Jerries might be pouring across it even now, to hit the defenders from behind.

"We could use that game trail I found and slip into the woods," Cole suggested.

Tolliver shook his head. "If those are SS troops coming at us from the bridge, these townspeople won't stand a chance. They'll murder everyone here."

Cole thought about the bodies of the villagers that he had found in the woods. Those men had been summarily executed. The general was right. If the SS captured the town, there would be more of the same. They couldn't leave the villagers to that fate. Not if they could help it.

"Sir, why don't I take Vaccaro and Frenchie down toward the bridge to see what good we can do."

Tolliver stared at him. "Three men?"

"Maybe we can hold them off long enough for this attack to fall apart," he said. "Give us some kind of fighting chance."

The general chewed his lower lip again. "Hold that bridge, Cole," he finally said. "And if you can, keep those SS bastards from blowing it up. We want that bridge across the river, but those Jerries sure as hell don't want us to cross so they'll do what they can to destroy that bridge."

"Yes, sir."

Gathering Vaccaro and Frenchie, the three of them loaded up on grenades, shoving half a dozen each into their pockets. Cole would have liked more ammo for their Springfields, but he and Vaccaro were already carrying every spare clip that was available. They had maybe fifty rounds each. Frenchie carried an M-1 with every spare clip they could find—maybe eighty rounds. Cole hoped to hell it would be enough. Their isolated unit wasn't getting any resupply.

The trio headed for the river and bridge at the

opposite end of the village. It seemed strange to be headed away from the fighting. But if there were SS troops down here, they wouldn't be out of the fight for long.

When they had arrived in the village earlier, he and Vaccaro had scouted out the bridge. Built of stone and timber, it seemed solid and impregnable as any medieval fortress. Frenchie had encountered the bridge when he had first dragged himself out of the river after the debacle upstream at Dornot.

The sight of the bridge seemed to bring back those memories. "If these are SS troops, I wonder if it's the same guys who chewed us up when we tried to cross at Dornot? I'm not eager to run into those guys again, I can tell you that."

"Let's see what we're up against before you start worrying about that," Cole said.

The three of them spread out across the road, rifles at the ready, straining to see toward the bridge. The village road sloped slightly down toward the river. The stone structure soon came into sight, looming above the muddy brown water.

They saw the Germans, who spotted them at almost exactly the same time. The Krauts had been swarming over and under bridge, running wires and planting satchel charges. Although the bridge was stone, it seemed to be held up in part by a web of crisscrossed timbers. Cole was no engineer, but it looked to him as if wrecking just one of those timbers would send the whole affair down into the muddy water below. That appeared to be what the Germans had planned.

At the sight of the Americans, several Germans dropped whatever equipment they had been using and started firing with their Mauser rifles. They were too far away to shoot accurately, but the bullets were too close for comfort, raising clots of mud as they hit the road or cracked through the air. Cole and the others scurried for the side of the road, where a low stone wall offered some cover.

The Germans on the bridge were more exposed. Four or five set about laying down suppressing fire while the rest of their squad moved to finish setting the charges.

Cole and Vaccaro got their rifles across the stone wall and fired, picking off three Germans with as many shots. The Germans had, in fact, been wearing black uniforms, so the rumors about them being SS were true. Frenchie was banging away with the M-1, quickly burning through a stripper clip, but he didn't seem able to hit anything. All three of them ducked their heads down behind the stone wall when one of the Germans opened up with a *Schmeisser* pistol and peppered the wall.

"That's some shooting," he said to Cole. "I didn't hit a damn thing."

"Aim low when you're shooting downhill, Frenchie," Cole said. "In case you ain't noticed, we ain't got a limitless supply of ammo. We want to get out of this mess, then you need to pick your targets."

He raised the rifle and dropped the German with the *Schmeisser*.

Studying the remaining Germans, looking for a target, that was when he noticed a familiar figure. Even at this distance, through the scope, he thought that he recognized the face.

Cole stared, incredulous. He was looking at the same German sniper that he had tangled with in the forest. The sniper's arm was patched up—one of Cole's bullets must have found him, after all—but he was still in action. The Jerry still had his sniper rifle, a Mauser K-98 equipped with a telescopic sight. Hell, this German had more lives than an alley cat. He must have let the stream carry him into the Moselle, and then reached the far shore to team up with the SS unit. A strong swimmer wouldn't have too much trouble with that, and the German looked strong as a bull.

Cole watched him through the scope as if taking in a movie, seemingly unable to do a thing about it. The German aimed the rifle in their direction, seeming to take his time about it.

Cole reached out and dragged Frenchie down just as a bullet struck the rim of the low wall—a space that had been occupied by Frenchie's head an instant before. The German sniper was still a deadly shot. Cole himself had never used a telescopic sight until joining the Army, and it had never stopped him from hitting targets. Then again, he had the eyes of an eagle.

"Keep your fool head down," Cole snapped at Frenchie.

Looking pale, all that Frenchie could do was nod in agreement. As Cole spoke, another bullet cracked overhead.

Vaccaro had joined them in crouching behind the stone wall, his hand on top of his helmet as if to hold it in place against the passing windstorm of bullets. He gave Cole a look. "That's some shooting. If I didn't know better, Hillbilly, I'd say that's the same Kraut sniper or maybe even his twin. I thought you took care of him."

"Weren't for lack of trying," Cole said bitterly.

"Now what?"

The rate of fire from the Germans on the bridge had increased, effectively pinning Cole, Vaccaro, and Frenchie behind the wall. But it was a long wall, running along the road down to the river. The road itself wasn't paved, but neither was it entirely dirt, being an amalgam of stove pavers, cobblestones, and dirt packed hard by centuries of use. Low clouds draped the hills beyond, and Cole could smell the dampness in the air and wafting up from the river. One thing for sure, they were not going to get any help from the Army Air Corps. Those planes remained grounded. The defenders of Ville sur Moselle were still on their own.

The one bright spot was that so far, the SS troops had not made any effort to advance and hit the American defenders from the rear. Instead, the Germans seemed intent on setting charges to destroy the bridge. Cole wondered if they would hold off to see if their comrades fought their way through. He doubted it. The SS didn't seem to care much for anyone, including the Wehrmacht.

Cole risked a quick sight check over the lip of the stone wall. More SS troops had come up, right to the edge of the bridge, while others were busy setting charges and running detonator wires back to the western shore of the Moselle. He guessed there were maybe twenty troops on the bridge now. Once they were done wiring the bridge, would they advance into the village to hit the Americans from behind? That was a distinct possibility. Cole wasn't sure how long the three of them could hold off twenty Germans— and who knew how many more might be waiting on the opposite river bank?

General Tolliver had issued orders to hold the

bridge, or to try and prevent the Germans from blowing it up. It looked like that wasn't going to happen.

Slowly, a plan began to take shape in Cole's mind. The plan wasn't much, but it was better than nothing.

CHAPTER TWENTY-EIGHT

"C'MON," he growled at Frenchie and Vaccaro. Following Cole's lead, they crawled on hands and knees behind the stone wall, following it down toward the river. The Germans were still concentrating their fire at the point on the wall where they had last seen the Americans.

"We get any closer and we can throw rocks at 'em," Vaccaro grumbled.

"Keep moving," Cole said.

The going was hard, with their hands and knees absorbing the roots, stones, and occasional shard of broken glass embedded in the muddy soil. Although they had left their packs back in the village, they were weighed down with canteens, ammo, and half a dozen grenades each. Cole also carried his big Bowie knife. It didn't help that the wall seemed to get lower the closer that they came to the river, cramping their arms and legs as they tried to stay low. If the Germans on the bridge spotted them, the gig would be up. Soon, they practically had to hug the ground.

Cole's plan was to reach a point near the river where they could see under the bridge. He wanted a glimpse of what those engineers were up to. He also had a vague idea that the three of them might be able to make life very short for the Germans stringing the explosives. Then again, the SS troops guarding the bridge itself might have something to say about that.

He glanced up, noticing that the sky was beginning to clear somewhat. The clouds hung low over the hills beyond, but no longer wrapped themselves around the peaks. It was just possible that Allied planes would get back into the air soon. That was fine by Cole—he'd had enough of the gloom and rain. He turned his attention back to the ground and kept crawling.

Finally, they reached the end of the wall. From here, the bank plunged down steeply to the swirling currents below. There wasn't any cover to speak of beyond this point.

"End of the line," Cole said. He chanced a quick peek around the end of the wall. The Germans on the bridge were still focused up the road, toward the point where they had last seen the Americans. This close, Cole could see the German sniper, tight against his rifle, waiting for a target. Cole was tempted to pick him off, but there were bigger fish to fry.

Beneath the bridge, he could see half a dozen SS troops working to lay satchel charges in the framework of the bridge. They stood on the timbers beneath the bridge, shoving the charges against the stone underbelly of the bridge. Other soldiers were busy snaking wires from the charges, edging along the timbers. The wires would run all the way back to the opposite bank, to a detonator.

Cole had not worked much with explosives, but he knew the basics from the rudimentary training that all GIs received. Both sides carried satchel charges for this very purpose: wrecking bridges, railroads, or destroying whatever resource the enemy could be denied. Considering the abuse these charges took being hauled around the countryside in combat conditions, it was a good thing that the explosives themselves were inert. You could drop them, set them on fire, and even shoot them without the charge going off. Setting off a satchel charge required a smaller detonator charge, which was rigged to an electrical device via a wire. In a sense, the arrangement used a method similar to an old flintlock musket, which required a "flash in the pan" to ignite the main charge in the barrel.

He suspected that an explosive bullet fired into the charge might do the trick, but Cole didn't have any of those for the Springfield. German snipers had used explosive bullets on the Russians, and vice versa, in defiance of Geneva Convention rules. Those two nations hated one another on the gut level. So far, German snipers had not used explosive rounds on Allied forces. Short of an explosive round or an electronic detonator, Cole had an idea for what might be the next best thing for setting off a German satchel charge.

"Just like the arcade at Coney Island," Vaccaro said, eyeing the soldiers silhouetted among the timbers. "We can pick them off and win the kewpie doll."

"You know the SS," Cole said. "They'll just send more. And once those sons of bitches on the bridge spot us, we won't be around to stop them."

"Once they have that bridge wired, they'll attack the village," Frenchie said. "Our guys and the villagers won't have a prayer, fighting in two directions."

Cole had to agree. The force on the bridge was well-armed and experienced. If Frenchie was right about them being the same unit that had wiped out the GIs crossing at Dornot, it was going to be a short fight. A likely scenario was that the SS troops would attack, and once the Americans were defeated and their Wehrmacht comrades were across the river, then they would blow up the bridge.

He looked toward far shore and could see the rest of the unit assembling. He tried to count the troops in their dark uniforms, but gave up after twenty. There were at least twice that many, along with the troops holding the bridge. There were a couple of Kübelwagen there, sporting mounted MG-42 machine guns. It became all too clear that the Germans intended to advance across the bridge and hit the GIs defending Ville sur Moselle. The Germans planned to blow the bridge, not hold it— but SS troops never needed much of a reason for an opportunity to kill Allied troops. The SS was hated and feared by the Allies, and the same might be said of the Wehrmacht. The difference came down to soldiers on the one hand, and fanatics on the other.

An officer on the other side stood up in his Kübelwagen and waved the men forward. Cole desperately wanted to pop him, but one officer wasn't worth the risk. The SS troops moved onto the bridge.

Vaccaro was also peering around the wall and saw the SS troops advancing. "Huh, I thought things were bad, but they just went to worse in a hurry."

Frenchie saw them coming now, and his knuckles went white as he gripped the rifle even harder.

"I reckon we're about to get caught between a

rock and a hard place. What else is new?" Cole gave them a crooked grin, then explained his plan to Vaccaro and Frenchie. "All right, boys, this is where it gets interestin'. When I give the word, I want you to pitch a couple of grenades at those sons of bitches on the bridge. Then give 'em hell. We want them to think that there are a lot more of us than there are. Frenchie, make sure you've got a full clip in that M-1. Shoot, and keep on shootin'."

The M-1 had the advantage of a convincing rate of semiautomatic fire, versus the bolt action Springfield—or the Mauser rifles the Germans carried, for that matter.

"What are you gonna be doing?" Vaccaro wanted to know.

"Me? City Boy, I'm fixin' to blow up this bridge with all them Nazis on it."

"We're supposed to hold this bridge, remember?"

"Ain't likely to happen now, so the best we can do is stop them SS troops from getting across and hitting our rear." He watched Frenchie put a fresh clip in the M-1, and set a couple more on top of the wall within easy reach. "Ready? Now!"

Vaccaro and Frenchie popped over the wall, throwing their grenades at the Germans on the bridge—one, two—then ducked down again. Two ear-splitting explosions resulted. The fragmentation grenades caught the Germans by complete surprise because they were still looking up the road at where they had last seen the Americans. Vaccaro and Frenchie began shooting into the mayhem they had caused with the grenades, forcing the defenders on the bridge to scatter. One of Vaccaro's rounds caught an SS soldier in the abdomen, causing him to double over and then tumbled over the side of the bridge into the river, where his body landed with an enormous splash.

But the ruse didn't last for long. Already, troops from the second wave of Germans on the far shore rushed forward to bolster the defense. The German sniper was the first to spot the Americans. Cole could see him clearly on the bridge, turning his rifle sights toward Vaccaro and Frenchie. Cole dearly wanted to put a bullet in him and finish what he had started in the forest, but didn't want to give away his own position. *Wait*, he told himself. The German was going to pay for what he had done to the villagers, and to those kids. He had something special planned for that Kraut sniper, along with the rest of them. Bullets began to smack into the stone wall or whine overhead.

Cole was still positioned at the terminus of the wall, out of the German line of fire. From here, he had a clear view of the underside of the bridge, where the Germans were finishing up the charges and scrambling to get out of there, now that the bridge seemed to be under attack.

Through the scope, Cole picked out a couple of Germans making their way along one of the timbers supporting the bridge. The timber couldn't have been more than a foot wide, so the Germans had their arms raised, gripping the bottom of the bridge to keep their balance as they crab-walked sideways along the timber. He could see the look of concentration on the Germans' face. The muddy river yawned below. Cole wouldn't have been eager to trade places with them. Tucked among the timbers over the Germans' heads, Cole could see where the satchel charges had been placed.

He could easily have shot into the satchel charges, but he knew that would not detonate them. He knew that a grenade could set off the charges. He had seen it done once, when a detonator failed, and the engineer had settled for lobbing a grenade at the satchel charge. The energy of the blast had set off the larger charge. He also knew that a bullet could detonate a grenade because it contained a different explosive, one that was under pressure and thus more volatile when exposed to the energy of a bullet.

The first German soldier didn't seem to have what Cole was looking for, so his crosshairs passed over him and settled on the next enemy soldier. *Bingo, bango*. He was in luck. From a bandolier across his chest, there dangled a couple of stick grenades. Detonators.

To his right, he heard Frenchie yelp in pain. The firing from the M-1 stopped. Although he was concerned about Frenchie, Cole did not take his eye from the rifle scope. Now, it was all up to Vaccaro. There wasn't going to be much suppressing fire from a bolt-action Springfield.

Seconds later, a bullet snicked the stone wall near Cole's head. Too close for comfort. Outgunned, he knew that the three of them couldn't stick around much longer.

He pulled his eye away from the scope long enough to glance at the soldiers on the bridge. He spotted his sniper friend right away because his uniform didn't match those of the SS troops. He had half-expected to lock eyes with the sniper, but to his surprise, the German was looking up, his rifle now pointed away from Cole.

What had drawn his attention? Was he shooting toward town? Had General Tolliver organized an attack on the bridge?

Cole got back on his scope. He had his own shooting to worry about, and this wasn't going to be an easy shot. He could sub the stick grenade in his crosshairs and he could see the German engineer, but the soldier was still shimmying his way along the trestle, with a web of timbers between him and Cole. This was going to be like shooting through a keyhole.

Cole slipped into his shooting trance. The sounds of the battle fell away. He was dimly aware of another bullet striking close, but he ignored the sting of stone fragments against his cheek. He didn't even pay attention to the trickle of warm blood on his face. All that mattered was this circular field of view. His universe came down to that rifle scope.

Anchored against the stone wall, the rifle felt steady as stone itself. But the German kept moving, moving. Cole bided his time, but soon the German would slide farther away, out of Cole's reach. Then the soldier paused. Cole's finger took up the last fraction of tension in the trigger, so that he was very nearly surprised when the rifle fired. Automatically, he followed through and kept up the pressure on the trigger.

What happened next was instantaneous. Traveling at twenty-eight hundred feet per second, the .30/06 round struck the German grenade, unleashing nearly three thousand foot-pounds of energy. It was like a bullet-sized anvil hitting the grenade at more than twice the speed of sound. Cole expected the grenade to oblige by exploding. The shockwave of the grenade in the confined space under the bridge would shatter timbers and hit the satchel charge like a flint striking steel, unleashing their own kinetic energy in the resulting detonation.

That was what Cole hoped, anyhow. But what he saw was the German soldier stagger, then lose his balance and pitch forward into the water. The grenade had stopped the bullet, all right, but it hadn't exploded or saved the soldier's life. Cole's plan literally sank into the river.

The second soldier looked around, desperately trying to determine where the shot had come from. He began to move even faster along the timber, precarious though it was. Cole could see a grenade stuck into the man's belt at his hip. He tried to line up the sights on it before the German was out of view. He had one more chance to get this right. More bullets struck the wall near Cole, but he ignored them.

He inhaled, exhaled, let his finger press ever so slightly on the trigger. The rifle fired—

Someone was grabbing him by the shoulders, pulling him behind the wall. Vaccaro was shouting something in his ear. "Down! Down!"

Instantaneously, the whole earth seemed to lift him up and then slap him back down.

Cole pressed his face down into the stone wall as the concussion washed over him. It literally took his breath away. Stunned, he raised his head to see that the whole bridge had lifted into the air, just like a blanket snapped over a bed. Chunks of stone and timber and bodies shot skyward. Through the debris, Cole could just get a glimpse of a plane racing away beneath the cloud cover.

As the bridge settled, pieces of it began to rain down. Some fell into the river, while others struck the river bank and road. Something crushed a portion of the stone wall and Cole realized that it was the spare tire from a Kübelwagen, blown nearly across the river. Another two feet to the left and it would have taken his head off. Despite the ringing in his ears, he heard screams from the direction of the river, but they died as suddenly as they had started. Cole ducked as more debris showered their position.

When Cole looked up, the bridge was a smoking ruin. Something had definitely set off the charges under the bridge in a chain reaction. The question was, had it been the rocket fired by the P47 Thunderbolt or had it been Cole's second bullet, hitting that grenade?

He might never know, and it didn't matter, anyhow. The bridge was wrecked and the SS troops were dead. Upon closer inspection, however, he could see that the bridge was not entirely destroyed. Some of the ancient stone and timber had withstood the blast. The bridge pillars still rose out of the muddy water. But where the center span of the bridge had been, Cole saw a gaping expanse.

He noticed the wreckage of a Kübelwagen, upside down, half in and half out of the water at the bottom of the steep bank. Sure enough, the front tire was missing—it was now embedded in the stone wall, having nearly taken Cole's head off. The officer, driver, and machine gunner who'd been on that vehicle must be in Valhalla right about now, Cole reckoned—or wherever dead SS went. Considering that nothing moved on the wrecked bridge, it was probably safe to say that the whole damn SS squad was in Valhalla, along with that German sniper.

Now it made sense that he had glimpsed the German sniper looking away. He must have seen the plane coming for him like a reckoning. Maybe he'd even taken a shot at it. Cole only hoped that the son of a bitch had felt at least a few seconds of terror when he saw doom itself headed right for him.

Cole looked over to his right. Hunkered down behind the stone wall, Vaccaro nodded at him. He had a dazed look in his eyes. Frenchie looked up from trying to wrap a rag around his bleeding arm. He'd been shot through the upper left arm.

"I was worried you two was goners," Cole said. The words sounded muffled. Somebody seemed to be ringing a bell in his head and his ears felt like they were stuffed with cotton.

"It's not for lack of you trying to kill us," Vaccaro

said. "That explosion was too close for comfort. Let's not do that again anytime soon."

"How's that arm?" Cole asked Frenchie.

The kid was using his teeth to pull the bandage tight. "Missed anything important," he said. "No broken bones. Hurts like hell, though."

"Being shot will do that."

Movement in the water caught their eye. They could see an SS soldier swimming toward shore. He appeared to be the only survivor.

Cole put his crosshairs on the German's head and shot him. The body sank beneath the muddy surface.

Frenchie stared at him, looking pale, but didn't say anything.

"Let's get you back into the village," Cole said to him. "I have a notion that Margot is goin' to fix you right up, one way or another."

Behind them, they could still hear the sounds of the fight taking place in town. There were single shots, interspersed with bursts of automatic fire. It sounded as if the battle for Ville sur Moselle had become up close and personal.

Cole spat dust and the taste of cordite from his mouth.

"You know what, Cole?" Vaccaro said. "General Tolliver is not going to be happy that you wrecked that bridge."

"Me? Hell, City Boy, it was that plane."

"I was there, remember? You shot at the same time that the plane hit the bridge," Vaccaro said. "That plane fired one rocket and you fired one bullet. The bridge blew up and killed all those SS. I mean—" Vaccaro sputtered to a stop, shaken by the destruction that he had seen. "I mean, what the hell? Either way, somebody made one helluva lucky shot."

"Lucky shot," Cole agreed.

CHAPTER TWENTY-NINE

LEAVING THE RIVER, they made their way back into town, following the stone wall for whatever cover it provided. They had no way of knowing how far the Germans might have advanced. For all that Cole knew, the town could have fallen and they were walking right into what might now be German lines. Behind them, a pall of dust and smoke still hung in the air above the shattered bridge. They advanced carefully, keeping an eye out for Germans.

They soon reached the center of town, where the situation balanced on a knife's edge. While Cole, Vaccaro, and Frenchie had been down at the river, the Germans had overrun the second line of defense. The first barricade that had been made up of everything from furniture to mattresses was still burning, sending pillars of smoke into the overcast sky. Maybe the smoke had gotten the attention of that passing plane. The air in town smelled strongly of burning household goods and gunpowder.

The fighting in town was now alley to alley, and house to house. Staccato bursts of fire were punctuated with the deep booms of hand grenades and single rifle shots. Somewhere, a woman's cry of terror ended in a blood-curdling shriek.

"The Jerries must have seen the bridge go up in smoke," Vaccaro said. "You'd think that they'd give up."

"Bridge or not, they'll still want to get across that river, even if they have to swim," Cole said. "As far as the Jerries are concerned, we're all that's standing between them and Germany."

"I didn't like that scream," Frenchie said. "Let's see how Margot is doing at the aid station."

Before Cole or Vaccaro could say otherwise, Frenchie was running up the street, his boots pounding across the cobblestones. A burst of fire hit the stones near his feet and Frenchie stumbled, but kept going. Cole and Vaccaro had no choice but to go after him, rifles at the ready.

The door to Margot's house stood open. The interior now looked more than ever like a hospital, with wounded soldiers and villagers occupying the floors and furniture. Most were too badly injured to fight. One or two stared with open eyes, far beyond any hope of medical care. Margot, however, was nowhere to be seen. From the second floor, they heard shouting.

"Upstairs!" Frenchie shouted, and went bounding up the steps two at a time.

A German soldier suddenly appeared at the upstairs landing. He aimed a rifle at Frenchie, who with his bandaged arm, could only fumble for his own weapon.

"Down!" shouted Cole, who was right behind him on the stairs.

Frenchie dropped to his knees, and Cole fired over his head at the German, who slumped in a heap in the landing. Cole shot him again for good measure.

An instant later, Frenchie was back on his feet and running into one of the bedrooms. No sooner had he disappeared from sight, but there came the sound of a gunshot from the room, then a scream.

Cole ducked around the doorway, keeping low. He saw three things at once: Margot holding a fireplace poker, Frenchie collapsed in a heap, and a German soldier swinging a rifle in Cole's direction. He fired at Cole, but the bullet struck just over his head. Cole fired his own rifle and missed. That was the last shot in his clip. He tossed the Springfield at the German, who ducked reflexively. Then Cole drew his Bowie knife and launched himself at the German.

In two slashing strokes, the fight was over. The

German fell to the floor, clutching at his wounds but still alive, and Cole kicked his rifle away.

He joined Margot, who was kneeling beside Frenchie.

"Winged me," Frenchie said through gritted teeth.

Cole could see that Frenchie was partially correct. The bullet had hit him in the arm that was already bandaged. But it was a lot worse than a flesh wound. Margot grabbed a pillowcase and attempted to stop the fresh bleeding.

"Dammit, kid. You could have waited."

"I was worried about Margot."

Cole glanced over at the German he had knifed. His eyes stared. He was gone.

Cole had never killed anyone with a knife before. He could clearly remember the way that the blade felt, slicing through flesh. That slightly wet resistance of flesh. The thought made him shudder. He was glad that the German was dead and not him, no regrets there, but killing with the knife was not something that he was eager to do again. Cole was a hunter, but he was no butcher.

Behind him, he heard Vaccaro pounding up the stairs. He came into the room, breathing hard. "All clear downstairs—at least for now. The town is crawling with Krauts." He looked down at Frenchie, took in the blood-soaked bandage. "Aw, for Christ's sake, Frenchie. What have you gone and done?"

Margot was busy securing the makeshift bandage tightly. She let loose with a stream of angry French, directed at her patient.

"What's she saying?" Cole asked.

Frenchie said, "She says that I'm an idiot, but that I'll live."

"That's one smart woman. You better hang onto her, Frenchie."

Margot bent down and kissed Frenchie full on the mouth.

Cole and Vaccaro looked at each other. Frenchie was a fast operator.

"I reckon that's for medicinal purposes," Cole grunted.

"Some guys have all the luck," Vaccaro said. "That is, if you can count getting twice shot in the arm lucky."

"Come on, let's get him downstairs with the others," Cole said. "Looks to me like Margot here has plenty of wounded to attend to."

With Cole taking the shoulders and Vaccaro taking the feet, they carried Frenchie down the stairs. Margot fussed over them, and they got Frenchie settled on a carpet on the parlor floor. It looked as if he was in a lot of pain, but that he was going to live.

Cole straightened up. He inserted a fresh clip into

the Springfield rifle. "Now if you will excuse us, mademoiselle, we got us some German ass to whip."

Vaccaro said doubtfully, "Maybe we ought to hang back here in case more Germans show up."

"Come on, City Boy. We ain't gonna hole up here. We're gonna take the fight to them."

Cole ducked low and ran out the door, giving Vaccaro no choice but to follow.

On the main street, everything was in chaos. They spotted Sergeant Woodbine and General Tolliver behind the village fountain, engaged in a hot firefight with a couple of Germans who were using an overturned vegetable cart for cover. Woodbine kept up a steady fire with his M-1, while the general banged away with a .45. The Germans had not spotted Cole or Vaccaro coming out of the makeshift aid station, but were focused on pouring fire at the men behind the fountain. In unison, Cole and Vaccaro raised their rifles and shot the Germans. Tolliver looked their way and acknowledged them with a nod.

Cole looked around, taking stock. Down the street, a German was shooting from the upstairs window of a house, using his vantage point to keep the defenders pinned down with his machine pistol. His suppressing fire was enabling other Germans to get through the barricades and spread out through the town. Pretty soon, Ville sur Moselle would be in German hands.

"This way, City Boy."

They ran toward the house sheltering the German, keeping close to the other houses for cover. Cole juked into the street and dropped to one knee, shooting into the window. Vaccaro kept going, tossing a grenade through the door of the house to clear out any downstairs defense. With smoke still billowing out, he barged through the door.

Cole fired again at the window, not sure if he had hit the German. His answer came a moment later, when he saw a muzzle flash in the window and a smatter of bullets stitched its way toward him. He rolled, desperate for cover, but he was caught out in the open. Another couple of seconds, and he would be in that German's sights.

The window suddenly exploded outward, glass and wood showering the street. The Jerry machine gunner slumped in the window frame. His head lolled forward, and his *Stahlhelm* clattered to the street below, revealing the dead soldier's blond hair. Then Vaccaro's ugly mug appeared in the window, and the City Boy gave him the finger.

Cole couldn't help but grin.

Without the machine gunner's suppressing fire, the Germans lost their foothold in the village. The attackers seemed to have reached some kind of high tide, but now the tide was receding.

Cole made his way toward the fountain in the village square sheltering Sergeant Woodbine and General Tolliver. From the get-go, that fountain had been a natural command post. Cole's dive toward the cobblestones had done something to his knee, and he limped toward them.

Tolliver straightened up from his shooting stance and holstered the .45, then put his hands on his hips, glaring at Cole. If Cole had expected some praise for helping to turn the tide of battle in the village, he could see that he was sadly mistaken.

"What the hell happened, Cole? You let the Jerries blow up the bridge! I could see the smoke and debris from here. It looked like Vesuvius erupting."

Cole wasn't sure who or what Vesuvius was, but he planned on telling it to the general like he saw it. He was a straight shooter in more ways than one. "That goddamn bridge was more trouble than it was worth, sir. A whole unit of SS was coming at us from yonder side of the Moselle. They wired that bridge to explode, and then they were fixin' to hit our position. Back home, that's what they call bein' between a rock and a hard place."

"Are you telling me that the Jerries blew up that bridge before they crossed it?" the general asked, incredulous. "That doesn't make sense."

"I reckon the Jerries planned to blow it up after they wiped us out and got the Wehrmacht troops across. I thought that I'd beat them to it. As it turns out, those SS troops were on that bridge when it blew."

"So what happened?"

The general stared at him. "Just how the hell did you plan on blowing up that bridge, son?"

"With a grenade, sir. However, I reckon that plane beat me to it."

Cole didn't see any point in a belabored explanation. General Tolliver was still staring at him, as if expecting more. Finally, he reached out and smacked Cole's helmet. He was grinning. "You are such a goddamn hillbilly, aren't you, Cole? I like that. I'm not happy about losing that bridge, but if a squad of SS went with it, I guess that's something."

He motioned Cole to follow him, and the two joined Sergeant Woodbine, who stood behind the fountain, rifle at the ready. But the fighting seemed to be over.

The Germans were now in full retreat, moving past the barricades and pulling out of the village. The remaining defenders might have whooped and hollered at the sight, if it hadn't been for the fact that they were so bloodied and battered. The fight for Ville sur Moselle had been tooth and nail at the end, leaving the defenders exhausted.

Through the smoke, they caught a glimpse of a Kübelwagen driving off. It might have been limping, if it was possible for a vehicle to do such a thing. Standing in the back, directing the retreat with a few shouts and a wave of his arms, was the German general.

Instantly, Cole put his rifle to his shoulder, thinking that he'd never shot a general. At least, not that he knew about. He couldn't pass up such a good target. The vehicle was no more than three hundred feet away and moving slowly. He placed the reticule slightly ahead of the general and moved it to match the vehicle's speed. His finger began to take up tension on the trigger.

He felt a firm hand on his shoulder. Surprised, he broke away from the rifle scope to find General Tolliver watching the German retreat. He gave Cole's shoulder a squeeze.

"Let him go," the general said.

"Sir?" Cole still had the rifle at his shoulder, ready to acquire the target. The wind changed direction and whipped acrid smoke at them, making Cole's eyes water. In another few seconds, the vehicle would go around the bend in the road and be out of sight.

"Stand down, son." When Cole didn't obey right away, Tolliver added, "That's an order. Those are Wehrmacht troops, not SS. The general is just doing his duty, same as we are."

Cole lowered the rifle, blinking the smoke out of his eyes, and when he looked again, the German vehicle was gone.

The final battle for Ville sur Moselle was over, and against all odds, they had won.

EPILOGUE

ONCE THEY WERE sure that the Germans wouldn't be back, the surviving defenders and villagers began to let their guard down. Everyone had about a quart of adrenalin running through their veins. Hands shook as they tried to smoke cigarettes or take a swig from a bottle. The aftermath of every fight was the same. Exhaustion would soon follow.

The fate of the defeated Germans was hard to determine. There couldn't have been more than a dozen men left with that German general. They would either surrender, find another river crossing, or fight to the end until they were wiped out once the Allied planes got back in the air. Nobody really cared what awaited the Krauts, so long as they left the village alone.

As the fires in the burning barricade died down, the people of Ville sur Moselle began to emerge from their homes to survey the damage.

An older woman saw Cole standing there alone and held out a basket of food and a bottle of wine. He slung his rifle and accepted the food with a grateful nod.

"The Germans are gone for good!" someone shouted in French. The ragged cheer that followed was feeble and short-lived. The ensuing silence was punctuated by the crackling from the fires and the sound of a woman sobbing.

"Mon deu," an older man muttered, looking around at the smoldering barricade, the shattered windows, and a few bodies sprawled on the cobblestones. Their peaceful village had largely been spared from the war —until now.

A woman cried over the body of a middle-aged man, who had died clutching his shotgun. Nearby lay a dead German. Cole walked over and looked down at the German. He was no more than nineteen or twenty, his blue eyes staring and a vivid red pool of blood surrounding him. Judging by the proximity of the bodies, it seemed apparent that one had shot the other.

Cole shook his head. He wasn't one to dwell much on what this war meant, or the cost of it, because his job was to *fight* the war. But it was hard to ignore this tableau. Cole did not think much about consequences in the middle of a battle but now he took time for reflection.

The young soldier should have had girls to make love to, lager to drink, an entire life to live, but all that was gone now. The older man might have had grandchildren someday to bounce on his knee and his plump wife to keep him warm on winter nights. Just two more lives lost in the wastefulness of a war in which millions had already died.

Tomorrow, it would be somebody else's turn to die. Maybe even Cole's.

He put his hand on his rifle and smiled grimly to himself. If he could, he sure as hell would make sure that some German son of a bitch would die instead.

"Sergeant Woodbine, put together a detail to clear out the dead," Tolliver said. "See if you can get any of the villagers to help. I want our men posted as sentries, just in case those Jerries do come back."

"Yes, sir," Woodbine said, and saw to it.

While the damage and loss were significant, Cole knew that it could have been much worse. He had seen how other towns in the path of the fighting had been utterly destroyed by artillery or Allied planes— usually as they tried to root out German defenders. Here, there had been no artillery shells or even tanks to take a toll. The fighting had been limited to rifles and a few machine guns and grenades. Still, it was enough.

Nearby, General Tolliver was talking with Vaccaro and some of the other men. He gave orders for them to report to Woodbine for sentry duty or burial detail. Then he came marching purposefully toward Cole, with Vaccaro following the general at a respectful distance.

"Cole, goddammit, why didn't you tell me the whole story about what happened at that bridge?"

"I'm not sure what you mean, sir." Earlier, Cole had given the general a brief rundown of events at the bridge.

"You told me that you attempted to blow up that bridge by setting off the charges with a grenade, but that the plane beat you to it."

"Yes, sir."

"You didn't explain that the grenade was still attached to a German engineer who was placing charges under the bridge. Vaccaro filled me in on that little detail, along with a couple of others. Vaccaro said you fired at the same time the plane did, so there's an even chance that your bullet took out the bridge. What have you got to say about that?"

"Lucky shot, sir."

"Cole, I think there is exactly one soldier in the United States Army who could make that shot, and I am looking at him. Even if you are a peckerwood."

"Thank you, sir." Cole grinned. "I reckon."

"From now on, though, don't go blowing up any bridges against orders. Not every general is as forgiving as I am."

"Yes, sir." Cole paused. "Permission to speak freely, sir?"

"Granted."

"We're lucky you showed up when you did, sir. You saved this village. You saved *us*. You stopped the Germans, bridge or no bridge."

Tolliver grunted. "You know what? I'm just a bean counter, Cole. For most of this war I've been a pencil pusher polishing a chair."

"I heard a rumor to that effect, but I wouldn't have believed it. I'd say you make a mighty fine general, sir. Then again, what the hell would I know? I'm just an ignorant peckerwood, like you said."

The general shook his head and walked off. But he was grinning.

Vaccaro had hovered close enough to hear the exchange, and he came up to Cole. "I had to tell him. He said that he'd put you in for a medal, but nobody would believe it."

"I don't hardly believe it myself. Let's go see how ol' Frenchie is doin'."

They walked over to the aid station. The rooms of Margot's small house now overflowed with wounded, with the furniture shoved out of the way or even carried into the street to make room. Other villagers had come to help. There were only a few GIs among the wounded—there hadn't been that many to begin with. Most of the injured were villagers who had come to the defense of the village or who had been caught in the crossfire. There were even a couple of badly wounded German soldiers. Although they were the enemy, they were clearly suffering and in pain, so it was hard to have anything but compassion for them.

Fortunately, an actual doctor was on the scene. With his shirtsleeves rolled up, he went from person to person, staunching wounds and administering morphine from the Americans' limited supply.

Frenchie was among the walking wounded. With his arm tightly bandaged, he was doing his best as a one-armed medic. More importantly, he was also translating between the wounded Americans and the French doctor.

"How you feeling, Frenchie?" Vaccaro asked.

"Hurting some," he said, wincing as he lifted his arm. "But I'm a lot better off than most of these people. I got sulfa on there and it's wrapped up tight, plus I had a couple swigs of calvados."

"Morphine?"

Frenchie shook his head. "Others here need it more, and we don't have that much. Besides, I'll be useless if I take a hit of that stuff. I'm going to do what I can to help the doctor."

"Where did he come from?" Vaccaro wondered, nodding at the doctor.

"Turns out he lives out in the countryside. He slipped into town once the fighting was over, to see how he could help."

Cole and Vaccaro nodded. Like most American soldiers, they appreciated the fact that in the process of fighting the Germans, they were also liberating the French, who were basically a defeated and occupied people. When you thought about it, Cole found it amazing that the Germans had conquered a country as vast and powerful as France in less than six weeks.

Americans ought to take lesson from that, he thought. You never wanted to get too comfortable or soft as a people. Then again, it was hard to imagine enemy troops conquering the Tennessee or Kentucky hills. More than a few Americans still owned guns and knew how to shoot them, thank God.

Still, it felt good to give the French their freedom back, returning a national favor that went all the way back to the Marquis de Lafayette and the American Revolution. However, the soldiers' opinions of the French weren't always positive because many had accepted the Germans and even collaborated with them. Cole found it refreshing to see the French doctor doing what he could for the American wounded.

Margot came bustling past with an armload of bandages, but when she caught sight of Frenchie, she paused long enough to press close to him, hip to hip, and the look that passed between them was unmistakable. If Margot and Frenchie were not already lovers, then they were about to be. There were enough sparks there to start a forest fire. For a moment, they both seemed completely oblivious to their surroundings.

The spell was broken only when Margot turned to Cole and said something to him in French. He looked at Frenchie, who translated: "Margot says that she hasn't seen you since you went into the forest to look for her brother this morning. She wants to know if you found any sign of them."

Cole could hardly believe so much had happened in one day. He had gone into the woods shortly after dawn. The gloom of the day had thickened, indicating that it was getting close to evening.

Along with Margot, Vaccaro and Frenchie both looked at Cole expectantly.

"I didn't find her brother," Cole said, after a moment's hesitation. "I did find Pierre, the village mayor. He and those other men were hell-bent on joining the Resistance, so I don't expect you will see them back anytime soon."

Frenchie interpreted, and Margot received Cole's report with an exasperated sigh.

"Ce vieil imbécile!" Margot said, although her voice held a tinge of pride. She asked another question.

"She said Pierre is an old fool," Frenchie said. "But what about Marcus and his friend?"

"Pierre told me them boys done run off to Paris," Cole said, and Frenchie passed on the news.

"Paris!" Margot exclaimed.

"Oui, Paris," Cole said. He told Frenchie, "Some Resistance fighters came by in a truck, and said they were going to help liberate the city. They asked them boys if they wanted to go along. I reckon they're halfway there by now."

Frenchie explained to Margot, who nodded, wiped away a few tears, and smiled. She said something that Cole couldn't understand, and once again Frenchie translated.

"She said those crazy boys won't want to come home once they get to the big city, but maybe it will be better for them there than in a little village. I told her that maybe they'll send a postcard once they get there."

"Gonna be a long time before any mail gets through," Cole pointed out. "But she can rest easy knowing her kid brother is on his way to Paris."

Someone cried out in pain, and both Margot and Frenchie broke away to help. Cole and Vaccaro gladly left the sounds and smells of the makeshift hospital behind and walked outside.

Back in the village square, Vaccaro turned and looked at Cole. "Those boys didn't really go to Paris, did they?"

"No," Cole said. "The Germans found them in the woods and killed them, along with Pierre and the others."

Vaccaro absorbed that news, then nodded. "So now, you've fixed it so that Margot is always going to think that her brother is alive somewhere, maybe off in Paris, too busy having adventures to write home. She'll always wonder what happened to him, but she'll have hope."

"I reckon she will."

"You're a good man, Caje Cole."

Cole slung his rifle. "Don't let word get out."

* * *

ANY CHANCE of the clouds finally lifting for good disappeared when a fog drifted up from the river. Just before nightfall, they heard the sound of vehicles on the road toward town. The remaining GIs scrambled to take up defensive positions, so tired that they felt as if they were running through concrete instead of the misty air. They had hoped against hope that the

Germans were done, but exhausted as they were, they prepared to fight back.

"Hold your fire, boys!" General Tolliver shouted, although he had drawn his .45. Like the others, he had detected a difference in the sound of the approaching vehicles. German and American motors had different sounds to them. But there was no ignoring the fact that they were also hearing the ominous clanking sound that could only be a tank or half-track. If a Panzer came up the road, they were done for. "Make sure it's the Jerries before you shoot!"

What came into sight was not a German vehicle, but a Sherman tank. The name "Beast" was painted prominently on the side, along with a caricature of a hairy monster. Maybe a werewolf? Tolliver stepped out into the road and waved. The tank hatch opened and the tank commander's head popped out.

Although Tolliver wore no insignia, he had the swagger of an officer. Two days ago, he had moved and acted more like the administrative pencil pusher that he claimed to be.

"Where are we, sir?" the tank commander shouted. "We've been following this road for two hours and we don't know if we're still within our own lines."

"Who are you, son?"

"Second Armored Division, when we're not lost."

"General Tolliver," the general said. Upon hearing that the officer in front of him was a general, the tank commander's eyes visibly widened. He forgot battlefield protocol and pulled his arm out of the tank hatch to salute.

"Sir!"

"You're not lost anymore, Sergeant. You are in American lines. We hold this village," Tolliver said. "You don't know how glad I am to say that. Almost as glad as I am to see that Sherman."

"There's more behind me, sir. What do you want us to do?"

"We are going to figure out a way across this river, Sergeant. And then we're going to kill us some more Germans."

"Yes, sir!"

* * *

A CHUNK of the bridge span was destroyed, but the villagers and local farmers were a resourceful bunch once Tolliver explained what he needed. The next morning, huge timbers and planks were hauled into place, bridging the gap created by the blast.

Cole went down there to see how the bridge was going to be pieced together, but he had another purpose, as well. He was hoping to find some evidence that the German sniper had died in the explosion. Several enemy bodies had been found in the debris on the bridge, and these had been carried to the side of the road leading to the bridge for burial. The German sniper was not among them. A few bodies had washed up along the shoreline, and Cole scanned these, but the sniper wasn't there.

Cole figured that the sniper had gone into the river and his body had been carried downstream. Cole doubted that anyone could have survive the explosion, but he couldn't shake the nagging feeling that maybe, just maybe, that German sniper had more luck than he deserved. The critter deep down inside him growled uneasily.

He heard a tank approaching, and stood by to watch it pass. The resulting makeshift bridge was rickety, and it creaked and groaned ominously, but it was enough for a single tank to pass across the Moselle.

One by one, the handful of tanks that had arrived in Ville sur Moselle made their way across the river. They were followed by Tolliver's Jeep and the remaining GIs, including Vaccaro and Cole. Frenchie had been ordered to stay behind and help the wounded until they could be evacuated to the nearest field hospital. By some miracle, West still clung to life and there was some hope that he would make it now.

German forces continued their retreat toward the Fatherland and the vaunted Western Wall of defense.

That, too, would fall in time as Allied forces pursued the battered Wehrmacht and SS troops.

After the intense fighting that had separated units and even individual men, some of the confusion was sorted out. Cole and Vaccaro found themselves reunited with Lieutenant Mulholland and were assigned to sniper duty. Orders came down for General Tolliver to rejoin headquarters and get back to supply and logistics, which Cole thought was a shame. But orders were orders, and as with most things in the Army, it was likely that there were some politics involved. But no matter. It was enough to know that somewhere back at headquarters, there was a bean-counting supply officer who had risen to the occasion to make a fine battlefield general, commanding like a god on earth.

The weather turned colder. Cole and the others awoke in the French autumn mornings to a layer of frost on their helmets and gear. The sun rarely shone, but the weather cleared enough for the Allied planes to unleash their holy wrath on the Germans. As they trudged west, Cole could begin to see the outline of real hills on the horizon. The country grew steep and rugged, with dense pine forests. He was reminded of the mountains back home.

"These are called the Ardennes," Vaccaro said. "Real mountains. I hope to hell we don't have to cross them. One good thing is that the Germans won't come back at us through there. The terrain is too rough."

Cole studied the brooding hills, some of them already dusted with snow from the coming winter. "We'll see," he said.

NOTE TO READERS

This story is based on the events surrounding the Lorraine campaign, or the final push across France made by the Allies in pursuit of the retreating Germans.

These Caje Cole books begin at D Day with *Ghost Sniper* and then move on to *Iron Sniper*, set during the horrific fighting and destruction of the Falaise Pocket battle that firmly placed Normandy in Allied control.

By the fall of 1944, the Germans were in retreat toward Germany. Two major boundaries played an important role in that fighting retreat; these were the Moselle and Rhine rivers. The Rhine is more famous, being the boundary line of Germany itself. Located in France, the Moselle is actually a large tributary of the Rhine that runs parallel, several miles distant. The river is known for being swift and deep as it passes through the French countryside, making it a substantial obstacle for American forces.

In order to thwart the Allied advance, the Germans sought to destroy any crossings once they had their own forces across. Many of the details about this final push across France come from *The Lorraine Campaign* by Hugh M. Cole.

Eventually, the Germans would manage to regroup and counterattack through the Ardennes

Forest in what came to be known as the Battle of the Bulge in December 1944. Cole finds himself in the thick of that fight in Ardennes Sniper. Red Sniper is set during the final days of World War II and just beyond.

With the big picture out of the way, a few notes on locations and events in Gods and Snipers will be helpful.

Located on this actual river, Ville sur Moselle is an imagined place, but it could represent any of the small French villages that sprang up around the bridges across the Moselle River. It's such a small village that it has largely been spared from the actual fighting until the Germans and Americans converge there at roughly the same time, both intent on the bridge across the Moselle.

Sadly, the fight at Dornot that Frenchie survives was based on actual events that occurred when American troops attempted to gain a foothold across the Moselle in September 1944. They encountered fierce resistance and there were problems in coordinating the attack, as described in *The Moselle River Crossing*. This 188-page report by the U.S. Army's Combat Studies Institute provides a detailed analysis of the battle at Dornot, in which nearly 800 American troops died. The battle took place a short distance upriver from Ville sur Moselle.

There are a couple of plot devices that some

readers may feel strongly about, but I kept them because they were so unusual or showcased Cole's prowess as a marksman. The first is that the German sniper dons WWI armor to protect himself from Cole's bullet. Such body armor existed in the Great War, but it was cumbersome and not terribly effective against rifle rounds. The story reflects that because the armor that Hauer finds in a barn does give him some protection, but it's not complete, as he finds out the hard way when the two snipers duel in the woods. I thought that the armor added an interesting twist to the story and gave me an excuse for spending countless hours researching the obscure topic of WWI body armor.

Moving on to the second plot device, could a bullet actually detonate a grenade and then in turn set off satchel charges? By all accounts, a rifle bullet could *theoretically* explode a grenade. The grenade setting off the satchel charge was actually inspired by an incident in the 1968 novel *Panzer* by Harold Calin, a popular writer of the day who was also a WWII veteran. His books (sadly, long out of print) are filled with the sort of details and descriptions that could only have come from someone who was there, so the grenade scene has some precedence. As for a marksman being able to hit a German stick grenade at any distance, it's just the sort of thing that a dead-eye like Caje Cole is capable of doing.

Finally, a word about the title, which was inspired by a quote from the wonderful Michael Shaara novel, *The Killer Angels*. Winner of the 1975 Pulitzer Prize, this fine literary novel describes the heroic 20th Maine at Gettysburg in 1863. If you haven't read it, please be sure to add it to your list. Shaara's son, Jeff, wrote a fine sequel called *Gods and Generals*, and I only realized the similarity after I'd chosen the title for this book. For me as a writer, the title always comes first and then the rest of the book seems to fall into place.

Writing can be lonely work, so I want to thank the many readers and acquaintances who continue to offer encouragement. A special thanks to my family for their support and to my small-but-mighty team of advance readers for their input.

As always, thank you for reading and putting up with all my faults and shortcomings in turning actual events into historical fiction. As Caje Cole might say, "I reckon it'll do."

ABOUT THE AUTHOR

David Healey lives in Maryland where he worked as a journalist for more than twenty years. He is a member of the International Thriller Writers and a contributing editor to The Big Thrill magazine. Visit him online at www.davidhealeyauthor.com or www.facebook.com/david.healey.books

Thank you for reading! If you enjoyed the story, please consider leaving a review on Amazon.com.